Also by Francesca Momplaisir

My Mother's House

THE
GARDEN
of BROKEN
THINGS

The
Garden
of Broken
Things

FRANCESCA MOMPLAISIR

Alfred A. Knopf, New York, 2022

THIS IS A BORZOI BOOK
PUBLISHED BY ALFRED A. KNOPF

www.aaknopf.com

Knopf, Borzoi Books, and the colophon are registered trademarks
of Penguin Random House LLC.

Library of Congress Cataloging-in-Publication Data
Names: Momplaisir, Francesca, [date] author.
Title: The garden of broken things / Francesca Momplaisir.
Description: First edition. | New York : Alfred A. Knopf, 2022.
Identifiers: LCCN 2021016262 | ISBN 9780593321065 (hardcover) |
ISBN 9780593321072 (ebook)
Classification: LCC PS3613.O5226 G37 2022 | DDC 813/.6—dc23
LC record available at https://lccn.loc.gov/2021016262

Jacket images: leaves © bumbumbo / Shutterstock; people based on a
photo by Thomas Barwick / DigitalVision / Getty Images
Jacket design by Ruxandra Duru

MANUFACTURED IN THE UNITED STATES OF AMERICA
First Edition

for my country
I never left you

for my people
especially those lost
in the 2010 and 2021 earthquakes

THE GARDEN *of* BROKEN THINGS

THERE MUST HAVE BEEN a woman bracing herself in a doorway, arms spread as if on a cross, palms against the frame to keep a house and herself from collapsing.

THERE MUST HAVE BEEN a radio playing, sound squeezed out of speakers first tilting, then tumbling off of the low table made from a plank of wood atop a dusty plastic bucket. There must have been windowpanes, mismatched sets of flower pattern plates shattering, mirrors slicing through reflections, fingers, and feet, drawing blood.

THERE MUST HAVE BEEN a desperate cook recoiling from the burn of coals flung far from fires, pots slipping off stoves, spilling rice into scalding piles, pans of uncooked meat, tough bones, and boiling broth sinking into dirt.

THERE MUST HAVE BEEN stick-figure children on scraps of paper stolen from sacred school notebooks, scattered drawings by scattered children on the shaking ground where they once ran safely.

THERE MUST HAVE BEEN lovers on a mattress as low as a rug on the floor, wondering if they had finally made the Earth move. Bent breaths between stifled moans coming, coming, not from the tangled lovers, although they cried as the low ceiling crashed on top of their bare bodies.

THERE MUST HAVE BEEN a stretched-out shriek of bottomless pain from the core of the confounded Earth cracking open.

THERE MUST HAVE BEEN shattered limbs, bodies flattened by dense slabs of invincible concrete. Bodies, so many bodies sequestered in closed caves with no room to breathe, only space for flies to flow in and out of crevices of flesh, making their way to infinite meals after the quake.

THERE MUST HAVE BEEN blood, so much blood, leaking from the crush, pooling, then flowing slowly to satiate the ground and gods that had not encountered liquid of any form in months. Greedy gods, each awaiting their turn for the blood to flow over their lips, then into the broken mouth of the ground itself.

THERE MUST HAVE BEEN a hungry grove of green trees, dry, tan leaves gathered at their feet, like children waiting patiently for soon-come kisses that would never arrive.

FOR ONE MOTHER, ARROGANT enough to think that she was the only mother, there must have been hours on all fours searching for the child she believed had been buried in the grove.

THAT SAME NIGHT, THAT only night, those only hours in the deep dark of searches suspended until the morning after, there must have been one mother, the only mother, she thought, fingers blindly clawing close to the roots of plantain trees in a grove that would always and only grow ghosts and graves.

One

I

There must have been a defeated family
torn along an unmendable seam
hoping that all of the damage could be undone

I blast the music to cover the sound of gunshots that fire only in my mind and not into the body of the boy beside me, who seems indifferent to his vulnerability.

Miles doesn't want to understand why his rebelliousness is not like the revolts of the white boys at his school. He cannot accept that, for them, there is no deadly consequence for minor misbehavior, no cops waiting to scratch the itch of their trigger fingers after first finger-frisking the young boy bodies who stand black, up against the wall before them.

It doesn't matter that we just got our first Black president. Miles is only safe with the music blaring in our luxury car in this neighborhood with me driving, daring the neighbors to call the law on an unarmed driver and a passenger visiting a delinquent dad at the cul-de-sac of a New Jersey suburb.

I repeat what I've been saying for months. "This has to be the last time, Miles."

"Yes, Mom," he drawls.

"You could have gotten yourself killed."

"Fuck, Mom."

"Are you kidding me?"

He rolls his eyes. "You can curse in front of me. We can listen to songs like this, but I can't use profanity."

"We're not having this discussion again." This is not the battle I want to fight. Bigger fish, bigger fish.

"We're not having any discussion." Miles puts his earphones in.

I yank them out. "I'm talking to you!"

"Just give me room to breathe. Damn . . ."

At least he is responding. Like the car vibrating, answering the bass of Lil Wayne's "A Milli."

I place my hand on his and squeeze. He squeezes back. He always squeezes back. No matter what, he always lets me hold his hand.

I open the moonroof and let the lyrics flow out, cussing at the unseasonably cold November air.

A milli, a milli, a mill
A millionaire, I'm a Young Money millionaire

Miles is enjoying the song with me. He doesn't smile; he doesn't have to. I know that he loves that we have a love of hip-hop in common. And that I play the explicit versions of songs without embarrassment. I'm not like other mothers, especially not the Ivy League–educated ones with enough degrees to award to our entire family of five: me; Yves, my nine-year-old—sorry, *our* nine-year-old; Miles, who always says that he's a parent and the only adult in our household; my mother, Yanique, whom I call "Ma" as do the boys; and my grandmother, whom we all call Ol'Lady. We never count

Bright, even when I was married to him. But he is the daddy, my baby-daddy. He hates it when I call him that, so I do, every chance I get.

I keep my hand on Miles's as we pull up to Bright's new McMansion in Bergen County, New Jersey. I park in front of the driveway (not in it), facing in the opposite direction of the other cars. There aren't usually cars parked on the streets. All of the houses have multicar garages. But it's the day after Thanksgiving, so the neighbors have had overnight guests. A bigger audience for me. I close the moonroof to keep Miles warm.

Before I step out of the car, I change out of my sneakers and into my Manolo stilettos. Bright is already outside in his driveway, arms crossed, armed to the teeth, angry armor on. I can't wait. I'm on the offensive, as always. Before he can start his rant, I go in.

"Loosen up, Bright. Unfold your arms. Stop being so pretentious. Living in the Jersey burbs doesn't make you white." I've come prepared for the biweekly entertaining argument. Today will be worse because of what Miles did last weekend.

"Go to hell, Genevieve!"

"I wouldn't want to crowd your space!" He's already weakened, off his game. My loud, explicit hip-hop, with all of the profanity and the N-word, always throws him off-balance. I focus on the contortion of his furrowed brows. He always takes the bait, enjoying the angry exchanges almost as much as I do. Well, not quite as much, because he's usually on the losing side.

"Just because I have some sense of decorum . . ." He's huffing now. "Blasting your music from your 'Range' doesn't make you 'Jenny from da Block.'" He raises his voice over the bass thump of my modest SUV. No crazy rims, no dark tinted windows, a subdued burgundy instead of shiny black or bright white.

"'Jenny from da Block'? That's so old, *Bradley*. You can do better than that."

"And you can do better than roll up here like some hood-rat—"

"What? I didn't catch that!" I cup my hand over my ear and lean in as if I'm straining to hear him over the music still playing in the car. Lil Wayne's words are muffled, but I'm bopping my head to the beat. I mouth the lyrics.

Bright looks like he's about to cry or slap me. He never does either. He never has. I pretend not to hear him say: "My neighbors and I thank you, once again, for the lesson in ghetto-fab. And, I'll remind you, once again, that this is the sort of behavior that has Miles acting out."

"And, *once again*, I'll remind *you* that . . ." I take a deep breath and speak through my teeth to keep from yelling. Composed, I enunciate, "Lil Wayne did not abandon *your* sons."

I stop for a moment and take stock of the house. Six bedrooms, Miles told me. I have never stepped foot inside. It's the house we should have built together, the house that Bright now wants my boys to live in with him. That is always the threat—to take the boys from me. I think but don't say out loud this time, *I wish a muthafucka would try!*

The music sounds louder as Miles gets out of the car. I see him out of the corner of my eye but I can't stop arguing with Bright. Before Miles can even slam the car door shut, he turns around and gets right back in.

I know that he will write about this incident later. In a rhyme or a song. There might be a sketch. I convince myself that he doesn't know that I go through his notebooks when he's at school. He composes more than he draws. I am never in his pictures. Only Yves, mostly Yves. And a man in profile or with his back turned, walking or running.

"That's on you, Bright." I throw a nod over my shoulder.

"Isn't it always my fault?"

"I see that you still haven't tried therapy."

"Just because you're a psychiatrist doesn't mean everybody needs therapy, Genevieve. When all you have is a hammer—"

"I have more than a hammer. I have a tire iron, a baseball bat, a hunting knife. And that's just what's in the car." I always refine my words beforehand, well-forged instruments, sharp and blunt, wielded to injure. I use them on Bright to keep from turning them on myself. I know me. I've done a million times what a doctor is never supposed to do—self-diagnose and psychoanalyze members of her own family. I know that attacking Bright keeps me from hurting myself. Not slit-your-wrists type of hurt. The negative self-talk stuff that sends me into the darkness. But the prophylactic of hurting Bright, this backward self-protection, never lasts. Neither does my poise.

I imitate Bright and stand with my arms folded. I look him up and down, formulating my next injurious barb.

"You have got to stop this, Genevieve."

"Stop what? Stop reminding you how you fucked up? I don't have to say anything about that. Your sons don't even want to see you. I had to force Miles to come here."

"The same way you're forcing him to take a vacation to Haiti?"

"You know damn well it isn't a vacation. We agreed on this, Bright. You asked for this."

"I said we should send him to my mom down south."

"To hang out with your thug nephews and end up dead or in jail anyway? Isn't that what we're trying to prevent?"

"Thugs? But you can come over here all ghetto . . . You always let him do whatever he wants."

"He doesn't *want* to go to Haiti. I am *making* him go. He needs to see what life is like for so many kids. What it could have been like for him or me, for that matter." I cringe as I say the words I've heard most of my life. The voices of my mother's and grandmother's friends scolding their children, threatening to send them to Haiti for good if they didn't straighten up, ring in my ears. I never imagined that I would be one of them. I never imagined so many things—marriage, divorce, motherhood, single motherhood, and now taking my first-born son to Haiti because the boy has been getting into trouble.

"You're taking him to the Caribbean!" Bright senses that I'm weakening.

I am, but I will never tell Bright that I am taking Miles to Haiti so I can be alone with my son, so I can get to know him. This is not punishment; it is a rescue. I need to get him away from here, if just for a week, away from this place, so he can breathe because he is away from danger. For a brief reprieve from my worry, and to love him without the interruption of the constant fear that he might be taken from me violently.

Bright insists, "At least in North Carolina he could visit some colleges, see a good example."

"*You* are supposed to be the good example. The man he should want to grow up to be."

"Not this again. . . . You could let them come live with me." Bright turns his head just in time to see his girlfriend's face in the upstairs window.

I see it too. "Time to change baby's diaper," I chuckle. "That's why your sons don't want to see you. I couldn't even drag Yves here!"

I can only suppress my anger in short stints. I push my pain down into my abdomen. I'm like a shaken soda bottle. I know that the cap will eventually pop off; the foamy liquid will explode and spill into a mess that cannot be put back in. But I try. I try so hard. I need to keep it all contained in these moments; otherwise, I'll start crying. Then fucking Bright will see me dripping all over myself. He'll relish the sloppy leak. So, instead of allowing my wounded self to rise into my throat, to breach the barrier of my eyelids and lips, I stamp it down into my stomach and let rise the toxicity of my venomous wit to taunt Bright into overflowing.

I am trying to hold myself together. But the flutter of the curtains, the gauzy image of a younger woman, threatens to knock me over and splatter me all over the driveway. I can't help but imagine him with this new woman or some other. I couldn't see it all those years ago, when I suspected but refused to admit inside myself what he was doing. My hurt and jealousy drive me to this sort of low-brow pettiness every time I see him except when . . . When we meet up to touch each other again, to pretend it's still early on in our relationship, when we were young and greedy for each other. I need to believe that he couldn't have, still can't be like that with, anyone else. But, standing here watching the blinds fold shut, I can see it all.

I've never met this new girlfriend. All I know is what little I see through the sheers on these trips to drop off the boys. Mostly Miles. Yves never wants to go. He doesn't know Bright. Bright was gone before Yves was born. It hurts to talk about that part, even to myself. I focus on the girlfriend.

Miles told me that she looks like me, but shorter. In my mind I make up the rest. Mini-me, five feet two, rounder, less attractive, a little bit younger. Most likely, she has a weave. Bright must hate that. Gotta be careful not to snatch out that horsetail while doing it from behind. That's what I used to enjoy most. What I still enjoy. Him pulling my hair while taking me, gathering my ponytail into his fist, yanking my head far back enough to kiss me.

I can't stand this any longer. I turn around and start to walk away. I feel the long locks I've been growing since before Yves was born sway in rhythm with the sound of my three-and-a-half-inch heels. I can feel Bright's eyes on my ass. I switch my hips just a little more to make sure he knows that I know he's looking. I look good, at least ten years younger than forty-five. I walk steadily, flaunting the length of my legs in skinny jeans. I pretend that I'm not cold in my cropped leather jacket. I need him to see that I am still on my game, even knowing that he has someone, yet another one after the other ones. I want him to look at how balanced I am in the shoes I buy especially for these occasions.

I stopped wearing heels as soon as we started dating, to preserve his ego. He's tall enough, a respectable five feet ten. But damn, what he lacks in height, he more than makes up for in looks. He is *fine*. Really fine. I am tall for a woman, instantly taller than him in anything but ballet flats. In pumps, I can practically drink soup from the top of his head, as the Kreyòl saying goes.

Head held high, I turn around and wave with my hand to

acknowledge the blurred figure in the window. I make a tight little gesture approximating a good-bye before flipping Bright off. I laugh at how trifling I can be. I recognize the look on his face. I need him to hate me for a moment, knowing that his disdain will give way to lust, then love. And my favorite expression—regret. No matter how viciously we argue, his eyes always dissolve into remorse for what he did to wreck our marriage. I pucker my lips in a tight kiss, just for fun. He is shamelessly panting for a piece, a nice hot slice of what he is watching walk down his driveway. He is probably hard too. I am ashamed to say that, despite how wounded I am, I feel desire every time I see him.

As I drive off, I turn up the volume. My heart thumps in my chest to the music. There's a lump in my throat. I let the rhythm take me outside of myself. Although it's now inexplicably colder than when we arrived, I open the moonroof to allow the sound to split the freezing air and the ears of his white neighbors, to remind them that he is Black—truly Black. Not the genteel well-connected suit-and-tie district *attorney* (not lawyer) who waves at them as he comes and goes, opens the car door for his girlfriend, walks the dog, puts out the trash (he still hasn't found suitable help), or fetches the mail.

I rap at the top of my lungs, as if that will somehow raise the volume even more. I dance in my seat. My hand gestures fly as I let go of the steering wheel, satisfied that I've succeeded at riling him up, putting a pounding in his pants. *Damn, that bitch is going to have amazing sex tonight. But he'll have me on his mind—not her. It's never anyone but me.*

Once the house is out of sight, I exhale, turn the music down, but not off. I squeeze the steering wheel with both hands.

I don't have to glance at Miles to know that he is mad at, embarrassed by, and disappointed in my behavior. I deserve it. I made the entire encounter with Bright all about me. Somehow, I'm never able to stop myself. It's like trying to keep a slit wrist from bleeding. No matter how much gauze and pressure I apply to the wound, the red still runs, spilling over and into every exchange, staining everything and everyone. On days like today, the bandages fall away altogether. I can't stop myself, even though I know that Miles is wearing white.

~⁀~

I don't say anything to Miles. I just drive west instead of east on the highway and watch his face change into a delighted grimace, as if he knows that we are going somewhere to buy his iPhone. I figure that it's easier to get it in New Jersey than deal with the wrap-around-the-block lines in Manhattan. I turn in to the packed parking lot of the Best Buy and realize that I underestimated the Black Friday demand for cheap flat-screen TVs, next-generation video-game consoles, unnecessary new appliances, and, of course, the latest iPhone. Not an empty spot in sight.

I place my hand on Miles's in the hopes that he'll take pity on me and say, "We don't have to do this today, Mom." But he does not. He smiles as much as a morose teenager who just saw his unlikeable father and vengeful, wounded mother, can manage. I accept it. This is penance.

Before I start stalking customers who are walking back to their cars, I reach under my seat for my sneakers.

"Gotta get ready to stand in line. But first . . ."

"Parking!" Miles finishes the sentence in chorus with me.

We are car-owning Manhattanites. We have turned the hunt into a game.

Taking pity on me he says, "You can stay in the car. I'll get in line and call you when I'm close to the front." He flips his phone open to make sure it is adequately charged, then flips it closed again, harder than necessary. I get the hint. I owe him this and, even though he is being merciful, he is exacting his due. I take what I can get—his unearned compassion.

I am grateful to remain in the warm car. I can release an even bigger breath. I never want the boys, especially Miles, to hear me sigh. A sigh means that I am letting go of something worrisome, uncomfortable, painful. I have been holding back this breath since we left Bright's. Truth be told, I was holding my breath the entire time we were there. Even as I was telling him off, I was holding back the fury that usually makes me cry. But not in front of the boys. So I am thankful for Miles's mercy.

Alone, I can accept that, once again, I am buying Miles something out of guilt. I am always apologizing to my boys, trying to make things up to them, even though it has been years since the divorce. Even though I blame the end of the marriage on Bright, I feel the need to fill the void he left. But I too am responsible for the holes. So I fill them with things, cover over the shallow grooves, pat down the small mounds of sorry soil and water with tears things that will never grow.

The boys aren't old enough for me to explain how and why things fell apart, how the marriage died. Not died as much as was massacred by what Bright did and his refusal to stay and work things out. To stay and make things up to me. To stay. To stay. To stay at all. With and for me. And, if not for me (did I mention I was still pregnant with Yves at the time?), then for

Miles, who was only six. For Miles, who got his first headache after getting out of the bath to find that Bright was gone. That Bright had refused to wait. For Miles.

Miles balled himself up in my lap, still wrapped in a towel, dripping bathwater and tears as he cried himself into a headache so intense, his body trembled. That was the first time I saw him in that state. I thought he was having some sort of seizure. I prayed then that he would calm down, and for the strength to soothe him.

If only Bright had stayed for ten more minutes. Less than that—five—for Miles to get out of the tub and maybe wrap himself around his father's chest, drip tears while pointing to the gift he'd bought for Bright's birthday. If only Bright had stayed for the three of us—more than that—four of us—to fold ourselves into one another, into the family I needed us to be. Since Bright did not stay, I cry and buy tangible apologies for the boys for what I know is and is not my failure to keep our family together.

That was not the last time Bright left us behind. I took him back, not once, but twice: first before I knew that I was pregnant with Yves and second during the pregnancy. The last time Bright left, right before Yves's first birthday, I let him leave. I didn't let him *go*. I still can't. But, I made him leave. That last time.

~

There is no parking! I pull over and sit in a spot on the perimeter of the lot. It's not really a spot. It's a space where I decide to stay, hoping that some rent-a-cop in a tinfoil truck won't force me to move while I wait for Miles to call. I turn on the radio to 1010 WINS news to get the traffic report in preparation for our trip back over the George Washington Bridge into Manhattan. I wait as they finish a clip commenting on Obama's first year in office. I don't want to hear this and turn it off.

I tilt my head back on the headrest and let the tears run. Times like this, I wish that there was someone to call, but there is no one. I have distanced myself from my friends. I don't have many anyway. How can I face them when I am now the fulfillment of a stereotype? A single Black mother raising two Black boys without a father. I can't bear their pity, knowing that they are embarrassed for me, even if they are angry at Bright on my behalf. Bright and I broke the pact to always be the Clair and Heathcliff Huxtable, Black lawyer, Black doctor, beautiful Black children.

But it's worse than that for me. I have broken a promise I didn't even know I'd made, the pact made for me before I was born, the pact Ol'Lady made with Ma, and that they both made with and for me. They cursed my marriage before there even was one. I was not supposed to get married. I was never to rely on a man, to enter into and maintain a relationship with one, never to fall in love, and, if I happened to fall in love with one, I was never to allow him to know that I loved him as much or more than he loved me. I was required to maintain the advantage, to make it apparent to others that I was in control, while letting him think that he was. I was never to get caught up in the matrimonial tradition of subservience expected of Haitian women, and women the world over. I was being punished for disobeying the matriarchs. I not only fell in love and got married, I did so with a man they didn't like or liked less than other men. I was supposed to love nobody but them. Talk about a mindfuck. It would take me years to help a patient unload that kind of baggage. So there is no way I can ever cry out to my mother or grandmother, even during my worst breakdowns. I must swallow my words into my acidic stomach and try not to throw up.

I never knew any of the men my mother and grandmother had been with, including my father. Ma never spoke about "the donor," which is what she called him during the rare times she mentioned him. Ol'Lady shared bits and pieces about her own relationships, especially her marriage of convenience, through which she'd become a permanent resident and then a U.S. citizen, and then a landlord. But the primary subject of Ol'Lady's stories were generic tales of her struggles to come to and stay in America with a young child. Ol'Lady reminded me often of the only reason to be with a man—only in an emergency, only when there are no other choices.

I was scared during each pregnancy after finding out the sex of the baby. Boys both times. Would Ol'Lady and Ma accept them? They wouldn't, couldn't, love them. I would never get rid of them. That's what I told myself. I told no one, not even Bright, until I was well into my second trimester, just in case. In case I was forced to make a choice. Between my male children and the women who raised me. Because I was never sure whom I would choose. They loved the first one, Miles. But would a second boy be too much? There would be as many men as women in the family. I was afraid that they would resent the equality, even if it were just in numbers. I was afraid they would cow the boys like they tried to do to Bright. But they love the boys almost as much as I do. I could tell that they still wanted me to have a girl next, even after Bright left. They would be happy for one even now. But they would drop dead from the shock that this girl would be Bright's. *"San wont."* "Have you no shame?" But, overjoyed that there was a girl, they would forgive me.

A secret that is not a secret: all of the women in our family in Haiti have had four, five, six boys before having an only daughter. Ma and Ol'Lady lucked out and had girls first, and, not wanting to tempt fate, they stopped having children. Ma likes to say that she put her "ass on ice" after having me. Ol'Lady never tries to hide the fact that she wanted more sex, but now that she is truly an old lady, there is no hope of pleasure besides her two fingers. I never recoil at her slightly vulgar honesty. It's what I grew up with.

I pull out my cell phone to make a call to no one, and then toss it to the passenger seat. I'll just talk to myself, and if I can't say good or at least neutral things, I'll tell my mind to shut up. I'll climb into my own lap, lay my head on my own chest, wrap my arms around my body, listen to my two heartbeats, alternating thumps like one. I won't think of Miles, or Yves, or Bright. I will shut out Ma's and Ol'Lady's voices and listen to myself breathe into my tears. If I can't choke them back, I will choke on them. The end. But I need to stop this meltdown long enough to get through this afternoon with Miles, who will only be momentarily comforted by his new device.

My New Yorker parking instincts tell me that a spot is about to open up. I wipe my eyes, so I can see. I hustle to get to a couple walking to their car. I am on them before they even open their car doors. Just as I pull into the spot, Miles calls.

"I'm coming right now." I pull the key out of the ignition.

Five hundred dollars later, with an even colder wind blowing in my face, I run with Miles across the sprawling parking lot back to the car.

I place my cold hand on his and keep it there the entire ride back to Manhattan. I always do this. I have a need to confirm that he is there, and I know that he needs reassurance too. We are both still haunted by Bright's desertion.

Before Miles was old enough to sit in the front seat, I would frighten myself by reaching for Bright's hand, which was no longer there. It is the same when I am in the car alone without the boys. I always feel their presence. The psychiatrist in me tells me that this is only normal. PTSD can persist for an entire lifetime. I also think that I am still carrying the burden of two of my patients, a couple who attempted suicide after both of them forgot to take their sleeping baby out of the backseat of their car in the middle of winter, believing that they'd already dropped her off at the sitter's. I never stop feeling that one or both of the boys are in the car with me when they're clearly not. I am haunted by my living children.

I pull up in front of the building Ma and Ol'Lady have owned since forever. They had it before I was born. It was Ol'Lady's first and then at some point she put Ma's name on the deed. They have been waiting to make sure I will never go back to Bright before adding my name too.

I try to let go of Miles's hand and he squeezes tightly before releasing me.

"You can go upstairs. I'll come up when I find parking," I tell him and unlock the doors. "Tell Ma and Ol'Lady I'll be there in a minute."

"Nah. You can go, Mom. I'm gonna hang out here for a while. Yves and I will walk home."

"You sure? You have your keys?"

"Wallet and ID too." Miles closes the door gently. He

finally listens. I have told him a million times that he slams the door like he's trying to take it off its hinges.

I watch as he climbs the few steps. I hear the door buzzer letting him into the renovated building that will be part of my inheritance. I dial the landline that Ma and Ol'Lady insist on maintaining.

"Miles is on his way up. No, I'm not coming. I can't find a spot," I lie.

I look to see if Ol'Lady comes to the window to assess the state of parking on Amsterdam Avenue. The building always amazes me—a renovated former tenement, a building that had been restored long before I was born, an elegant, pre-war six-story that merits but is too small for a doorman. Ol'Lady lives in the one-bedroom on the very bottom floor, with Ma right above her, although they really live together. Ol'Lady is almost always upstairs, which is where she lived first. She only gave it up when Ma had me and therefore needed the two bedrooms.

I know only bits and pieces about how Ol'Lady ended up owning a building on Amsterdam between 105th and 106th on Manhattan's fully gentrified Upper West Side. Just what she told me, which was quite a lot for a little girl, even a teenager. But this was all part of the education, or should I say indoctrination, into the cult of womanhood. I still marvel at what must have happened for a young Haitian immigrant, a Black woman, to own anything in the 1960s, let alone Manhattan real estate so close to an Ivy League university. Sometimes I can't distinguish between what Ol'Lady actually told me and what I imagined and then repeated to myself over the years. But I know the truth, even if it is made up.

I see a young Ol'Lady holding a wet washcloth, rolling a bar of soap that is nearly the same color as the thigh of the old man she is bathing. He is pale and his skin holds no hint of the race he long ago denied to acquire and hold on to wealth. He doesn't actually deny his race. He merely fails to correct the people who assume he is white, the way I don't correct people who mispronounce my name. By the time she comes to work for him, the old man looks even whiter, with thinning hair revealing a pallid pink and freckled scalp. Ol'Lady knows his secret. She knew men like him back in Haiti, half-castes claiming that they were pure French, as if there is such a thing as "pure" anything in the Americas. Ola—she is still going by her given name at the time—lets the old man believe that he has pulled the wool over her eyes along with everyone else's. She plays the fool while her gentle but unrefined hands and just-come-immigrant eager-for-work mannerisms soothe him.

She lets him soak and then rolls the washcloth over his wrinkles until he is overwhelmed by the thrilling shadow pleasure running down and through his two missing legs, which were amputated decades ago. Ola does not recoil the first time he guides her hand to the still functional bulge between his stumps. Hers are the tender brown hands of an understanding arrivant from Haiti, playing at the pleasure of fondling the stiffening swell of an old man. Ol'Man, as she calls him once she learns enough television English, is grateful for Ola's newly refined fine fingers and what he perceives is her desperation. She makes the best of her situation as an immigrant with no papers and a girl child to raise. Ola accepts his renaming her, a woman of twenty or so, "my old lady," which she understands means wife. She makes herself comfortable with the knowledge that he wants to possess her like the properties he owns from the Upper West Side to Harlem. Ol'Lady strokes him to release until he marries her, changes her last name too, sponsors her green card, then wills her one of the buildings he owns.

I understand why Ol'Lady believes that men want possession of, not relationships with, women and that marriage is, at its best, a chance for two self-serving individuals to use each other to achieve their own ends. At least Ol'Lady has some frame of reference with a modicum of a strange truth for how marriages play out in the world. Ma doesn't even have that. All she told me and still tells me is that she fucked only married men because she wanted to have a baby without the threat of a man trying to possess either her or her girl child. Married men understand that sex is just that and have too much to lose to try to claim illegitimate children by immigrant nurses.

I think about parking and going to see Ma and Ol'Lady. They would take care of me. Without acknowledging my hurt, they would press down on my wounds, tell me to put my big-girl panties on, to tie my head-tie tightly, and keep it moving. I could never cry in front of them. I didn't need to. They knew, even if they didn't want to admit, let alone talk about, how men had taken advantage of them.

I lift my head off of the steering wheel where I've been resting it and stare at my reflection in the passenger-side window. My eyes have already begun to swell with water waiting to fall. As I drive west to my apartment on Riverside Drive, I can barely see the stoplights, pedestrians, or other cars through the gauzy curtains of my tears. It is a miracle I find parking in my condition, let alone a coveted spot a few steps from my building.

I turn off the ignition and compose myself so the doorman won't see me crying—again—like he has witnessed so many times before, during, and after the divorce. My sneakers allow me to run without stopping, through the door held open for me, across the marble floors, straight to the elevator. I press the wrong button, then quickly remember that I am going to the apartment, not my office, which is in this same building. I am so thankful to have the elevator to myself so I can sob without the discomforting, pitying stares of neighbors. I just want to get into the apartment and into bed.

I let the door slam behind me. I stop at the entryway to the kitchen and kick my sneakers off. (*Damn! I left my shoes in the car.*) I smile a little, tears still streaming down my face. I do not look in the mirror. I'm remembering how Bright stared at me coming and going this afternoon. He called me "Jenny," which he knows I hate more than any of the other versions of my name. In college, med school, at the hospital, everyone always uses the English pronunciation of my name instead of the French, which ties their tongues into knots. But I tolerate that because the butchering of my proper name is even worse. I'd never let anyone call me Jenny, except Bright back in the day. Jenny is what he always called me during sex early on in our relationship. Five years dating, and engaged from senior year of undergrad through med school. Then married before my residency because, uh-oh, Miles was coming cuz Bright had cum. Ha, ha! Laugh to keep from . . .

Crying because I have hurt Miles, kept my true love for him from him, tucked it away to fill the hollow parts of me.

I feel my mind tipping. I am on the verge of the loud, ugly bawling that always scares me. The kind that makes me think of my patients, not the ones who come to my private office.

No, not them. The ones in the hospital whom I am called to see at two in the morning. The ones who made their final attempt, and having failed, entered the dark pit out of which they might never climb. The ones too far gone to even whimper, to know anymore that there was something they should be crying about, down too deep to recognize their pain because they have become their pain. The ones who didn't even feel the bleeding that would never stop, the leak that would never kill them.

To prevent my infinite sinking into the abyss, I wipe my runny nose on the sleeve of my leather jacket. (I hope I haven't ruined it.) I throw it on the couch, where it lands heavily like an obese cat. I unravel my scarf as I make my way to the bedroom. I don't bother taking off anything else and climb into bed. My merciless body resists the sleep I need. My body wants Bright, is what I tell myself. I am the one who needs him. It is too soon since our last time. Although I want to have him more often, I don't want to deceive him or myself that we could ever be together again. I just want to indulge in the temporary fantasy that we could be. I don't want him to think that our fucking is lovemaking. I simply want familiar sex that does not require the learning of someone else's body or desires, or the teaching of my preferences.

I pull my jeans and underwear down over my knees and reach into the nightstand for comfort. The vibrator sputters and then dies.

I fall asleep with my hands folded between my inner thighs.

2

There must have been tears, so many, too many,
and never enough for a boy
Yes, there must have been a boy

I wake up from a tiring nap in time for the start of our decent into Toussaint Louverture International Airport. Haitians leave out the *International* part. No one comes here on vacation except Haitians, not since the seventies. It isn't even a layover to anywhere else. It is a place people want to escape from, not pass through, let alone stay. Except for those who "just want to help." Begrudged do-gooders, who take and leave behind. They condescend, objectify, give hand-me-down handouts the people are too poor to turn down but too proud to take home. They earn their missionary wings, Greenpeace designations, peacekeeper pats on the back, to assuage their imperialist guilt. They study for scholar credits, dig wells, plant saplings, give lectures to struggling farmers about sustainability, and do their parts saving the environment.

I hold back tears as the airplane breaks through the clouds turbulently. I am grieving. For what? My poor country, which I am powerless to help beyond regular remittances to my cousin? No. It's because I've had to bring Miles here to let him know that it is okay to let go, to let the tears flow. That it's okay to fall, because I am and always will be here to catch him. Have I told him? Explicitly? That it's okay to cry? Does he know? Does he know? Does he know? Should I tell? Should I tell? Should I tell?

I try not to choke up, so I can say the words: *If you hold it all inside, you will explode, in the worst ways. Your grief will bubble over, manifest itself dangerously. You will hurt yourself beyond how it hurts to cry.* I know. I know. I know. But does he? I can't say. A word. To my own son. Because I am mourning the worst, which has not even happened yet.

I turn my head toward him and stare at his profile, which is backlit by the sunlight sliding along the airplane's wing through the window. Miles sits up a little straighter, not because his seatback is now upright in preparation for landing, but to lean forward to listen to the flight attendant reciting the landing monologue in French, Kreyòl, and then English, in that order. I wonder how much he understands of the Kreyòl beyond what he is able to decipher based on the French that comes before and the English that comes after. Ma, Ol'Lady, and I tried to teach him our native tongue, to no avail. It was impossible with Bright, a unilingual anglophile, in the household. Miles had what we all consider the misfortune of Bright's presence in our home for over five years, which necessitated speaking English so "Dad won't feel left out." Yves has a better chance of mastering Kreyòl since he has spent most of his time with Ma and Ol'Lady since birth, absent Bright. They speak only Kreyòl to him, to both boys.

The sun lights up Miles's eyes, which glow like glass almonds. The centipede sideburns crawling toward his squar-

ing jawline make him look so much like Bright. I neither love
nor hate the resemblance. I adore his emerging smile as we
descend toward Haitian soil. I look at him for so long that
he turns to face me directly. He doesn't ask me why I'm staring so hard, but my serious face reinforces the fact that this is
not supposed to be a fun trip. It is for us to get to know each
other again and teach him not to take things for granted, to be
grateful for the kind of life he lives. And, although I can't say
this to him, it is to save his life and mine, because if he dies, I
will too.

The lectures I heaped upon him back home in New York
are undermined by the gold and silver sand framing the bejew-
eled blue-green ocean below. Does he know? Does he know?
Does he know? That I am pulled under by a riptide, released
on this exquisite shore that is home and not home.

I wish that he could see and appreciate the dry hills dot-
ted, not covered, with greenery. The ailing alopecia mounds
mean nothing to him now, but he will soon learn what happens when soil has no roots to hold it in place.

I continue focusing on his face with a maternal gaze that
does not reveal my awe of his innocence, naïveté, and purity.
Mine is a stare of unconcealable and inconsolable worry over
what might happen to him back home in New York, if this trip
fails to make him cry. He used to all the time after Bright left,
before Yves was born. And then Yves arrived, and everything
seemed to change. There was joy. There still is. But Yves was
here. And Miles felt that he had to be strong because "I'm not
a baby—only babies cry" and "I am the man of the house,"
until adolescence dragged the baggage of hormones and mood
swings and a sadness that makes him sleep far more than even
a teenage boy should. Not wanting to wake up early (as is nor-

mal) but not even staying up late. I still wake up before dawn to check on him. He is always down, snoring, not crying into his pillow, not releasing in any way that one might expect, that I am hoping. He only woke up once in the middle of the night and that almost got him killed.

I had to scold him, but it was pointless. It always is. My hand-wringing reprimands have failed to penetrate his adolescent façade of boyhood bravado, indifference, and insolence. So, we are here—almost. A trip to heartbreak that I hope breaks him like something that won't bend. I'm still upset over his near expulsion from school back in October after getting caught in the school stairwell holding a friend's flask. But I am grateful for the two-week deferred suspension "to commence after, not concurrent with, the winter holiday," like a jail sentence. I accept the extended time off that has stretched his holiday break into January so we can make this sojourn.

I am no longer angry at him even though he has been suspended for it. And he did something so much worse after that—that thing that could have gotten him killed.

no dreadlocks no cornrows no twists no willful 'fros no
wild hair of any sort no beards mustaches sideburns no
facial hair nothing that makes you look like a grown
man no ripped jeans no sagging pants no big belt buckles
designer or otherwise no ball caps no hoodies no do-rags
no bandannas no skullies no head gear to hide a perfectly
neat nicely trimmed haircut no tattoos visible or hidden
no earrings diamond or cz no piercings no body mods
at all ever no chains gold silver real or fake no Jesus-
pieces no nameplates Cuban links no rings bracelets
anklets no jewelry flashy or not no kerchiefs no blue no

red no black nothing that looks like blood oxygenated
or not coagulated spilled or dried no colored clothing
that could be mistaken for gang affiliation no high-tops
Timbs fat laces Jordans no sneakers no boots no footwear
that changes your walk no hard walking never ever run
never a toy gun not even a thumb and pointer pointed
simulation no cell phone no wallet no umbrellas short or
long no cane or crutches nothing that could be mistaken
for a weapon no polished shoes no ties no crisp shirt no
suit that might signal wealth earned or stolen nothing
that might imply you-think-you're-better-than . . .

I didn't think I would have something so big to be thankful for on Thanksgiving. I was too busy relishing the fall.
I noticed the leaves turning before I saw him. He had been
changing right in front of me and I had missed it. I blamed
the changing seasons for their moodiness, for making me miss
what was going on inside my home, inside my child. I blamed
the trees, not my blindness, not my denial, not my dismissive-
ness of Miles's disposition, which had gone from adolescent
angst to full-blown depression. I saw the rain pinging off the
maples in the park across the street before I noticed how he
bowed his head, hiding tears. I had forgotten to take his face
in my hands, to lift his chin, to look in his eyes, to wipe his
face. I should have known that the rushed "I love yous" on
the way out the door were not enough. I let careless "What's
ups?" and "How did it gos?" pass for interest in his day, in his
life. I wanted to know. Honest, I did. But the fall, the early fall,
with its peridot turning to topaz, its morning chill, its crystal
dew on browning grass, got all of my attention and I didn't

realize that Miles's smiles were accompanied by no gleaming eyes. There was love but rarely any laughter from him, even for Yves, who had been able to bring his brother's berating chuckles out during competitive gaming.

I blame myself for missing his voice deepening one more octave, his beard coming in curly on his chin in an untrimmed goatee. Truth be told, I hadn't been looking at the trees. I had been looking at myself.

I had been standing at my full-length mirror, making sure that I was still me. That I was still attractive enough, desirable enough. That I hadn't been the reason for Bright's affairs. I saw his infidelity, but it was only one woman in a wax-and-wane pattern, like the warming and cooling of autumn air. He only wanted me in the fall and winter, when I could warm his bones spooning on lazy Sundays, nurturing but not romantic. He was home more because of the cold, which is why I'd been lost in the cool air, loosening leaves that floated to the ground like burning scraps of paper in a fireplace.

The first call from school came while I had been staring at my figure, catching a glimpse of the bag I'd been packing for one of my seasonal trysts with Bright. Rendezvous twice, maybe three times, no more than five times a year, depending on the timing of the overnight. If the liaison was New Year's Eve, I counted it as part of the following year.

I didn't blame Bright in my heart, although I'd told him that everything was his fault. Miles's drinking. (Even in my inattentiveness, I didn't believe that he'd just been "holding" the flask for a friend.) The gum, mouthwash, lip balm, the condoms. Had I left these things in my designer duffle? Had they fallen out when I came home smelling of hotel soap and sex? They couldn't be Miles's. Of course not. Of course not. That's what I told myself while I watched flames fall from wet branches through the window on a cozy weekend morning. I was thinking about Bright's arm flung over my waist. His heat and hardness against my body. The citrus and sandalwood from our shower together at the hotel the night before and the scent of tender things.

I blamed everything on the leaves, on Bright, on the almost frosty breeze, the autumn rain. I missed it all until my car keys went missing. Then I had to call Bright for something other than sex, and I hated that. I hated him except when I loved him in high-end hotel rooms on the East Side of Manhattan.

I checked Miles's room and his phone was nowhere to be found, which wasn't a bad thing. At least I could call him, which I did. There was no answer the first time, so I called again. I kept on until he picked up.

The cops let Miles answer my call as long as his hands remained visible.

"Mom?" His voice cracked on speaker.

They took the phone from him before he could say anything else.

"Ma'am? We're going to bring him home, but the car will be impounded."

"May I please speak to my son?"

"He'll be home soon enough. About the other boys . . ."

"I'll call their parents, if you tell me who they are." I glance at the school's phone list that I keep on the refrigerator door.

"We couldn't reach them," the cop explains. "The other boys can call their people from the station."

Their "people"? As if saying "their moms and dads" would have been too humanizing. At least they'd said "people" and not something else. At least the boys were alive.

"Can you go and see what you can do, Bright? I'll get their parents and they'll meet you." As a U.S. District Attorney, Bright has connections from federal to local politicians, from the State Department to the mayor's office, which is why the cops brought Miles home.

"I'm not going anywhere. Miles needs both of us now," Bright insisted.

I rolled my eyes. The whites had turned red.

The officers brought Miles home in zip-tie handcuffs and a sweater over his clasped hands to save us some embarrassment.

Although I didn't want to leave Miles alone in the apartment with Bright, I rode the elevator down with the officers. I watched as they left, ignoring the questioning curiosity of the doorman and a faceless neighbor. I stood in the lobby looking through the glass doors. All of the leaves looked black in the pre-dawn darkness. Only my reflection stared back at me. I questioned the woman I saw, asking her things she should have known. She wiped my tears with a trembling hand. I finally recognized her.

It was me. It was only me.

No friends with dreadlocks who wear sagging pants, do-rags, piercings, high-tops, who walk hard, whose people have not taught them hands on the dash, do not run, drive, smoke, smile or mean-mug, whisper or scream, don't move, do not fucking move, hands where I can see them. No friends, no friends. Please no friends.

There is no point bringing it up at all or ever again since the argument is the same as always—his friends got him in trouble. It's always the same exchange. I never want to argue with him. I know that I am to blame. But I have to say something.

"It's always them—your friends. You need different friends, Miles!"

"What do you know about friends, Mom? You don't have *any*! Not one. You just want me to be lonely like you."

Should I tell him, again, that I do not want him to be friendless like I am? That I wouldn't wish my lonely on anyone.

"You think those boys are your friends? Friends don't leave you to take the blame for everything. You have no idea how lucky you were. In the Bronx at two in the morning? You don't even have your permit yet. What were you thinking? Drinking *and* smoking? And you never cleaned my car, by the way!"

I quickly shut out the part of me that wishes he'd been punched once. Just once. But I wanted him punished, not murdered. The police would have never stopped at one blow. They would have taken turns beating him up, stopping only to thrash the other boys with him. Four Black boys choking on weed, the private-school children of well-off parents. What pissed me off more than Miles's foolishness was that I had to call Bright in the middle of the night and listen to him blast me for being a bad parent.

"I had to call your father! Do you know how that felt? I had to listen to *him* criticize *me*! Do you have any idea? I'm about to lose my mind worrying about you with my car keys missing. And then I had to fucking call him!"

"It's always about you, Mom."

"Don't you dare." I clenched my teeth, unable to calm myself down. I screamed, "It is never about me! Not one day since you and your brother came into this world. And I wouldn't have it any other way. I just need you to think." I wanted to poke him on the forehead. "Just think about the consequences for all of us if something had happened to you. Yves would have died. I would have died along with him. Ma! Ol'Lady! Straight to the grave without a pit stop at the hospital."

"You don't really care. If you did, you wouldn't spend so much time trying to show off in front of Dad. How am I supposed to feel when you still want the attention of the person who has hurt me the most?"

I was in shock. I was breathing hard, the air freezing inside me. There was nothing I could say. I didn't want to go cold on him. I wanted to remain warm and open and soothing, so he wouldn't run away and disappear into himself. He had to know. I had to tell him. *None of it matters. Nothing else matters. What's important is that you're home. You're here. You're still here. And so am I. Always.*

Even now, remembering what he did arouses my anger. I calm myself and my anger falls away like melting icicles on a string of electrical pole wires. It becomes a puddle around my feet, a pool around my ankles, a pond, a river, a lake, an ocean, a riptide rolling over me, dragging me down, down, down. I am charged with keeping him alive, but I need to be rescued from the warming water inside and around me pulling me down, down, down. I am failing at the one job that I can't fuck up. I don't know how to keep him safe from the sharks on the outside ready to rip into him, or from the hurt of feeling less loved. I want to save his life and teach him how to save himself, the boy on the inside who wants to die. This is too much. For one person. For one child loved more than anyone has ever been loved. For one parent who needs help to come quickly. I will keep asking Ma. And Ol'Lady. I will keep asking them for help, so no one has to die.

I am just as worried now as I was then. Even in the air, the water is rising. I have to keep it in. I have to push it down, lest I drown inside myself. I look over at Miles and I wonder, *Does he know, does he know, does he know? That he gets it from me?*

As the plane floats lower and lower, I look away from him and out the window. I am absorbing the things I have not seen in years. I will explain the sites to Miles later, maybe on the drive to La Tranblè. I can't tell him now, but I can explain away the trembling of my bottom lip with the excuse that going home makes me emotional. I can tell him, if he asks, but he won't.

He turns toward the window because he doesn't want to look at me. He doesn't want to argue but he still whines, "Why can't we stay at a hotel? I don't want to stay with people I don't know."

"I've told you that this is not a vacation." I need him to see how good he's got it. I have always validated his feelings about the divorce but he needs to understand that things could be a lot worse. "You'll see what I've been telling you all along about how other children your age live. How much of the world lives. You are privileged—spoiled, even. You have choices."

"I have to make better choices," he says, mocking me.

I don't react. "You'll like my cousin Mimi."

"Is she your real cousin or just someone else I have to call 'Auntie'?"

"She's not blood but she might as well be. She's nice. Different," whatever that means. "Mimi is fierce. She runs the plantain grove, manages everything, including the men who hate being told what to do by a woman." I pause and take a breath. "I'm not sure what you'll make of my real cousin Ateya. She likes to think that she's the boss of everyone, including Mimi. For better or for worse, Ateya will give you a real taste of Haiti. And Ti'Louse, you've seen her in pictures. The little girl—"

"You never had . . . I know." He rolls his eyes not because he's jealous but because I am being repetitive.

"You'll see."

"Will I see all of my sneakers you keep giving away?"

"Seriously?" I raise my voice enough for him to hear my irritation but not enough to make any of the passengers turn around. Softer, I say, "I've told you about Ateya and the suitcase. How we tried to get her on the plane to New York." He doesn't even pretend to be listening. "Children's antics. If I hadn't gotten in with her, we might have had a chance," I say, smiling. "I'm talking to you, Miles." I poke him gently on the shoulder. He ignores me.

I'll tell him later when we get to the village. For now, I talk to myself, remembering.

"Get in there," I whispered to Ateya.

"How are you going to carry this with me in it?"

"You're right. Let's put it in the back of the car first, and then you get in."

"They're going to know."

"How are they going to know?"

"I just know. They're going to know."

"You're just scared."

"No, I'm not."

"Okay, then stop saying they're going to know. I think we should use the bigger suitcase. It's a nicer color too. Blue instead of that ugly brown," I added.

"Who cares about the color? I'm going to be inside."

"Let's go."

We put the empty suitcase on the folded-down third-row seat of the station wagon. Ateya unzipped it and flattened the already densely packed carabella fabric. She left a few layers for me to cover her with before I zipped it up.

"Wait. We forgot snacks. And water."

"I can't eat in here. I'll dirty the fabric."

"Ma won't care about the fabric once she sees you in New York."

"What if the zipper breaks on the way?"

"You sound scared. I think I should get in there with you."

"No. I keep telling you, I'm not scared. The suitcase will be too heavy if we're both in here."

"But I want to be with you. Isn't that the whole point of this? So we can be together."

"They're going to know."

"No one's going to know."

"I'm older than you and I know things about grown-ups that you don't."

We always had the same argument about age. A two-and-a-half-year difference seems like so much more when you're five and nearly eight.

"You might be older. But I'm smarter. I've been in school since I was born."

I could feel her rolling her eyes.

"Fine. Get in."

"I knew you wanted company."

"I want to go to America. I want to live with you and Tati Yanique."

"Remember, it's cold there. We won't be able to play outside all the time."

"Snow. My mother talks about it all the time: 'You can't get me to go live in that ice for all the money over there.' She talks as if she has seen it."

I imagined that the suitcase would be brought with us into the plane's cabin, somewhere in the back. I could sneak bags of peanuts and a can of Sunkist to her. The thought of suitcases being flung roughly, carelessly into a dark baggage hold never entered my mind. I never thought about where suitcases disappeared to. I would have tried to figure out a way to make sure the bag was handled carefully. I would have misspelled "fragile" on a wide piece of tape and stuck it on.

"There's already a bed for you, on top of mine."

"You told me."

"You think you know everything." I started a whispered quibble.

"Be quiet."

She never even called our names. She didn't even look for us. Ma just unzipped the suitcase.

"Get out of there. Both of you." Ma was on the verge of

tears. She did not let on that she was relieved that she had found us in the suitcase and not Ateya's mother, who would have whipped her with the always-handy *igwaz*.

～⁀～

Miles is cranky now. "I just don't want to stay with those people. They might not be strangers to you, but they are to me."

"Ateya would not be a stranger to you if I'd sent you to Haiti for the summers like Ma and Ol'Lady sent me. Actually, Ateya should have been with us in New York. Ma begged for that. But Ateya's mother wouldn't let her. I would have had a companion, since you always remind me that I have no friends."

"Hotel?" he says snidely.

"Anyway, we won't be spending much time in the village. And as little time with Ateya as possible. We'll mostly be out and about in the capital with Mimi." I start to point out what looks like a miniature statue down below but I stop. I don't want him to see things from afar where they look small, unimpressive. "You'll see" is the last thing I say to him until the plane comes to a full stop on the tarmac. I tour the city with my eyes, and I feel tiny by comparison—with my pocket-size pain and the short history of my little life.

3

There must have been women
in the before and the now
bound by blood and better than blood
carrying heavy truths like parcels
they dare not lay down

I am ashamed to say that I don't know much of Haiti's history. I don't even know my own son, so why would I know about my country? I don't have enough knowledge to be able to school racist critics or convey to my children in a meaningful way. I know Toussaint Louverture, Jean-Jacques Dessalines, Henri Christophe. I have heard the name Défilée but I'm not sure where she—the only woman—fits in. I recall Pétion only because the town of Pétionville is home to the elite and affluent of the greater Port-au-Prince area. Between Pétion and François Duvalier is a blank. I don't even know who was president, or king, or whatever, during the Dajabón massacre. I only know Trujillo. I know about Haiti's repeated occupation by America. After Duvalier *père* and Duvalier *fis*, I know Aristide, then Préval, sort of, then Aristide again. In between Aristide's three stints, I know little to nothing, even though I have been traveling here every year except the years Miles and Yves were born. I know about travel-prohibitive circumstances that delayed my and Ma's visits—embargoes, antigovernment protests turned into tires-on-fire riots, military coups, hurricanes, mudslides, tornadoes, and whatever else Ma and Ol'Lady discuss or what makes CNN, BBC, or *The New York Times.*

I know American and European, even Asian history better than my own. I am American despite myself and Ma's and Ol'Lady's efforts. It is clearly not enough to send one's foreign-born progeny to one's homeland. There must be focused and dedicated inculcation that depends on one's own education. What Ol'Lady knows but never tutored me in, the blank bits between the massacre and François Duvalier. Maybe it is all a blur for her too, since everyone died in office (assassinated, committed suicide, executed), was overthrown, or rendered powerless by the American government. They are all the same leader, just in different bodies. It is all the same history repeated again and again. Ol'Lady is not one for redundancy.

Another reason for this trip—I want Miles to know more than I did, more than I do. Every time I visit Haiti, just as we're about to land, I look out of the window at the elegant bronze statue of Neg Mawon. It is no different now. I am still taken by the Maroon, who takes a knee with his head tilted backward as he sounds the battle cry through the conch shell raised to his lips. I almost hear him calling me, calling me toward him, calling me forward to fight beside him. He is a reminder of Haiti's history of rebellion, of Maroons descending from the mountains to war against colonizers and slavers. The statue testifies on behalf of the self-liberated people fighting alongside uniformed soldiers with swords and enslaved men and women wielding weapons from their work in the soil.

I turn my attention to the Palais National, less of a palace, more of a plantation house, a rickety replica of America's White House. It is a place of trickery, fraud, and falsehood that makes a mockery of the Maroon kneeling directly across the road from it. The Maroon would never bow down to anything white. If only he, they, were here now.

My eyes reel in tears as the passengers applaud the safe landing. The flight attendant launches into another monologue that falls on deaf ears as seat belts click and chatter rises. Miles unbuckles his seat belt prematurely and I tug at his shirt to keep him from standing up. This is less for his safety and more to keep him from blocking my view of tall, wild grass, struggling sugarcane, and plantain trees involuntarily stretching drying green fingers upward. The tough, defiantly growing brush that rings the fenced-in tarmac is a stronger barrier than the failing chain link, whose barbed wire has long lost the bite of its rusting cats' teeth.

"Let them all get out first," I say to Miles without looking at him. I still want to see outside, where ripples of invisible hundred-degree heat move with the sunlight. I want to wave to the warmth, although I know it will be cruel. I want to return the greeting of the grass and the banana leaves waving their welcome in the artificial breeze produced by the plane's whispering engines.

I remain silent while gathering the things strewn about me—my deflated neck pillow, pointless airline magazine, a book I didn't even try to read, and guilt-inducing snack wrappers. Miles only has his earbuds and phone to put away. I know that he has packed his notebook but he won't write or draw in my presence. This trip will give him a lot to fill his pages.

I hurry up a bit because Miles is becoming impatient. I get up and exit our row just as the last passenger wheels a suitcase so tiny it could have been a child's. Miles grabs our bags from the overhead bin and drops my rolling case at my feet. I am not expecting him to speak, especially not as he glides through the aisle and floats down the wobbly staircase to the dusty tarred ground. Although I am wearing sneakers, I steady myself as I climb down the flimsy metal slope that passes for stairs. On the last one, I land myself slowly and softly, as if the earth might give way beneath me if I step too quickly or too hard.

Miles is far ahead of me, racing toward the flat-roofed building where he assumes there will be American-grade air-conditioning. I look forward to his shock at the frail fan-blown breeze inside the terminal. Should I tell him? Should I tell him? Should I tell him?

When I catch up with him, he looks at me but does not speak. Having gotten his first taste of Haiti, he is wondering if he will survive this trip.

I trail behind him, not because I can't keep up. I want to watch him discover. First, the immigration line that he can't zip through because he is the foreigner here. His passport garners envy but not privilege. With a dark-brown hand whose palm is almost the color as its back, the immigration officer gestures for us to come forward. He takes our passports and landing cards. He looks up, clearly surprised by where we are staying, not in Port-au-Prince, not at a hotel, but in La Tranblè, barely a village and more a string of struggling hovels, in the town of Croix-des-Bouquets, on the outskirts of the city. He smiles cynically as if he knows that the very American teenage boy before him is in for the shock of his life, that Miles will ask to turn right back around and go home before we even reach our destination.

The officer looks down again and examines my passport as though this is the first time he has ever seen one. He flips through the pages, I assume to see where I've traveled. It is arrogant of me, but I assume that he wants one—an American passport. A passport to everywhere, anywhere. No visa required by most countries. I assume that, despite his status, gatekeeper to his homeland, he longs to leave, to see that place *lòt bò an,* over there.

After working at the airport, he would never dare travel in a tiny, overcrowded motorboat illegally ferrying people who look like him and manned by someone who could be him. He would want a fresh paper ticket, the kind that "those ungrateful Americans" wrinkle and then attempt to smooth out when they get to the front of the line. I assume, perhaps wrongly so, that at times he is inclined to turn them away, send them back to America, deport them, have officers escort them— strong hands gripping straining arms, dragging them to the plane, dumping them inside, slamming the door shut. Even someone like me, who speaks Kreyòl with no accent. With natural hair, dressed unassumingly—leggings, a T-shirt, dusty sneakers. Maybe he is mad that I didn't dress up, that I don't think his home worthy enough to warrant a dress, not a new one, a decent pair of shoes, a little scuffed, worn three or four times, a little gold necklace, matching earrings. He must think worse of Miles. One earbud in and another out as if the officer's words, words the boy likely can't understand, are only halfway worth listening to. Perhaps Miles's height is even more of an insult—a teenager, six feet two, broad shoulders, well fed, skin on the lighter side, proof that he has never worked in the sun, fingernails more pristine than any girl's, proof that he has never worked at all.

I attempt to ingratiate myself to the officer. *"Merci,* Papi," I say, and he smiles a little. I have acknowledged his seniority, allowed him some dignity, shown him the requisite deference. He hands me both passports. I say good-bye with a gesture that is almost a curtsy.

Miles looks at me and shakes his head at my obsequiousness, something he has only seen me do in front of white people—the headmaster at his school when he was caught with the flask, the police officer who brought him home a few weeks later. And, that same night, to Bright, who rushed over, stood in the foyer of the apartment, and scolded us both, mother and son, for acting up, acting out. I was barefoot, not even in slippers, so Bright was taller even without his authoritarian stance. My posture said, "Pardon, Papi." I almost cried. Miles almost apologized to me but held back until after Bright and the police left. That was the night I decided that this trip was necessary.

Miles stands up straighter, as if compensating for my bowed stance. He wants to run away from this scene and sprints ahead of me again as if he knows where he's going. The luggage belt in the baggage area is broken, and two men are swinging suitcases that are piling up on the floor. Our luggage is easily identifiable, a matching set of three new but cheap red bags, no little ribbons tied to the handles, no shrink wrap holding contents in tightly like shapewear around a thick woman's waist. Miles looks around for a trolley and finds that they are all taken by short, skinny, elderly-looking porters, who are stronger than they appear. Just the look on our faces when we spot our bags and two of the men compete for the promise of a generous greenback tip.

I spot Mimi in the crowd outside of the terminal and wave. The porter leaves Miles and me to trail him, quickly following Mimi to the truck.

I hand the porter ten dollars after he loads the bags into the pickup. The gratuities are always best when passengers arrive, USD in hand. Departure bills are in *goud*, left over from their vacations.

"*Merci*, Papi," I say. This time, I do not nod. I am not asking for service; I am paying for it.

I wait for him to leave. With our bags secure, I hug Mimi. "Mimi? *Chéri?*" I hold her for a long time. Out of the corner of my eye, I see how uncomfortable Miles is. The armpit of his crisp white tee is wet and the outline of matching, equally new Airforce 1's are already coated in saffron dust. I grab his hand and pull him into the hug.

Mimi rushes us into the truck before we are swarmed by the extended hands of wheelchair-bound amputees with their handlers, diminutive, underfed adolescents who would rather beg than steal, although they have likely stolen during the bad times, when hurricanes or coups have kept even Haitian *dyaspora* returnees away. Mimi rolls up the windows that she kept down so as not to waste precious petrol on air-conditioning for herself. She can see that Miles is melting.

"There's water," Mimi says to Miles in English, to show that she knows enough English to carry on a decent conversation with him. Then to me she says, "You see how nice the truck still looks?" She looks around, then strokes the leather seats that are still slick from the excess Armor All.

"I noticed even outside." She clearly washed the truck this

morning. The wet tires turned the road dirt into a light muddy film that has formed on the hubcaps.

"You-know-who chastised me . . ." Mimi rolls her eyes.

"You can say her name. He's not even listening."

"As if I wouldn't wash the truck before picking you up . . ."

"I can only imagine what she must have put poor Ti'Louse through. Ateya must have been at her worst, or is it at her best, ordering my little girl around to prepare for our arrival." I say "my" as if my words have the power to grant my wish.

"No worse than usual, which is to say terrible. She's still beating Ti'Louse," Mimi confirms. "I intervene when I'm around. I can't always be there. Maybe when she grows up . . . She's just nine but eventually nine will turn into nineteen and who will Ateya slap around then? Hopefully, Ti'Louse won't even be here at all."

I can see Miles is still holding his breath as we make our way through the crowd of disappointed hands that leave fingerprints on the pristine glass. He isn't used to the smell that I love—mildly acidic, tinged with smoking charcoal burning in from futile attempts to cover over the odor of wet gully trash. He downs a bottle of water without pause. He has no words, not even "Thank you."

"*Mal élvé!*" I shout at him for being rude.

"*Merci,*" he suddenly remembers to say.

Mimi smiles a genuinely generous smile. She is elated, which makes her already high-pitched voice whistle. She keeps her eyes fixed on the cars in front and around us as drivers nose their way into crowded intersections with nonfunctioning traffic lights. Mimi holds the truck's steering wheel tight. She wants to show me how much she values the truck I shipped to Haiti right after Yves was born, nearly nine years ago. It looks newer now than it looked back then. In New York the decade-old truck appeared decrepit compared to sleek new models that seemed to float on tar-tamed roads.

"There are patties too," Mimi says without even a glance at me. She must stay focused, lest she lose her place in the tussle homeward or hit any of the cars mere inches from ours.

"I'm sure Ateya has something prepared for us," I say with no animosity.

Mimi tries not to roll her eyes at the sound of Ateya's name. I understand what she does not say. It will take a lot out of both of us to keep our mouths shut, our ears perked, our legs swift, and our arms at the ready to scoop Ti'Louse away from Ateya's anger, which flares up especially when any of her daughter's protectors are around.

"Well, I came to do battle with Ateya this time. I'm not playing with her. If she touches Ti'Louse . . ." I pause and grunt, "That woman will see. She does not want to mess with me. I'm already in a bad mood."

"She wouldn't do much with you there."

"It's been a while since she last saw me. I was docile then. Not anymore. Not after what I've been through these last few months. If she even raises her hand in my presence, I will pounce on that woman. What she does to her own daughter. That's why I haven't been here in so long. Have you ever known me to stay away for a year? I just can't stand to be around Ateya. She doesn't want Ti'Louse but she won't give her to me." I calm myself down by stuffing my mouth with a crusty patty. There are as many crumbs in my lap as in my mouth. "I've messed up your clean car, Mimi."

"That's okay." Mimi turns her head to catch a glimpse of Miles. "Is he always this quiet?"

"He's mad at me."

"I can tell he doesn't want to be here."

"It's all his fault. Doing stupid things. Here you can do foolish things and only your family will discipline you. Over there, the police come for boys like him."

"Relax. Don't make your blood pressure rise."

Although we are moving slowly, the truck bumps over a particularly bad patch. I hear the suitcases jump and land.

"There is a bag for each of you," I say to Mimi. "One for Ti'Louse and one for Ateya."

"You're asking for it," Mimi chirps, a long, drawn-out sucking of teeth that makes her seem more feminine than she ever wants to be. *I'm manning a pickup truck,* her broad, raised shoulders convey. Mimi relaxes a little as we hit a less crowded stretch of road lined with plastic and tin market basins, some poised on women's heads and some on the sticky ground at their feet. I smell the *fritaye* of goat *tasso,* sweet and green plantains, and pickled habanero peppers. The smell of the greasy meat mingled with vinegar floods the back of my tongue with a pool of tangy saliva. I want to get out of the car, but I know that Mimi won't let me. Sensing my inclination, she places her hand on top of mine on the armrest.

Is Miles jealous or hurt as I sit in the front seat with someone else touching my hand? I can see a little bit of his reflection in my side-view mirror. Everything is wrong with the arrangements in this car. Miles is sitting where Yves usually does, so I can see and reach our little boy easily when I'm driving. Sitting in the passenger seat, where I never sit, I can see the emptiness behind the driver. A slight panic rises in me, then settles as I remember that Yves is back in New York, not lost at the Port-au-Prince airport. I want to reach for him. I should have brought him with us. Miles would be less annoyed, distracted by Yves's need for attention.

"You can nap, baby. It will be a while before we get to La Tranblè. The rest of the road is like this, so you won't miss anything." I contort my arm and reach behind me to touch his knee. He opts to stay awake, fighting the will of his eyelids. He seems unfazed by the sights, having seen the sanitized images of our surroundings in paintings, pictures, and postcards. He has no desire to embrace the grittiness of this chaotic reality.

I, on the other hand, want to walk through the market. I know that I would make it to the end faster on foot. I settle for watching the bustle through the truck window that I don't dare roll down lest the smells overwhelm Miles's senses. Through the sunroof I am gifted an unobstructed view of the sky above that is different from the sky back in New York, with its choking high-rises. It is bluer here, lower, clearer despite the smoke from coal that is used to fire pots and burn trash.

The windshield allows a view of the passengers jumping out of a jam-packed *tap-tap* truck. In bright paint the words DIEUX DONNE are emblazoned across the open arch where now-ripped-out doors once closed. The vehicle does not stop to let people off, as if the seconds it spends rolling will save it time on the journey. Practiced passengers skip out of the moving vehicle and land on their feet. They scurry, then stand in front of the vendor selling the wares that they desire.

Dust-covered secondhand clothes droop on wire hangers affixed to wooden walls of half-built storefronts. The T-shirts exclaim the logos of cheap but coveted American brands. Piles of Chinatown knockoffs have made their way here and compete with native straw handbags in neighboring stalls. There are no signs of the Salvation Army boxes, family-sent barrels, and dilapidated suitcases that the imports came in.

On either side of the road, produce merchants hand out single samples of ripe *keneps* for customers to test. The sellers shoo away the repeat tasters, who snack their way through the market for a day's meal. The bright colors of halves of avocados, papayas, and guavas boast their freshness to attract and reassure skeptical shoppers. A persistent doubter shakes an avocado to see if the seed will bounce around inside, a sign of ripeness. Above the honking of frustrated drivers, I hear the aggressive haggling between buyers and purveyors over limes and mangoes.

Women—there are rarely men in the markets—smooth out *goud* and greenbacks before handing the bills to impatient outstretched hands. Merchants spy on their neighbors, from whom they might borrow or demand repayment at the end of the day. There are no real profits. Goods and money make their rounds in a circle of bartering that allows everyone to survive. No one counts themselves as better off unless they are the recipients of remittances from abroad. Even then, it is hard to determine who's collecting more than whom, who comes from a family of naturalized American professionals and whose people work as undocumented nannies, gardeners, maids, or janitors. Haiti's insatiable economy revolves around loans, gifts, charity, and unrewarding, unrewarded hard work from the country's inhabitants and U.S. immigrants alike. I am a part of it as much as it is a part of me.

The road clears its throat of the congesting traffic. The crowd of cars seems to have disappeared to give us passage along cracked but open lanes. We breathe out breath that we did not even realize we were holding. For miles, unkempt greenery, corn stalks, and scattered plantain trees pass our windows. Vines of hibiscus and flamboyant hug the iron gates that fence in dispersed homes with things worth stealing. Stray goats leave behind stony black pellets and shy away from oncoming cars and cameras from diaspora tourists like me. The odd skinny cow lumbers in barren plots that cannot be called fields. The powdery dirt trails us everywhere we go, as do discarded containers and the piquant odor of charred waste. As soon as I cough, I turn around to see Miles's reaction to this alien atmosphere. He looks tired more than anything.

"He can sleep," Mimi says. She wants to gossip—*bouyi ʒin*—mainly about Ateya's snobbishness. Unlike me, Mimi tries not to talk about how Ateya treats Ti'Louse lest we both start crying. We know. We've seen and heard it.

"You know she never brought those supplies to the clinic. She wants the doctor to come and get them from her. Just so she can say that she made a doctor come to her door begging. I never ask her for anything. Anyway, she knows I don't need whatever she has. You always send me my own. And I have the truck." Mimi laughs loudly, then, remembering Miles, she covers her mouth with one hand. "Ateya will never ever forgive you or me for this truck. I should already be dead from the evil looks she casts at me every time she sees me driving. I'm surprised you can't feel her hatred all the way in New York. If she could cast spells, the *wanga* would reach you over there." We both laugh without sound, our bellies tightening, our eyes watering.

"And you? When will you have a special someone?" I ask, knowing that she won't say. Even with me, she acts ashamed. "Love who you love, Mimi."

She can't answer. She is still lonely. Not because she

doesn't have someone, but because she can't, won't, may never have a true someone. Even though everybody knows that she loves women, she could never be with one openly.

Even the vodou priestesses and their indoctrinated acolytes still cover over their sexuality under the guise of bisexuality, walking around with their men during the day, while they lie with women at night. Their way of life is known, excused as part of their religion. But, outside of that coterie, a circle into which Mimi tried to enter and then ran away from, *madivine* is a thing of whispered, disparaging gossip. *Madivine. My divine,* I translate to myself. How can that possibly be wrong?

"What about you? Have you and Bright reconciled?"

"Stop playing, Mimi! You know better."

"What? Are you sitting on a bucket of ice like your mother?" With a wide smile on her face, obviously not wanting to make any noise, Mimi laughs with her shoulders. "Are you sure you don't have a baby girl in there?" She reaches over and pats my belly with her right hand.

"You see how flat my belly is? Sexy, right? No babies. Never again."

"I'm hoping you'll have another one before you leave Haiti this time," Mimi says, speaking both of our minds.

"Maybe this time . . ." I say. I do not speak the rest.

I do not want to break my own heart again. I do not want to put myself through what Ma and Ol'Lady went through with the women on Ateya's side of our family. All I want is to help one little girl, one unwanted. Why not give away what you don't want?

Ol'Lady tried to take Guit, Ateya's mother, decades before, the first time when the girl was six. Ol'Lady came back over and over and over again with tears in her eyes, on her knees, with inducements, promises of protection and education, arguments about the plight of girl children wasting away in Haiti, wanting to save her sister's daughter.

Years later, Ma tried to rescue Ateya, lying on the ground red-eyed, crying, trembling. She tried other tactics, went to spiritualists outside of the village, slept in a cemetery as instructed, poured *kleren,* bought expensive rum and poured that out too. In New York, she kept an altar to honor Ezili Danto with a statue of Mary holding baby Jesus in her arms. Ma went to mass, genuflected, crossed herself with holy water, tithed. She paid thousands of dollars to vodou practitioners and sent even more money to Ateya's mother. Ma flew to Haiti every year and returned empty-handed, heartbroken, and more fearful for Ateya every time.

Although Guit did not allow Ma to take Ateya to the States, she pulled Ateya from the market stall and sent her to school. But Ateya had to study something useful. An education in something as frivolous as foreign languages was impractical for a child who would never travel. Mathematics or accounting would only teach Ateya how to swindle Guit out of inherited land. Learning to heed the needs of trees, to persuade hard ground to yield a valuable crop, was the way to wealth. Ateya took charge of the family's land, which had been passed down from generation to generation of women.

"I will try again to get Ti'Louse out of Haiti," I say to Mimi. "I'll remind Ateya why by yelling into her good ear."

"You are absolutely awful!" Mimi chuckles.

"I'm not playing around. No more wasted lives. No more

damaged, disdainful women. We can't afford any more stupid or crazy in the family."

"Well, I'm not really family but I'm both of those things. I guess it's contagious."

"Don't say that, Mimi. You've got your head on straight. And you're one of us. For better or for worse."

"For worse, I guess, since no one ever tried to take me to America."

"Ma asked Guit. I asked too."

"You should ask me. I have no children. I'm just growing plantains. That's all I'm good for." She looks me in the eyes to show me how serious she is, and how sad. "I have to resign myself to my position in this life, in this place. 'Stay in your place' is what Ateya constantly reminds me. I guess she's right."

I squeeze Mimi's hand reassuringly, apologetically.

Mimi turns away from me and focuses forward to make the turn onto the crumbling road that is the last dilapidated leg of our journey. Despite the truck's strong shocks and off-road tires, we feel every rocky rise and fall. The bumps and dips jolt Miles awake. Mimi creeps along the edges of the road to minimize the bouncing but still the luggage springs up and down. Petrol sloshes around in the three gas cans kept for emergencies. Intuitive, self-protecting gas station owners are prone to close up shop at the slightest hint of trouble— shut-down shortages, marches escalating to riots, embargoes, coups, house parties turned street-fest ra-ra, bed-wetting bandits turned gangsters. Mimi has even more gasoline at the back of her one-room cabin, and some deceptively buried at the entrance of the plantain grove. There is enough to burn down the enviably irrigated garden that Ateya tries to run like a plantation.

Mimi parks behind her house and unloads the suitcase I point out to her that is hers. "Ateya doesn't need to know," she says, winks at me, and smiles with a beautiful row of perfect teeth. I know that her looks are the reason women and men alike cannot stand the thought of her as a lesbian. Her hair would grow in long coils if she let it. Round hips, buttocks, and calves could clasp men in their grips if she let them. With smooth skin flaunting the red coloring from Haiti's original inhabitants, she has the type of face immigrant men come home to claim and take back to the States. What a waste of a woman, is what they say—*yon fam kap gaspiye!* To appease them, she allows one lucky man to spend the night at her place once a year. Just fingering and suckling, during which she imagines she is with someone else. She never gets pregnant, so the gossips whisper that the reason she doesn't like men is that she is barren.

Mimi jumps back into the truck and drives downhill. It is as easy to see the grove from up here as it is for anyone down there to see the truck approaching. I see the dog first, then Ti'Louse bringing up the rear. Ti'Louse stops running and I immediately see why. Ateya is standing at the front door, arms akimbo, mouth open, shouting. Ti'Louse halts but does not turn around. She stands in place because she knows that protection is on its way. Mimi keeps her eyes on Ti'Louse while I fix my gaze on Ateya and smile my greeting through the windshield.

Miles sits up tall, then bends his neck so he can get an unobstructed view of the place that is not a resort. He is about to sink back into his seat when he catches a glimpse of the plantain garden. I hear him inhale and exhale, as if the sight of the green with its hovering mist has arrested and then freed his breath. He places his hand on my shoulder in a gesture of thanks and relief. He has found one place in this whole new world where he wants to be. For the first time in a long time, I see pleasure and anticipation on his face. I know that the sight of the grove will soon feature in a poem or drawing.

I am grateful to be witnessing this moment of inspiration.

Two

4

*There must have been
a cut-out life
of a stick-figure girl
sketched on scraps
longing to be redrawn
in an unknown place*

The day before Genevieve arrived, Ateya practiced restraint by not hitting Ti'Louse.

"Ti'Louse!" Ateya hollered for her daughter, who came running breathlessly. "This house isn't going to clean itself! We're expecting guests tomorrow, as you well know."

Ateya held back the tongue-lashing, relishing the sight of the child's chest rising and falling in sync with a heart thumping with fear. There was no pity for the body that stood shrinking into a shape smaller than it already was. She looked Ti'Louse over, from matted head to ashy toe, from trembling knocked knees to a rickety neck that looked like it might give with one good tug of her kinky hair. As she stared at Ti'Louse's respectfully lowered eyelids, Ateya kept a record of the wrongs she would punish Ti'Louse for after Genevieve's visit. She thought of how she would surprise her only daughter with a wrathful whipping for just standing there with no tray in hand.

"What are you waiting for? Go and bring me some ice water!" Seeing Ti'Louse wince, Ateya cunningly withheld the slap that the child was expecting. She waited for Ti'Louse to put the cup of cold water on the dresser before yanking the girl's scrawny arm. She didn't hit her daughter, not then. She liked keeping the girl in a constant state of nervous tension. She held on to Ti'Louse's wrist as the girl shrank.

That morning, Ateya had done the same on her ride home from Port-au-Prince—she'd tried to make herself small so she would not look like someone who had an entire plantain grove flourishing on family property and money coming from two sources.

She'd worn her pauper's costume to the remittance office to pick up the money Genevieve had sent from the U.S. Her dirty bra had shown under the spaghetti straps of her grease-spotted dress. Underneath, the pockets of shorts had wads of bills hidden from would-be stick-up boys. She'd tucked a few bills between her breasts that she could present to a robber, who would believe that that was all she had. In her hand, she'd clutched just enough cash to pay for her ride back home to her village, just outside of Port-au-Prince. On her way to the bus station, she had waited for the men sitting along the road to catcall, not because she was pretty or shapely, but because they knew that she had fresh bills picked ripe from an American tree. She'd felt their eyes following her as she squeezed herself into the back of the truck that had been converted into a *tap-tap* to transport riders. She'd remained alert, suspicious of any whispering passengers, especially young men, whose lips she tried to read.

She had fooled no one with her guise. Her posture always betrayed her. Even as her dusty flip-flops slapped the heels of her feet, she'd walked proudly, knowing that she had an enviable wardrobe at home.

As soon as she stepped off the *camionette*, touching La Tranblè soil, her oldest son extended his hand to help her walk. She rolled her eyes at how predictable he was, pretending to care about her safety, waiting for her to offer the few *goud* in her bra before hitting her up for the big money he knew was hidden in the pockets under her dress. She pulled her hand out of his and once again lamented her plight. Here she was, with a thirty-year-old man, a reminder of her reckless adolescence, during which she'd believed the boys who'd courted her had been interested in love or at least her body— her large, round breasts and behind, her hair made longer and silkier by relaxers, or the way her spandex skirts made her waist look smaller and her hips wider. It had taken five sons and five heartbreaking desertions to realize that the boys and at least one older man had only been concerned with what she could offer them. A few crisp U.S. dollars. Dry goods from any barrels that might arrive from New York. Even a hot plate of food on those nights they might secretly stay over in the back room of her mother's cement-block shack. Sex with her had been a fringe benefit of their pursuit of their true object of desire—a coveted passage to the Promised Land itself.

In the end, realizing that her mother would not allow her to give away anything but her body and her naïve and hopeful heart, the men had wordlessly abandoned her and their sons.

Ateya's mother would then quip that the men had walked all over her daughter. The name *Ateya* meant "the ground," after all.

Ateya had not thought about sex since having Ti'Louse, her last child, a girl finally, a child she thought of as her punishment for allowing herself to be used, for a naïve and hopeful heart. After giving birth to what her community had labeled the devil's child, black as sin, darker than boiled blood, Ateya finally gave up on the lying lovers who only wanted like-new *pèpè*, pocket money to spend on their real girlfriends, and freshly prepared food on a regular basis. After eight pregnancies, six living children, five sons, countless grandchildren, and a gag gift of an ugly navy-blue-black little girl, Ateya laid her emotions in a corner, hardened her heart against her sons, and beat her only daughter with random objects and deliberate words.

"This yard is such a mess. The house must be even worse," Ateya said to herself. "Ti'Louse!" she hollered.

"*Plètil, Manman,*" Ti'Louse squeaked in response.

Ateya didn't bother showing her annoyance that both the girl and the dog came running. Ti'Louse, the girl, had adopted the dog's name as a one-year-old, toddling behind it on her unsure legs. The neighbors thought it fitting that an ugly baby would take the name of a dirty dog rather than the other way around. Now that she was nine years old, only gossipy elders remembered that the name had first belonged to the dog. Everyone else had forgotten, ignored, or didn't care who was being called. The name finally belonged to the girl, as did the dog.

Ateya slipped off her shorts with the money still in the

pockets and raised her arms to remove the dirty dress. She didn't have to turn around or speak for Ti'Louse to know to bring a small basin of soapy water, a washcloth, a clean moo-moo, and slippers.

"Don't make me tell you twice. This place had better shine before Genevieve gets here tomorrow."

"I'll do everything. I promise," Ti'Louse found the courage to say. Normally she would have nodded her understanding silently.

"Tell me what went on today," Ateya commanded as she splashed water all over the floor. She should have gone outside for her sponge bath, but she had Ti'Louse to wipe the floor. "*Di mwen.*"

"Everybody kept walking outside the house waiting for you to come back from *la ville.*"

"Come stand on this side. You know I can't hear you." Ateya let out an exasperated sigh at having to correct the girl and everyone else, to remind people of her partial deafness.

"I heard someone talking about how much money the pastor would get from the church collection basket on Sunday," Ti'Louse said loudly but in a mild, deferential tone.

"*En hen.*" Ateya rolled her eyes while stretching out an ireful chirp. "Well, the joke is on them. I'm not going to church at all this month. Greedy bastard. He can come and stand at this door and not one *goud* will come out of my pocket." Her message for the pastor had also been meant for any neighbor who might have been banking on a loan.

Ti'Louse knew better than to reply.

Ateya never appreciated that she had someone who antici-pated her every whim. Why should she show gratitude for the presence of someone to whom she had given life? God was not grateful for his people; he barely tolerated most of them and only blessed those who feared and obeyed him.

She knew that she had not trembled enough before the throne, nor sufficiently submitted herself, to have earned only partial benevolence. She had a modicum of wealth from New York but never got to experience the place from which the blessings poured. She was allowed hearing in one ear, not two. She had a comfortable bed but got little sleep because that one ear kept her awake with the sharpness it had developed to compensate for the deaf one.

While Ti'Louse went about wiping, scrubbing, and washing, Ateya leaned back on her headboard and closed her eyes.

The lights turned off at last, she slid under the sheets, placed her head on her pillow, and allowed her ear to bring her the goings-on in the yard the way a child might bring home pebbles or sticks. It brought her the usual—the high-hat din of lovemaking, the whispered arguing of her neighbors. She could hear dust settling on her dresser and the breeze from the fan in the room next door. Like a nocturnal predator, she could even hear moss growing, mist rising in the dark, the tiptoe of forest animals. But lately there'd been something new, a growl that did not come from any animal she had ever heard. No flesh, blood, and bone thing could make such a menacing sound. It even made the ground beneath her tremble. She believed that this thing had come for her life and hers only. It was so frightening that it scared her to sleep.

The morning of her benefactor's arrival, Ateya nudged Ti'Louse with her foot to wake the girl up. It might as well have been a kick. She was about to step on the groggy child, who had not awoken from her pallet on the floor early enough, when Ti'Louse sat up.

"You let me wake up before you?"

Ti'Louse jumped to her feet but kept her eyes lowered.

"You don't say *bonjou*? You must be my man. Did you wake up next to me in my bed? You fresh little girl!"

"*Bon* . . ." Ti'Louse started to say.

"Don't you dare speak to me before you wash your mouth!" Ateya grinned at the fresh anxiety she'd inspired in Ti'Louse. "When you finish, go and call Mimi for me."

Ateya sat on a shaky plastic chair in her front yard watching Ti'Louse handle a broom that was much too tall for a child, especially a growth-stunted little-bit who looked six although she was about to turn ten. Ateya did not even make a move as if she might have thought about helping the girl. God helps those . . . She only thought of her daughter as a curse put on her by angry wives whose husbands she'd slept with and had had children by over the years. Wives had tolerated the affairs because of the spoils their husbands would bring home after trysts with her. She'd finally learned that the wives had hoped that she would be granted a visa to the U.S. and take one of their husbands with her. A few years and a full green card later, the husband would return for his real wife and then happily ever after.

Even if none of their aspirations materialized, Ateya was not a woman the wives worried about. She was unworthy of their scorn because she was not a threat. She was no man's addiction. She was not the one husbands snuck off to meet, risked their marriages for by spending the night, or made a mistress of. She was stand-up sex—rarely, a quick lay on a mattress. Just enough to tide a man over, so he would not have to rub himself against a wife's unyielding thigh. She was just tempting enough for a man to dip a spoon into the pot on her stove but not to sit at her table for a proper meal. She was an incidental piece. The one a man would snack on, a few shelled peanuts tossed into the mouth just because the bowl was there, and he was bored.

The last time Ateya allowed herself to be used, she'd been deceived by a light-skinned man who'd failed to pass on the one valuable thing he had—his color.

Ateya, all of her neighbors, church brethren, and the extended community had been shocked and then frightened at the dark baby, whose skin was indistinguishable from her black hair. The philanderer rumored to be the father was a mustard-beige-skinned man with pink lips and *good hair*. Ateya herself had doubted the paternity of her baby, although she knew that she hadn't slept with another man for many years before. When she looked at her infant, all Ateya could do was place one hand over her mouth and shake her head. Then, like any other mother, she took her baby to her breast and loved her. It wasn't until her time of sequestering had expired and she started taking the baby outside that she realized how disgusted people were at the sight of the bundle that curved like the shell of a snail in her arms. Seeking acceptance and forgiveness from her neighbors, Ateya joined in the loathing of the child. By the time the baby girl was running behind a dog whose name had become her own, Ateya was spanking Ti'Louse for just being.

Had Ateya been honest with herself and allowed her irrepressible maternity to be made public, she would have admitted that Ti'Louse was, in fact, very, very beautiful, like the first Black dark-skinned dolls made in the seventies. A baby doll over whom tar had been poured. People couldn't stand to look at Ti'Louse, not because she was ugly but because she was so painfully pretty. However, centuries of conditioning and self-hatred had convinced them that the revulsion they felt at the sight of her was because of how dark and, therefore, unsightly she was. Somewhere down inside where Ateya had hidden her love, she knew what repelled people when they looked at Ti'Louse. An honest, self-loving people would have said that the girl was gorgeous. If they had let themselves acknowledge Ti'Louse's beauty, they would have insisted that it had been wasted on a girl so dark, that she had stolen it from a lighter-skinned girl who could have put it to good use. With a knowledge pressed as far as her brain stem, Ateya understood that their loathing was actually envy.

Ateya looked up and saw Ti'Louse and the dog obediently running toward the road. Even with a companion, Ateya always insisted that Ti'Louse wear jeans when going out of their *lakou*, the yard around which a loose circle of haphazardly constructed cement-block huts cowered. Jeans were hard to pull down, and, given her size, Ti'Louse was easy to snatch up. The tight, stiff denim sent to Ti'Louse by her godmother, Genevieve, made Ateya worry less, but did not calm her fears entirely. In this regard, Ateya let herself feel for her daughter, without shame for her protectiveness.

Ateya was less concerned when Ti'Louse was with Mimi. No one would dare touch the little girl when she was with Mimi, who could hold her own despite her girly voice and curly hair. Ateya knew that Ti'Louse was excited that Mimi was coming over because the little girl wanted her hair combed. Mimi was the only person willing to make sense of the steel-wool-textured hair that broke combs, splintered brushes, resisted grease, and fought and won against a hot press.

Mimi was an oddity for many more reasons than loving Ti'Louse enough to touch her tenderly. Mimi was also the only woman in La Tranblè who could drive, who had never been known to have a man, and had no children. Ateya knew that Mimi would walk the short distance down the hill rather than drive the used pickup truck Genevieve had sent to Haiti to haul plantains from the family's grove. Mimi was the only one allowed to touch the vehicle. In addition to paltry monthly sums from Ateya, it was her payment for her labor. She even slept in it on some nights, fearing vandals and robbers known to dismantle and sell a car for parts overnight.

"Bonjou, matante mwen yo," Mimi called out in salutation to the elder women in the yard, who'd poked their heads out of their windows and doorways to see who was coming. No one responded except Ateya, who stood up to receive Mimi's embrace.

"You remember that Genevieve is coming, right?" Ateya didn't even try to hide her fear and disgust, born of resentment and jealousy of her cousin.

"Yes. Today's the day," Mimi responded. Ateya could see on Mimi's face what she really wanted to say but didn't dare. *You've told me every day since you found out. Forty days and forty nights, including Christmas, New Year's, Little Christmas, and today.* Instead, Mimi repeated, *"Oui,"* in a squeaky soprano that did not match her size. She was tall, with a large, masculine body frame contrastingly overlaid with the thick curvature of a goddess. Her voice matched her pretty face, which was framed by soft baby hair that never kinked. Men didn't know what to make of her. She was bigger, taller, not to mention stronger than most of them but with delicious cinnamon skin and salivation-worthy curves. She never wore dresses but her tight jeans and sleeveless crew-neck T-shirts showed off her hefty hips and heavy breasts.

"Before you pick her up, don't forget to stop by the *boulanje* for the bread. I don't know why that woman loves bread so much. Just like her mother and her grandmother. The only thing those people love more than bread are other women's daughters." Ateya sucked her teeth.

"I was thinking about taking Ti'Louse to the airport with me."

"Mimi, I told you not to bother yourself with thinking. It doesn't suit you. Just do. Preferably what you're told." The insult rolled off of Ateya's tongue like any ordinary phrase. She wasn't angry at Mimi for asking. The word *airport* with the name *Ti'Louse* in the same sentence confused and angered her. More than that, it scared her.

Looking at Ti'Louse, with comb and pomade ready for Mimi's nurturing hand, Ateya could not tell herself that she was as envious of her daughter's chance to go to America as she was of Genevieve's ability to offer such an incalculable gift. Ateya reasoned that she was the one who'd given the gift. She'd given Ti'Louse to Genevieve as goddaughter. And, to Ti'Louse, Ateya had given the spoils of that position, which included a formal education and Genevieve's love.

Ateya wasn't without human bequests of her own. She'd been given Mimi as a playmate when they were children, in exchange for hand-me-down clothes and seamstress lessons. Decades later, those rewards had been upstaged in the grandest way. When Genevieve learned that Mimi had learned to drive, she sent her the prized pickup. True to form, Ateya suppressed her anger and rationalized that she was the true beneficiary of Genevieve's gift because it was she who would benefit most from the like-new truck sent from America.

She never wanted to learn to drive; she wanted to be chauffeured around. She wanted a driver hired by her rich family in America, whose remittances supplemented the profits from the plantain plantation over which she reigned.

More than that, she didn't want to be thought of as mannish like Mimi. Labor was not for a lady like herself. She didn't want to be so close to the plantain grove, waiting for the yard boys and death-defying men to load huge branches with plantains fanning out like heavy green fingers.

"Did you wash the truck, Mimi?" Ateya asked.

"Yes," Mimi said, suppressing a frustrated sigh.

"I'm going to fry *tasso* tonight," Ateya said temptingly. She knew that it was Mimi's favorite.

"I'll eat when I come back. But if it's ready by the time I finish with Ti'Louse's hair, I'll take some with me."

Ateya looked at Ti'Louse sitting comfortably, quietly, and happily on an upside-down bucket between Mimi's legs. She wanted to throw her dirty slipper at the little girl.

5

*There must have been
a hardened heart,
crushed in a cupped hand,
a pile of crumbs,
a gathering of glass splinters,
a small heap of big hurts,
hoping for wholeness*

Ateya didn't say another word to Ti'Louse. She let her daughter be after getting her hair done. She didn't even yell at her to put away the comb, brush, and pomade. Ateya needed to save her strength for her silent war with Genevieve. She held back even after Mimi left to go to the airport.

But when she saw Ti'Louse running toward the sound of the truck returning with Genevieve, Ateya couldn't hold back any longer. Standing in front of her house, she only said two words. That was all that was needed.

"*Ey! Vini!*" Ateya screamed at the child to come back into the house, but she only succeeded at getting Ti'Louse to freeze.

Angry and embarrassed that she had been disobeyed,

Ateya didn't yell to Ti'Louse again. She stood in front of her house motionless and at a loss for words.

Ateya didn't know what to do with her hands, so she let them hang at her sides until her heart went on its way again and slipped into the middle finger of her right hand. She forced it to throb there with a steady beat by twisting her hand into a fist. As the truck crept closer, she carefully placed her fist on her waist in a precariously poised half-akimbo. She was so focused on controlling her heartbeat that she could not move even to reach Ti'Louse, who stood mid-sprint after her attempt to run. Ateya's eyes bored holes into Ti'Louse's back. She imagined the crooked-toothed smile on Ti'Louse's face, a crowd of teeth in her mouth like a packed church of white-clad worshipers who hadn't yet arranged themselves properly in their pews.

Ateya understood that the girl was less afraid of her because of Genevieve's arrival. Having a protector nearby gave Ti'Louse the courage to be defiant. Ateya let her be. In eight days, she would regain full control of the child, and she would make her pay for a week of disobedience. Ateya's anger did not require any misdeed by Ti'Louse to ignite it. Her hatred for Ti'Louse was ingrained. That morning's mistreatment had been no worse than usual, just the start of another day of unprovoked disdain.

Chin in the air, Ateya refused to budge from her doorstep. She feigned very mild interest in the arrival of her visitors from America. She would not give Genevieve the satisfaction of seeing her run for a greeting from thieving kin. She certainly didn't want her neighbors to think that she was thirsty for the gifts that swelled the suitcases being unloaded. She wanted them to know that this was no special occurrence—

that she received special things and important people all the time. She called out to Ti'Louse again, but the girl still would not turn around, let alone turn back. Under her breath Ateya said to herself, "I'll let you have this one. Watch what happens when they're gone. It's going to be you and me." In retaliation for her mean thought, the throbbing in her finger pricked her like a pin and threatened to go roaming wildly again.

She held back her vengeful thoughts to steady herself, but she could not suppress the jealousy piercing talons into her fingers when Genevieve joyfully jumped out of the big-wheeled truck like a euphoric athlete. Ateya was waiting for Genevieve to come to the doorstep but, instead, Genevieve bent down and picked up light-as-a-leaf Ti'Louse and swung her around. Ateya was so upset by the lingering embrace between godchild and godmother that she risked raising and folding her arms over her breasts. She lifted her chin even higher, turned the corners of her lips downward into a pronounced frown, and rolled her eyes into her head. As far as she was concerned, Ti'Louse and Genevieve were showing off like exhibitionist lovers who had left the blinds raised and curtains parted.

She felt the second prick in her still-balled fist when, from yards away, she heard Genevieve repeating the words "I love you. I love you. I love you." She did not hear but assumed that Ti'Louse was repeating the same into Genevieve's neck in English, to communicate gratitude for the pricey school where she had started learning English.

The heartbeat rolled its way up Ateya's arm, passed her shoulder, and took a leap across her clavicle to pound its way to and throughout her left lung. It hardened there and then splintered into shards of steel, slicing her breath into quickening gasps. She clasped her hands tighter over her chest to hold back the arrhythmic panting.

With her good ear turned toward them, Ateya strained to hear the rest of the exchange between Ti'Louse and Genevieve but she would have to leave her perch to do so. If she had heard, she would have slapped the girl for whispering: "Did you come to get me?"

"Later." Genevieve hushed her reply. "*Pita.*"

Ateya groaned as the pair unknotted themselves and started walking toward her. If her heart had been like a normal woman's heart, she would have felt a twinge, then a tear, then a rending that would never be mended. This she would have recognized as jealousy, the anger of a mother whose child had been taken—heart and all. Instead, she felt a ping in her fingers that soon spread to her hands and arms. Her heart was telling her what she could not understand—that she longed for Ti'Louse's love and that she missed the child who was still with her, alive.

Ateya had never lived with someone else's soul inside her or been in another body but she knew that her heart was not like other hearts. With her good ear to a strong, smooth chest, she had heard the double-time timpani of a man who would soon leave her. She understood well that a man's heart did different things. But even while he roamed, his heart stayed put in its proper place, supplying the rapid rate of his panting with blood, feeding him air for breath. Her own heart had an erratic tempo, too unreliable to even be called a beat, too unpredictable to be captured, which made men believe that she could never love them, certainly not as a wife, not even like a mistress. Hers was a throwaway heart. It was a piece of flyaway trash that was never in the same place and, therefore, left men unmoored with nothing to hold on to. Men, she reasoned, wanted a heart they could find easily, if just to break it carelessly.

Ateya was sure that her heart was not the same as other hearts. She often wondered about the women she watched, women who loved as predictably as they walked, with rhythm, driven by the steadiness that came from the inside, giving them a proper military-worthy march with the corresponding swish of the hips. The cadence of their gait tick-tocked, a steady swinging of a pendulum in time with an inner beat. Her walk was off kilter, not because of the vertigo of being deaf in one ear, but because her heart dragged her to painful places she did not want to go. She stumbled along behind it, a recalcitrant child holding an impatient parent's hand.

When she was younger, her heart had made her cry at inopportune times. Later came a lopsided laughter so sinister, it made her lovers want to run. Around domino tables, other women's husbands forewarned their brethren about that laugh, informing them of the high cost they would pay for the satiation of their lust. But fiending for a fast fuck, some had had to learn for themselves just how contagious crazy could be. They never stayed long enough to catch her illness.

It wasn't her free cackle that made them run, nor the unbalanced mind speaking through it; it was the heartbeat they couldn't find in its usual place. It was worse for those few men who gave a damn about anyone else's pleasure besides their own, who determined to stay long enough to find the place where her orgasm should have pulsed. They couldn't manage the untamed tension of a body too wild to throb between the lips below. They didn't trust what they felt there. Instead of the tightness of a close, closed space, they found a hollow so slippery, they struggled to pull themselves out. Shaking off a euphoric fear, they left immediately after ejaculating. Although they longed to know where the sloping, water-slick cavern led, longed to find what was lodged so deep it had to be treasure, they would not risk being caught and held while searching. They weren't afraid of falling in love or that she might. They dreaded falling into the bottomless, soundless place where her heart should have beaten.

How to describe a heart that went wherever it wanted when it wanted and without permission or the courtesy of a "So long," "Take care," "Go to hell," or "Good-bye"? A rogue heart that could escape its proper place at the center of her chest and roll like a boulder, bouncing angrily down a hill into her stomach. It might break apart its willful self into jagged rocks of different shapes and sizes, scatter and bore them into every joint, where its pieces would pulse erratically, painfully.

She had known it to regroup itself, come together whole, soft, fleshy, drenched in blood, and then, without notice, slip into one of her calves, stretching her skin into an unbearable bulge that made her limp. She would trip over her own feet and fall when it left that spot, flew past her chest and throat to reach its favorite place—her head.

Oh, it loved every part of her head—the blood vessels along her temples, the space behind her eye sockets, where it tried to supplant her eyeballs to see what she saw and maybe fall in love when it wanted to, not when she directed. It wanted to see the things that drove her longing and made her weepy—a man, a tree, an ice cube in a glass of water. And when it grew bored with the outside world, it would leave to find an underexplored and therefore exciting place in her body, leaving her struggling to find her sight again.

Her heart could flatten and spread itself across the inside of her forehead, then slip to the spot where the nape of her neck began, turn forward to scrape the bone around her long-closed fontanel, which it tried to crack to expose her brain. It loved to harden itself into metal, clank like a spoon in a tin cup, a butter knife banging against a glass bottle, or skip like the scatting of a glittering jazz singer.

Done with these tricks, it might make itself small and tight and smooth and round, a pebble speeding down her legs to her feet. It might be a marble in her big toe or a stubborn splinter in her heel. It might soften and swell around a perfectly healthy ankle or travel up to her thigh. Rest in her hip and fall asleep in the cradle of her pelvis.

No, her heart wasn't like other hearts. It was a traveler and a shapeshifter, an unknowable, uncontrollable, defiant thing. Its beat did not bend to serve her. It coiled around her insides, wringing her into submission. If emotions truly came from the heart, there was no hope for Ateya's battles with her feelings. She could only follow their whims. But firmly into her adulthood, she skillfully pretended to be in control.

As usual, Ateya focused outwardly on what and whom she could manipulate. She didn't like that something had made her feel out of place, made her question her decisions, if just her choice of what to wear. She couldn't figure out why she felt underdressed. Genevieve wasn't dressed up at all—black leggings, a T-shirt with the Haitian flag that read HAITI, redundant and clichéd, sneakers already rimmed with dirt. Her hair was pulled back into an ordinary ponytail, only its length and the fact that it was natural enviable.

Ateya wiped her palms on her sundress as if to iron out the wrinkles and wipe the stains away. She hated that there was nothing she could do now. It would be ridiculous to go and change into something clean. She would use the excuse that she had been cooking to explain her ensemble, which was topped off with a damp head-tie framing her sweat-beaded face.

But why the discomfort? She had never tried to compete with Genevieve over clothes before. She was as grateful as her envy allowed for Genevieve's generosity. Ateya had more new clothes than anyone in her yard, which she flaunted at church, where she went for that express purpose. Not only herself but also Ti'Louse. She wanted everyone to know that she was so blessed that she could even afford to be charitable with her unattractive child, who could not be made pretty even dressed up.

As Ti'Louse and Genevieve walked toward her hand in hand, Ateya eyeballed the pair, taking in Ti'Louse's crisp jeans, lace-collared shirt, shiny sandals with a missy block heel, and neatly twisted hair. She did not understand why but somehow Ti'Louse looked prettier standing next to Genevieve. In that moment, Ateya decided never to let Mimi style Ti'Louse's hair like that again. It looked too much like locks, like Genevieve's hair.

"Gen." Ateya took a few steps forward to reach Genevieve, who had not let go of Ti'Louse's hand. She kept her arms crossed over her breasts to receive her cousin's greeting. Ateya felt something inside of her body start to give. She squeezed her arms over her chest even tighter to press down into an inaccessible place whatever was loosening, whatever was longing. She reasoned that the loosening was due to Genevieve's perfume, a few dots dabbed behind her ears that would make the fake embrace worthwhile. Genevieve would leave the rest of the bottle of this new fragrance behind. Ateya took another step forward and turned her head slightly to accept Genevieve's kiss on each cheek. They weren't really kisses, no lips touching skin, just puckered chirps on the side of the face into the air.

"Go inside and get your godmother a bottle of water," Ateya said, looking down at the top of Ti'Louse's head.

"No need. I'm fine," Genevieve said too quickly. Feeling Ti'Louse loosening her grip, she held the girl's hand a little tighter.

"Then get one for your cousin. I'm sure that Miles . . ." Ateya said, deliberately (mis)pronouncing *Miles* like the Kreyòl word for *thousand*. It was her way of mocking the affluence that she always felt was taunting her.

"Miles had some in the car." Genevieve had prepared herself for such battles of wills, but she would hold back for Ti'Louse's sake.

Ateya didn't bother forcing the issue. She knew that she had the upper hand because Genevieve would once again beg to take Ti'Louse to the States.

Ateya called out to her oldest son, who had been hanging around all day in anticipation of the gifts—really the money—Genevieve would bring. Ateya hated his obvious desperation. He might as well have had his hands cupped, one on top of the other, to receive castoff coins.

Visibly annoyed, she led the way into the house through a curtain of wooden beads that separated the kitchen from the small sitting room where she received guests. She gestured for Genevieve to sit on one of the clear-plastic-covered chairs, but Genevieve declined and remained standing. The low ceiling made her look taller than she was. The top of Miles's head nearly touched the painted concrete ceiling above.

"Ti'Louse!" Ateya hollered harshly.

"*Oui, Manman.*" She was sure to acknowledge Ateya's command.

Again, Ateya stared irately at the back of Ti'Louse's head, watching the girl tugging at Genevieve's hand like a toddler. She led Genevieve and Miles to the room that had been prepared for *etrangé.*

Like most buildings in and around Port-au-Prince, Ateya's house was perpetually under construction. She had already added on two rooms, including the guest room her visiting cousins would occupy, and a second story was in progress. The upstairs—there weren't actually any stairs yet, just a stubby ladder leaning against the outside wall—would take months, if not years, to be finished. On the temporary roof, sturdy steel poles stood upright in freshly poured concrete like candles on a birthday cake. For now, it was all just for show—another display to remind her neighbors of her almost-wealth. This flaunting was unnecessary. Hers was the only painted house in the yard. There were even fickle flowers out front that chose when to bloom and when to wither, irrespective of the season or precipitation. The house boasted a proper kitchen with an indoor stove, next to which a functioning refrigerator proudly stood gulping power from the outdoor generator that protruded from the side of the house like a mechanical growth on the side of someone's neck. The finishing touches were the mesh screen door that kept out most of the mosquitoes and the gleaming windowpanes with thick curtains that blocked out sunlight and prying eyes.

More often than not, the outside eyes were trained on the room next to hers, which housed yet another "daughter-in-law" with little ones in tow. The jealous girls were always peering in to see which of their rivals occupied the bedroom, on which nights, and for how long. It was pointless. Ateya's sons were never allowed to stay the night or even drop by for daytime sex. Ateya loved her sons, but she didn't like them. They were men like all of the men she'd ever known, in the yard, in the world. They had the same greed and usurious tendencies. Out of pity she passed on to their women and children the maternal affections that she could not show them. She did so begrudgingly, stingily, but did so nonetheless. She couldn't judge the girls who'd given her sons passage through their bodies. She had done the same, as evidenced by the fact that Ti'Louse was the same age as several of her grandchildren.

As she leaned into the slanted doorway of the guest room, Ateya looked critically at the two poorly made twin beds that squatted on locally constructed wooden frames. At least the oscillating fan was in its proper place in the corner of the room. The spider-like base wobbled on the unleveled floor, only held upright by its electrical cord, which looped into the single outlet in the wall. Her guests would have to choose between charging their phones and sweating through the mosquito-owned night. She watched as Genevieve pulled a pair of rum-colored leather slippers from her wide tote bag and then gestured with her head for her to come to the other bedroom.

Although she did not want to show it, Ateya was eager to unpack the large suitcases, whose flaps were already flipped open; their contents appeared picked through but not removed. She sat down, giving Genevieve unneeded permission to do the same. Bent over the bag filled with girls' clothing, Ateya clicked her tongue. "You've brought too much, Gen. I won't even talk. You never listen. You always come with these big suitcases, big enough to bury the dead. People would kill for such nice coffins." Ateya cast a glance toward Ti'Louse, knowing what the girl was thinking.

"Never mind that," Genevieve said. "What's most important is that the kids get their school supplies and the clinic gets everything they need. At least, as much as I can carry."

"I haven't even given them what you sent last time."

"What do you mean?" Genevieve pretended not to know that Ateya had withheld the parcels.

Ateya felt a twinge of shame. First, she would never bring the medical supplies to the clinic. On a whim, she would send for one of the attendants to come and fetch from her whatever she felt like handing over on any given day. She liked to see the stained white lab coat flutter as a gangly twenty-something man, who looked more like a teenage boy, ran down the slope into the yard to get what she'd decided to give. More than once, she'd given a package so small and light, the courier had shaken it to make sure it wasn't empty.

"Give me whatever is left over from last time and I'll take it with this batch as well." Genevieve shook her head and tried not to sound too annoyed.

Ateya enjoyed how cowed and humbled Genevieve always looked during these trips. She had seen that same look on Genevieve's mother's face decades ago, when scenes like this one had played out in the same room: gift-laden suitcases opened on a sheet on the dusty floor, ruffled dresses in clear plastic sheaths, bottles of cheap perfume and lotions for distribution among the women in the yard, stacks of boxes of latex gloves, neatly coiled tubing, syringes, alcohol pads, folded hospital gowns, bandages of all sizes. A short, chubby Ateya would crawl into an empty suitcase at night and sleep like a puppy on a pallet. Even when she grew older, and could no longer fit, she would make a fort around her mattress in the room she shared with one of the pregnant cousins who rotated through the household. Since her mother would never give, Ateya had hardened herself against disappointment and balled her longing into fists.

As Ateya led the way to the yard, she called out to her son, "Go help them put the things in the truck."

"No, I'll take Miles with me." Genevieve turned her head in the direction of the bedroom assigned to her and Miles. "Let's go, Miles!"

Miles adjusted his eyes to the sunlight outside. He lumbered toward his mother with dropped shoulders, signaling his exhaustion, which was at odds with Ateya's son, who had come as soon as he'd been called.

"Go and help your aunt," Ateya started to say to her son again.

"No. I told you Miles would go," Genevieve insisted.

"Can I please stay, Mom? I'm so tired and it's so hot." Miles drew out the words. His whininess was at odds with his deep voice.

"That's fine. Mimi and I will go," Genevieve said, looking up at Miles.

Ateya turned to her son again. "Well, what are you waiting for? I told you to help them." She watched as the young man loaded the suitcases of supplies into the pickup.

Genevieve cut her eyes at Ateya and then said, "I'll take

Ti'Louse with me." She spoke authoritatively, not asking for permission.

"I'm going back to bed," Miles groaned. "I have to charge my phone too."

Ateya regarded him smugly and then turned her eyes to Genevieve. She didn't have to say anything. Hers was a pitying look at a woman who had no control over her own child; whose child could say "no" outright and whine and plead. There was no way this woman could handle Ti'Louse. She would spoil the girl. Ateya would not suffer that.

As the truck pulled back out of the yard, Ateya rolled her eyes and uttered under her breath all of the things she had been holding back, especially the sharp words she'd wanted to hurl at Genevieve.

6

*There must have been
wounding words in muted ears,
open holes that once housed
a heart's hums*

I don't ask Ateya for permission to take Ti'Louse with me to run our errand. I simply take Ti'Louse's hand and walk quickly to the car. I can feel the heat of Ateya's stare on my back. I don't turn around. She has said nothing to make me do so. We have made a temporary exchange—Ti'Louse for Miles. Ateya has one of mine and I have hers.

Ti'Louse uses both of her tiny hands to try to open the rear passenger door of the truck but it is too heavy for her. I place my hand over hers and pull, allowing her to feel strong and victorious at having conquered such a big obstacle. I lift her onto the step and let her climb onto the seat. In the U.S., I would have put her in a booster. I should have sent one for her even for the rare times that Ateya lets her ride with Mimi. I reach for the seat belt to buckle her in but decide against it because it slices across her neck and might choke her. I'm still worried that she might bounce around without some sort of restraint. I tell her to lie down instead. She stares at me with eyes that say, "I want to look out the window."

"Promise me you'll hold on to this." I grab the leather strap that is attached to the seat in front of her. Surprisingly, it is long enough for her to hang on to. "Don't let go." I place my finger under her chin to force her to look me in the eyes. I smile my approval. "You okay?" I say and kiss her on the forehead.

She looks at me with pleading eyes again, this time with water rising in them. She pats the seat next to her. "Stay with me," the gesture says. "Don't leave me," her watery eyes implore.

I close the door without answering her. I am about to sit in the front seat when she says out loud, "Take me with you."

"You shouldn't sit in the front seat, baby girl. It's not safe."

"You're such an American," Mimi says with a chuckle.

I get out and walk around to the driver's side rear door. As I open it, I say, "Is this better?" I am barely seated when she lays her head in my lap. "Don't you want to look out the window?" She climbs into my lap. She is now high enough to see outside.

"*Allons-y!*" Mimi says in French with a heavy tongue. "Let's go!"

Ti'Louse's body wobbles in my lap as I try to hold on to her skinny waist. We manage to make it up the hill that leads out of the compound without her falling off. Every time she starts to slide forward, she immediately scooches back into the curve of my body. She is more interested in me than anything outside.

She stares at the road, the people, the motor taxis, empty parcels of land, everything we pass, but makes no queries, utters no observations. She has learned not to speak unless spoken to and, even then, a misinterpreted response might earn a slap across the face. A bloody nose. A busted lip. Another slit in an unhealed heart. All for answering a rhetorical question or asking for clarification of an order misunderstood or an explanation of a newly seen thing. In the absence of conversations, she has developed an untainted imagination. She has told herself everything, not knowing that any of it is false or not real. She makes up her own world. I wonder what she's thinking. I only know that she has seen something interesting by watching her expressions. She doesn't point like a younger child might, or giggle, groan, or hum. She is seeing new things but her face says that she has just discovered something she had missed about an object, a place, or a person she has seen before.

I wonder what it would be like to live in my own made-up world where everything is what I say it is. But I know that the outside things that I cannot control are intrusive and fearsome.

The clinic is within sight, with its weathered, pastel-pink-painted cinder blocks and white window bars. As the guard opens the high gates, I feel Ti'Louse's breathing sputter. I am startled when she says, "She did not take me here when my fingers broke." She extends her left hand to show me the knuckles that have healed in slightly crooked curves.

"For using her left hand," Mimi explains. "I rewrapped them. That woman would have let them fall off."

"Who broke your fingers?"

"She did." Ti'Louse never names her only abuser. When she's speaking to others she only says "she" and everyone knows who. Ti'Louse only says *"Manman"* when falteringly responding to Ateya's questions.

"Who didn't bring you here?"

"*She* didn't."

When the truck stops, I am careful not to grab her injured hand to help her down.

"It doesn't hurt anymore."

Mimi hauls the two large suitcases of supplies out of the truck. The gate man runs to help. He gleefully takes both suitcases and walks as quickly as he can. He feels rich to be the bearer of such large, bulging parcels. He wants to be a part of this gift-giving, this offering. Another man opens the double doors for him and holds it open for us. He extends his hand to take one of the bags but is immediately rebuffed by his colleague. Mimi instructs both wiry men to go call the owner of the hospital.

Hôpital Croix-des-Bouquets has been here since I started coming for the summers. Back then it was a source of pride for the town and for Ma, who proudly pointed it out as we drove to La Tranblè one of the first times I visited. Ma had stolen supplies from the hospital where she worked in New York to help stock the clinic. It wasn't stealing, she said, if you were giving to the poor.

I remember the last time I really focused on this place. That year, Ma did an about-face when it came to leaving me behind. She stayed the few days as she had planned and, although I was supposed to stay for three long months, she rushed me back to New York with her. Ma and I were scared. Everyone present that day was shaken. I had never seen, let alone experienced, anything like that. The group of communion party guests, which included most of the village, feared that Ateya's father had killed her and believed that if not that day, it was only a matter of time before he beat her to death. The fact that her mother, Guit (short for *Guitar*), didn't protect or help her confirmed what people surmised—that the next time Ateya would wear a pretty white dress would be at her funeral.

At least she didn't die. At least.

He didn't have to hit her for her to fall. The ground beneath her feet, tiled like in rich people's houses, still soapy from the morning's sloppy mopping and her slick-bottomed new shoes, would have gotten the best of her eventually. But he had to show the power that his little wealth had bought him.

A restaurant is what everybody called it, even though it was really a bar with tables at which no one ever sat. The folding chairs were as unsteady as the barstools, so patrons always leaned against the high sawdust plank bar top. That would have to hold. No one could afford spillage of watered-down drinks for the undiscerning and the quality, five-star stuff for those who considered themselves upper class because they were less poor than their comrades. That day he poured his best for those who'd brought misleadingly thick envelopes for the bash.

Four slanted tables topped with plastic floral coverings lined the freshly painted wall. It was hard to tell if the tables were off kilter or the floor was uneven. The wall did all of the work of keeping both from collapsing under the weight of aluminum platters of saucy chicken and beef, eggplant legume, rice and red beans, rice with *djion-djion*, yellow rice, white rice, plantains, roasted pork butts, and the Haitian version of macaroni and cheese. After the food was consumed and drinks got more and more watery, a servant brought out an ornately frosted three-tiered cake that formed the bodice and bell-shaped bottom of a doll's ball gown. A tiny crown of artificial flowers lay gently on the blond ringlets of the plastic ivory doll that looked edible itself.

As the servant crept gingerly into the room, Ateya ran toward her, begging to carry her cake. It was her cake. Although the doll looked nothing like her, although the cake dress was prettier than the one she was wearing, she was confident that she could successfully carry the cake the few feet to the table. Guit followed behind Ateya to reassure everyone that nothing would happen to the masterpiece. Ateya's father followed to ensure that the money he'd borrowed to buy such an elaborate and enviable confection would not be wasted. Ateya had just made it to the table when it collapsed, tipping the cake toward her. She stumbled backward from the weight but Guit caught her daughter before she could fall.

The cake splattered on the ground. As Ateya's father's fury rose, he lunged toward Ateya to slap her across the face but, at the last minute, he closed his large open palm into an enormous tight fist and boxed her on the side of her head. The lightning strike knocked both daughter and mother on their backs. Before noticing its source, the attendees gasped at the blood dripping on the imported dresses that would be irreversibly ruined. Their gasps turned to wails when they saw Ateya lying on the floor with blood pouring from her ear.

While she was still unconscious, the guests whispered their consensus that any father was entitled to dole out a blow, especially after laying out so much money for such a grand event. *But,* they whispered, *he didn't have to hit her that hard. Not that hard. Is she alive? Go and see. No, it's bad luck to die on your communion day. I thought it was good luck since you had just repented. Is she dead? No.*

No one rushed Ateya to the hospital or called for a nurse or a doctor, not in the moment nor in the days after, nor ever. Even after Ateya lost hearing in the damaged ear, Guit did not dare ask the father for carfare, let alone money to pay a clinic.

Ma begged to take Ateya to the clinic but Guit refused. She said she preferred to use the money for necessities. Ma didn't just bow, she kneeled before Guit to let Ateya come to New York with us. Guit screamed all night, accusing Ma of trying to steal and enslave the child. Her no's rang in Ateya's remaining hearing ear. When we left, Ma received a promise that she could continue paying for Ateya's schooling beyond high school so the girl would learn some skill that would make her self-sufficient. Guit died before she could see the sprouting of plantain trees in an invisible grove that made the neighbors in the *lakou* believe that Ateya was insane and desperate as well as deaf. They figured that if someone could be knocked senseless, she could be knocked crazy too.

This place is not run by a foreign NGO, which is why I bring the supplies here. It's more of a clinic with a few rooms for overnight and longer stays. The only air-conditioned room doubles as the town morgue.

Mimi, Ti'Louse, and I stay long enough for the nurses to document the inventory, offer us water and cookies, which we decline, and thank us more than necessary. I shake the owner's hand, a gesture that makes Ti'Louse frown.

We take our places in the truck on our way back. Mimi drives. Ti'Louse sits in my lap in the backseat. I ask Mimi to stop along the road to buy *fritaye*, chicken, pork, goat meat accompanied by plantains, all pan-fried until crispy and topped with *piklise*, pickled peppers, cabbage, and carrots. The oil from the food mixes with the vinegar from the spicy condiment and the savory smell permeates the air around us. Mimi will not allow me to eat in the truck so I must ride with the paper bag parcel of delicious food for the entire drive. Out of spite, I put the greasy bag on the seat next to me.

Ti'Louse smiles at my pettiness. I wrap my arms around her waist and she places her hands on top of mine. I examine her poorly healed hand as if I could fix it by staring. I do not kiss it like I would have done to Miles or Yves. I don't know how she would react if I did.

When we get back to the house, Ateya is waiting for us out front again. As we walk toward her, I take Ti'Louse's broken hand. Ateya's face drops. Tears start to form, and I realize that I have never seen her cry as an adult. These must be tears of guilt. She knows that I know. I should kiss the hand now.

7

There must have been
an invisible grove of seeing trees,
a guiding path of dry leaves,
steering the feet of a lost wanderer
searching blindly for a way through life

Ateya didn't bother arguing with Genevieve. She had no reason to fear that her cousin would abscond with Ti'Louse since Genevieve had left Miles behind to sulk and sleep. She even waved a half-hearted good-bye that no one saw. When she was sure that the truck had made it out of the yard, she went into the house to satisfy her curiosity.

She just wanted to look at the boy. She had never had the privilege of watching a man sleep. None of her lovers had ever lain down, let alone spent the night. Her children had not been allowed the luxury of daytime slumber. Despite what the neighbors said about the grove being the domain of toiling, half-living men, it was her boys who'd tended the plantain harvest when they were younger. But, as they grew older, her sons became lazy because of hired help and their allotments of rich remittances. Even now, whenever they were in her presence, she would always find something for them to do, never allowing them to sit down, and certainly not sleep at her house. She thought of rest as an indulgent activity.

Ateya's manner of mothering was different from Genevieve's in every way. Ateya had just witnessed it. Genevieve cajoled rather than directed, asked rather than told, convinced rather than commanded. When none of those gentle gestures worked, Genevieve let Miles be, as if any other action would be as futile as trying to make him grow taller or change the color of his eyes.

Ateya ran her eyes over the length of Miles's body on the bed. He was more manly than most of the men in the village. His command of his physique, height, muscles, even his jawline, spoke of a confidence of someone who never had to worry about the bare necessities or even luxuries, who was pampered and carefree with no real responsibilities. She didn't try to look beyond the surface or ask herself if anything lay beneath. His secure repose even in a place he had never been before was an insult to her. Even here, with poverty all around him, he could relax, knowing that not only would his needs be met abundantly, but if for some reason they were not, he could always leave and go back home. Why had Genevieve brought him here? No doubt as punishment. Ateya's daily existence, which she regarded as quite comfortable, certainly far better than ninety percent of the people in her village, was his jail sentence.

Ateya wished that she could sleep like Miles. She could barely do so at night, and so napping in the middle of the day was as unimaginable as it was enviable. At bedtime her hearing ear kept her awake so she could anticipate and avoid the danger that never came but that she would forever dread—a second blow to her silent ear. But recently, she'd begun to fear something worse, the lowing of some unborn thing. Quiet yet piercing, it even made the lobe of her dead ear vibrate. Afraid of seeing in addition to hearing the shapeless, growling, prowling thing intruding on the stillness of her nights, she'd started sleeping with a pillow over her head and a blanket over that. However, she found no relief nor protection from the accompanying tremor.

She longed for the nights when the most frightening thing had been the hush of dirt settling in the graves of the grandmother whom she had never met and the mother she had tried to hate. She had a feeling that the peaceful floating of dry plantain leaves to the feet of the trees, the hush of the grove she had cultivated, would soon be gone. It was the sound of fronds landing that told her when the fruit was ready for harvest. Although her hearing kept her awake at night, it had served her well. Coupled with her education in agriculture, her right ear's ability to sense and assemble sound gave her everything she needed to coax the fingered hands of plantain trees out of the ground.

Charming fruit from stony soil was the raising of the dead; at least that's how her neighbors had seen it. They'd been further convinced of this when Yanique had brought white people to run an irrigation line in what would be a lucrative field of plantains. The yard folk concocted lore that soon became their truth about *zonbi* brought to trick them into seeing what was not there, what had never been and could never be. Arable land in dry country where it rarely rained was the deception of witchcraft workers from America. It was not that her neighbors were dumb—far from it. They simply refused to believe in what they had never seen so close to their yard before. They had only passed such things on the roads leading out of La Tranblè to Croix-des-Bouquets. Palm trees were the norm and therefore plausible. They ate from squat cashew trees strewn randomly about the yard. Low-growing garden plants regularly fed them—eggplant, all manner of beans, tomatoes, hot and sweet peppers. These became richer as water flowed underground and into the spigots that soon sprouted behind their houses. But even as they reveled in its gifts, they refused to concede that the grove was real. The contradictions in their beliefs manifested in earnest as they believed in the yield but not the source.

Every night while slipping into sleep, Ateya tried to ignore the words that seeped out of the dreams of her incredulous neighbors. She heard what was never spoken out loud and learned things she did not want to know—their hopes, fears, and sins, and what they thought of her. Through sealed windows and closed doors, over the gritty hum of dying generators allowed to run for only minutes at a time to charge phones, she heard their envy and felt her own. She envied them their sound slumber and wondered what nighttime was like absent the noisy silence that plagued her. What was it like to only hear her own voice inside her mind? To fall and stay asleep and think her own thoughts, uninterrupted by the meddling of whispered things? She sometimes wished that both of her ears had been damaged, that she was completely deaf. That would have been a mercy.

———

"Miles," Ateya said. Then in an exaggerated and slow Kreyòl, "Are you hungry?"

Miles groaned as he sat up. "What?"

Ateya repeated herself and enunciated so he could understand her. Genevieve had always said that her boys understood Kreyòl. Ateya guessed that they only understood it when they were fully awake and alert.

"No. *Non, merci,*" he replied, trying to get his bearings.

When he stood up, Ateya rolled her eyes, no longer admiring but disgusted by this boy, whose privilege stood out like his head and shoulders in a crowd of her townsmen.

As she walked to the kitchen, she could hear him dragging his feet behind her. He mumbled something about the heat as he walked past her to go outside. She's the one who'd needed air. She had sweated out a meal in a narrow, windowless kitchen in preparation for his arrival, and he was complaining about the heat.

Ateya proudly lifted the iron lid, exposing the beautiful product of her hands, *legume beregen,* eggplant stew with a mix of vegetables. She had not only cooked the food, she had grown every ingredient. She replaced the lid and raised another, revealing a pot of rice blackened with the water from dried mushrooms, *duri avec djion-djion.* The steam from the rice rose with the smell of the stew, and the feeling of pride and satisfaction threatened to morph into joy Ateya didn't think she deserved. Her heart, now lodged under her right breast, nearly stopped when she smiled. Feeling herself soften, she regrouped so she could make it through the day. Not that she would break down. She never did that because she never allowed herself to go up in the first place.

Ateya rubbed away her smile, an unfamiliar, unsullied delight she hadn't felt in years and no longer understood. She only knew danger in pleasure. She did not search herself for the origin of the warmth that flashed over her, soothing and light, like ash from a dying fire. That feeling was her and not her. It was outside and inside her at the same time. It was the something and someone she fought for control of her emotions. She thought of it as her weak second self, her vulnerable self that constantly threatened to cleave off and start a fire, a life, of its own.

Instead of stirring the *legume* again, Ateya went outside to the yard, where Miles was now standing. She let him follow her as she walked toward the plantain grove, from which petrichor and coolness emanated. Desperate to know the source of this delicious relief, Miles quickened his step and soon passed her. She let him stride ahead until he reached the muddy boundary between the yard's dry dirt and the moist soil of the grove.

Anyone who was watching them would wonder, once again, why Ateya was so in awe of an empty parcel that grew rocks from dust and nothing more. She would always be regarded as someone tipping into senility, a woman who pretended to raise a thriving plantain harvest from desiccated earth. They could not, would not accept that there was something soft and lush and warm and rich before them. They saw what was familiar. Two common coconut trees, dry-leafed, with hard-shelled fruit that fell to ground that would not give. A smattering of mango trees was believable only because of the green stillborn fruit hanging from the branches like tears. They preferred to dismiss the oasis at the end of the yard as a mirage. A true story written off as an old wives' tale, history as wispy folklore, a puissant spirit as an ordinary ghost. A hardened woman with no supple second self inside her.

Because she had allowed the community around her to be her mirror, Ateya sometimes doubted her reality. She was dismissive of her own depth, afraid of the parts of herself that were intricate and layered, suspicious of what she *knew* and trusting the simple stuff of made-up stories. In the midst of the faithless, she would sometimes imagine that the leafy, generous plantain grove was nothing more than an oppressive, sweltering wasteland.

She would find relief when someone else would see what she saw, what she knew to be true. A stranger might walk into the yard from the road and inquire about the source of the cool breeze, the smell of loam, the welcoming wave of green arms. If Mimi and the laborers had just loaded the pickup, the stranger would want to know about the water that was needed to yield plantains as long as a forearm. The visitor might be tempted but also afraid to step into the grove, which seemed to fade away, then reappear before the eyes. If they were with a child, they might let the youngster dip a toe across the border, into the beauty their adult eyes simultaneously saw and disbelieved the more they stared. Sensing that the grown-up was becoming overwhelmed, Ateya would lead them away and send them back up the gravel slope onto the steady ground of the road. The child would always want to stay to run through this idyllic and wondrous hide-and-seek place that they trusted wholly.

Miles's wide-eyed curiosity confirmed for Ateya that, despite his size and defiance, he was still a child. She empathized with his curiosity about the neat rows of wide-leafed plants, soft soil, and air so misty it intimated rain. So she gestured her permission to enter with a quick nod and watched as he stepped forward and then disappeared into the green. She knew that he would be safe. It was only a few acres, barely enough to get lost in. As long as he followed the mossy grid and the intermittent spigots of the irrigation line, he'd be fine.

She would not go with him. Enviously peering into the barely penetrable leafy path, she would try to convince herself that the grove was only fit for filthy laborers and wandering children. Every once in a while, she would nearly succumb to the allure of the smell of wet loam wafting through the angry dirt yard. But to keep from yielding to dangerous pleasure-seeking, she always closed her eyes at the border.

She only went in when she separated herself into two halves—the self she showed to others and the other she kept hidden. Her hardened self would watch as her irrepressible, yielding second self escaped from her body and ran into the grove.

When she was a child, she used to squeeze her eyes and press her feet into the dry ground to keep her brittle self in place. If she allowed that self to stare at the diversion of the thrilling green, both of her selves would enter, and neither would return. Both halves of her would wrap arms around a plantain tree and disappear into it. Even now, she coveted the courage of those who fearlessly flung their complete selves into the embrace of trees. These were the brave or foolish ones, unafraid of the grove's green breath, confident that they would emerge more whole than when they went in.

During her weakest moments, Ateya would release that soft self. More stalwart as a grown-up, turning a blind eye, allowing her other self small freedoms. Her hardened self would wait patiently but anxiously, afraid of her soft self being seen leaving or reentering her bricklike body. *She* was never allowed to enter. *She* had never tasted the dew, had never dug her toes into the earth, never leaned against a tree, sighed into the mist to breathe. But she would give her softened self enough time to enjoy itself. This is the self she would sometimes send forward to find Ti'Louse, to join her in a game of tag rather than drag her back. This other self, the child that Ateya had never been allowed to be, would chase Ti'Louse, who did not know that her imaginary playmate was actually her mother.

A familiar panic suddenly rose inside Ateya. Worried that she had lost track of time, she separated and sent her soft self to find Miles. She felt treacherous going after him because she had never been in there with anyone except Ti'Louse, so Ateya turned back and ran out of the grove into her own waiting arms. Her hardened half absorbed her second self into the rigid body that did not understand love. She barely had time to gather herself before she heard the pickup creeping down the bumpy rubble road with the trio of Mimi, Genevieve, and Ti'Louse. She called after Miles to come back, not a commanding cry, but a compassionate one that conveyed her empathy for how heartbreaking it was to separate oneself from the caress of loving trees.

Miles emerged with a gratified smile on his face, conveying his enviable transformation. Ateya would not let herself smile back. Instead, she frowned and beckoned him to come forward with his head bent down toward her. In a gesture she had never known herself to make, she wiped the moisture from his forehead. She looked over her shoulder to make sure that no one had seen her in the posture of innocence and self-lessness. When she released him, she felt lost and so she held on to what was familiar—a brittle body and equally rough ground. As her believing self struggled, she felt her heart split like a wink releasing a tear.

She didn't know why but she started to cry.

8

*There must have been
doors closed to long-ago loves
crossed arms forbidding hugs
closed mouths rejecting kisses
open graves waiting, waiting*

I didn't think you were coming back," is how Ateya welcomes us.

"We almost didn't," I respond.

She stares at Ti'Louse with a harsh look that exclaims: *What did you tell that woman? You better not have said anything. Our business is our business. Let go of her hand. Get inside now!*

Knowing that Ateya's gaze could be followed by a lunge and a slap, I drop Ti'Louse's hand and gently nudge her toward the front door. I have no strength to fight.

It is hard to imagine that Ateya is the same person I couldn't wait to spend time with as a child when I was banished to Haiti for the summers.

When Ateya got pregnant for the first but not the last time, I didn't think that Ma would send me to Haiti ever again. I can't remember whether she didn't let me stay long or if I had chosen not to stay the entire summer. But Ateya was incensed.

"I can't believe you're only staying for just two weeks."

"I can't believe you're going to have a baby!" I reached out to touch Ateya's belly, but she recoiled.

"Make it three weeks. Please."

"I have summer school," I lied.

"And?"

"And a job . . ."

"Friends, boys?"

"Neither, really. Definitely no boys."

"You want to sit on your phone, in your own room, in your nice house."

"Apartment. With Ma and Ol'Lady, don't forget."

"We could go to Port-au-Prince every day. I guess you don't want to spend your summer taking bucket baths, riding tap-tap in the backwoods with your backward cousin."

"That's not true!" The part about spending time with her wasn't, but the rest I could do without.

"Go ahead and rush back to your pretty bathroom, working shower, neat streets, air-conditioned buses, smooth roads."

"Roads? I don't even drive. And I take the subway. Everywhere."

"It's better than this place. That's what two weeks tells me."

"You could come with me."

"Not anymore or ever." She looked down at her stomach. She was seven or eight months along, but she looked like she was about to give birth at any minute.

"You know we could have gotten away with it." I looked at her mischievously.

"Here we go again. . . . You know damn well. It was your fault we got caught anyway."

We were arguing again, half joking, about our mad plan to get her to New York.

"You should have taken charge, Atè. You were older."

"You were more stubborn. And braver. Smarter but also more conspicuous."

"I just wanted to keep you company in the suitcase. I didn't want you to get scared."

Ateya sighed like she always did when we had this discussion. We both wished the plan had worked.

"Then your accident . . ." I said, looking away, so I wouldn't stare at her ear. I still couldn't look straight at her without showing pity.

"It wasn't an accident, Gen. He wanted to cripple me. I think he knew that my mother was seriously thinking about letting me go. He must have known that I wouldn't be able to fly with my damaged ear. Not even to get it fixed."

"You give him too much credit."

"Blame. Not credit."

We remained quiet for a while. Silence was still easy between us then. We were both on the verge of tears.

"You should have stayed out of the bag. I could have made it by myself."

"The car never even got a chance to pull away."

"They were looking for you! Even if your mother believed the lie about why I was nowhere to be found, there's no way she would have left you behind, silly."

"Your mother was never going to let you go."

"I know. But it was fun to dream, to plan, to act like I had a choice, or that I could make something happen."

"You have a choice now," I said, looking at her conspiratorially.

"To do what? I'm too far along to do anything," she said in a low voice. "And I also have the plantain project." This she said with the gravity of a pastor charged with leading his flock to salvation.

"Growing stuff isn't a bad thing."

"You still want to be a doctor?"

"Of course! What else?"

"You can tell me the truth. I won't say anything to your mother or mine."

"It's true. I still want to be a doctor."

"And you can. And you will. I know it. Maybe you'll deliver my next baby."

"I won't be a certified doctor for another ten years. Are you going to wait that long?"

"That's perfect. I don't want to have another one anytime soon."

"Do you remember that pretty *marabou* girl? The one Mimi had a crush on when we were little?"

"We all had a crush on that girl. The entire town did."

"So pretty for a brown-skinned girl," Ateya and I said in unison, dissolving into tearful laughter.

"She has three already! She's only a couple of years older than I am."

"You're just as pretty as she is, so be careful."

I reached for Ateya again. This time, she let me pat her stomach.

"You'd better watch out or he'll kick you."

"How do you know it's a boy?"

"That's what all of the women in the yard say."

I placed my head on the mound.

"You're really asking for it now," she said, placing her hand on my cheek. "Gen?"

"Yes?"

"You're going to be a godmother."

"No, I'm not. I don't want a boy. I'll wait for a girl. And I'll take both of you with me. Plus Mimi."

Ateya took in a deep breath and let it out slowly. I felt her stomach rise and fall.

"You've been practicing." I lifted my head to give her room to breathe.

"Two weeks? Really?"

Standing in front of Ateya's house now, even with anger flowing between us, I want to hug the girl she used to be. I don't think she remembers us—how close we were. Then again, how can she remember? It was five sons ago for her. Two for me. And a tug-of-war for a girl, her girl.

Ti'Louse leaves my side and runs past her mother and into the house before she gets hit.

I want to see my son, to make sure he survived the few hours spent with Ateya while I was gone. Light from the setting sun elongates my shadow on the ground in front of me as I cross the yard.

I find Miles sitting on the bed in our room, pad and pencil in hand.

"May I see? Please?"

He turns away from me. "I know that you look at my stuff."

"All moms do. How else do you find out what's going on with our children? Teenagers aren't exactly forthcoming."

"You could just ask."

"But would you answer?"

"Can we not talk about this?"

"No, let's talk."

"I share stuff with my closest friends."

"The ones who get you in trouble?"

"I make my own decisions, Mom. Anyway, who else would I talk to?"

"I don't trust them."

"You don't know them."

I stand over him and catch a glimpse of a page saturated with trees and wide leaves. He has drawn the plantain garden. There is an outline of a man with his back turned. The shadow, which is not filled in, is poised to walk. Its hand is extended, as if reaching for someone else's hand.

"Never mind," I say.

He puts the drawing down and tries to call home, to call Yves, to let Ma and Ol'Lady know that we made it but, in addition to having no reception, his phone is nearly dead. The electricity here is feeble but at least it has not been shut off entirely since we arrived. Even when the power goes off, Ateya refuses to use the generator because of the price of fuel. The air-conditioning unit in the window has probably never been touched since Ma sent it here when I was a teenager. Ateya has held on to the tradition of frugality Ma and Ol'Lady say was passed down from her mother and grandmother. Before we got here, I warned Miles not to bother asking for it to be turned on.

I know that a brownout will roll in at some point in the days to come and Miles is going to flip out. He has never been without electricity except for once, but I'm not sure that he would remember. I haven't been deprived either, for the most part—only the blackout of 1977, when Ma dragged me out of the apartment to go to the Food O Rama on Broadway to loot rice, of all things. Not that we needed it. She just wanted to get something free and to send that free stuff to Haiti.

The second time I experienced a blackout was in 2003. Although Bright wasn't living at home then, he was still using the apartment as a walk-in closet from which he would snatch clothes he left behind—a few shirts, a tie, one or two suits—and leave to go to wherever it was that he was living back then. It was August, so it was still light out well past eight o'clock, which reminded me of something Ol'Lady used to say: "Love may be blind, but my love sees just a little bit." A little light stuck around, so we could see just a bit if we weren't afraid to look.

When dusk finally died, giving way to an evenly dark sky with no stars, I could still see shadows, mine and Miles's, as we took turns standing in the beam of a flashlight. I wasted a deep breath and pushed my stomach out. My shadow was an uppercase *B*, boobs and belly. Miles and I laughed so much that both our stomachs shook. He was chubby then, but not yet self-conscious about it.

"Do you remember the blackout when you were eight?"

"I was almost nine, Mom. Yves slept through the whole thing."

"He was only two. Two and a half? He wouldn't have remembered even if he had been awake."

Miles tries to call home again. I know that he is more eager to speak to his brother than anyone else.

"Still no signal?"

"Shit! I mean 'shoot'!"

As he curses at the red battery symbol on his phone, I remind him again with a side eye about our agreement—no cursing in my presence or in front of any adults and no slip-ups in Haiti, for sure. Despite my reprimand, we both laugh, remembering our shadows back then. Our chuckling settles into smiles as we think about how Yves never even knew there was a blackout. He is ours. Just then, out of nowhere, the power goes off and we are in the dark. It's for less than a minute. We laugh again, a nervous echo into the quiet, dark night outside our door. I unplug the fan to give Miles an hour to charge his phone and he promises that we'll keep the fan on for the rest of the night.

I walk out of our room to try to catch an elusive breeze. I step into a timeless twilight. The humidity mocks me. I feel like I am breathing through the damp washcloth in my hand. I touch my face in the dark and find that it is still wet, but not from sweat. I am crying tears that come upon me hard and fast. I hold my breath so I won't heave or allow my scream to escape and alert Miles. As suddenly as the crying came, prayer falls from my tear-sodden, quivering lips. Then, as if someone has slammed the back of my legs with a big stick, I drop to my knees.

I haven't kneeled like this since my wedding day and I haven't prayed since Bright left me holding a wet and trembling child in my lap and another inside me. But here I am, in the middle of my mother's country, on ground so rocky I will be bleeding when I stand up. Better me than Miles. Although the Haitian proverb says differently: *"Pito ti moun kriye, gran moun pa kriye."* "Better that children cry so grown-ups don't." The belief is that it's better that a child cries from a corrective beating than for an adult to cry because the child has done something irrevocable. I'd rather be the one crying, praying. I can handle it. Better me than him. And better here than in New York.

I am still afraid for Miles, even though we are away from home, away from the danger that he seems determined to drown in. He represses his emotions the way someone holds down vomit to keep from throwing up. He has the same look of fear I saw on his face the night he came home from joyriding. It is the look I've seen on the faces of my patients, rape victims with wide, bloodshot eyes that they lower when they are speaking to me in whispers between heartbreaking yelps. Someone, something has touched Miles in a way that is wrong, invasive, demeaning, terrifying. Someone has stroked parts of him that no one except a lover should, when he's old enough, or a mother, when he's young. I know that look. I have seen it on his face before but without the tears. That terror of being touched, even for just a minute, by someone who never should have touched, someone who knew that Miles was a child who had done no wrong. But that self-loathing someone despised my son, not a spoken or even a conscious hatred, but something instinctive, automatic, and therefore most dangerous.

Miles witnessed a stop-and-frisk while walking, not driv-

ing. Before he even reached puberty, he watched the light pet-
ting that escalated into a full-on up-against-the-wall assault of
bodies in skins as dark as his. He didn't tell me until he could
no longer hide behind the plausible "I'm fine, Mom, really"
that I believed because I needed a lie to hold on to. The truth
was slippery, wet blood spilling from irreparable wounds that
I could not heal. I held back tears from "the talk" that brought
Bright back to sit down and explain with me what no parent
should have to explain to a twelve-year-old. From the time
Miles was a talking toddler able to name all of his body parts,
we told him about inappropriate touching, the need to tell, the
fact that the one touching would get arrested by the police and
go to jail. But this other talk was not the same.

We had to explain that there would be a new touching, one
that would be scary but permissible, that it would hurt inside
and out, and that the one who touched would not get arrested
by but actually *be* the police. Although the law allowed this,
the pat-down, the stroke, the strip, the frisk, the fondling
would feel as invasive molestation.

Years later, when he arrived at the door with the officer,
Miles saw my fear in full. He had seen a more subtle, contained
version of that look on my face every time he came home after
sunset—even if it was the early darkness of a pre-solstice fall.
This was different. I was crying, holding on to Bright to keep
from falling, grabbing Miles into our grip to soothe and apologize to him even though he was in the wrong. Miles shed a
few tears mainly because I was crying. Bright's eyes were dry
but bloodshot. We were all hurting but I knew that Miles's
pain was greater than ours in that moment. This drive wasn't
one of the rapid-succession rebellious acts that would get him
in trouble with us, safely, only with us. This time he'd delib-

erately put himself in danger out there where the punishment for taking childish liberties could mean the taking of his life.

This told me everything I already knew—that Miles is both afraid and willing to die. The fear of how it might happen worries him and us. In the cruel arm of a chokehold or a curled hand around an unholstered gun. In doubtful eyes questioning the ownership of the Range Rover. Presumptuous eyes misjudging pocketed hands for concealment of an instrument of harm. The reactive jerk of an arm signaling resistance. The tears rolling over question-answering quivering lips mistaken as an attempt to spit into a clean-shaven face. Every move made misinterpreted as a reason to beat or to kill.

I had to admit, having seen that look of shame and despair on many faces before and even in the rap song he still listens to, that my son wanted to die. Not like that. He didn't want to die like that, no matter how much pain he was in, how disappointed he was in me, how angry he was at Bright. He didn't want to die like that. Better by his own hands. But he would never hang himself. Self-lynching was still lynching. He would choose some painless, peaceful method, since it might be Yves who found him. He would choose to look asleep, so his passing would be easier for me to explain to his brother. Miles would choose a reversible method in case he was found too soon, lying on his back with tears still streaming out of the corners of his eyes, down the sides of his face. If he survived, he would want to wake up in a hospital. To see me wounded and apologetic. To see Bright broken and speechless.

"God, please, don't let anything happen to my son." I am still on my knees in the heat, in the dark. In my country that is home and not home. A place that is even less home to Miles. "Please, let this trip work, Lord." All I want to do is my job as a mother, the one that started when he was in the womb, my sole purpose since he was born, the one thing I cannot mess up. I must keep him alive. Alive—not educated, not clothed, not entertained, not even happy. Life is all that matters. And the idea that someone might want to take his life, to harm the thing I love the most in the world, that someone might want him dead, is impossible to bear. But I bear it like millions of other mothers everywhere every day. That someone might actually *do* something to make him die raises my rage, turns me into something dangerous, dark, unrecognizable yet inbred, shockingly unfamiliar yet as natural as blood. "Lord, please, give me everything I need to be a mother."

I jump at the sound of the alarm on Miles's phone going off. His charging hour is up. I dust off my knees and run inside to silence the sound so it won't wake him up. His notepad pokes out from under his pillow.

As I unplug the charger to get the fan whirring, Miles says, "It is steaming in here," which startles me just a little bit.

"It's just as hot outside, so don't bother going," is what I say in the same tone I would use back home to warn him of external danger. I want to protect him, even from the heat.

I lie down on the narrow mattress that smells new, even through the sun-dried, starched sheets.

"What are we doing tomorrow, Mom?" Miles whispers, aware that the door is open.

"I'll take you around as long as Mimi's not too tired. She told me that the pickers are coming to the grove in the morning. I see you've already discovered it."

"I wish I could sleep there."

"Ateya would have a fit if you even suggested that," I say, raising my voice slightly.

"You know what? I miss Yves."

"Me too. I know he misses you too. He misses us, but mostly you."

"I'm sorry, Mom," Miles says.

"I'm sorry too. But you have to do better, be better for him."

"I don't mean to—"

"I know."

"No, you don't."

"Trust me, I know." My voice is nearly inaudible out of consideration for Ateya.

I know that she hears our whispers and, although she probably can't make out what we are saying, she can hear the affection in our voices. I hope it is contagious.

Suddenly, bare feet are pitter-pattering on the ground outside our door. Ti'Louse runs into the room. Before she can catch her breath, she drops to the ground in front of my bed and pulls a mat from underneath. I can't let her sleep on the floor, so I reach for her stick of an arm and pull her toward me. For the first time since I arrived, she hesitates to come to me. I can feel her fear. She knows that if Ateya wakes up to find her here, there will definitely be a scolding or, more likely, a beating. Either will be tempered because I am present to intervene.

We will worry about the consequences of our closeness in the morning. For now, Ti'Louse burrows her tiny body into mine on the twin bed not meant for sharing. But there is plenty of room for a grown woman and an undergrown child. If not for her moist skin touching mine, I would scarcely know that she was there. As she falls asleep, she inhales and then sighs. I miss Yves a little less.

Miles's voice is soft and kind. "Good night, little sister." Either he misses Yves more than I thought or he welcomes the possibility of having another sibling. "Good night, Mom."

~᷒~

Two lithe-bodied boys stand at the door to the room, waiting for me and Miles to wake up. At their feet are four bright plastic buckets of water for our showers. I gesture for them to come in and they slip silently into the room so as not to wake Miles. Ti'Louse trails them, holding a tin cup that I will use to ladle the sun-warmed water over my sticky body. The boys leave as quietly as they came in, their moist bodies assisting their glide. They look like they need the shower more than I do, although my skin feels simultaneously damp and dusty. I can't tell if I am wet from nighttime perimenopausal hot-cold sweat or from the humidity. Although he isn't here, a fleeting thought of Yves runs through my mind as the culprit, since he still wets the bed every now and then. I pinch my nightshirt and lower my nose to take in my scent but there is no distinct smell to reveal the source of the moisture. Ti'Louse stands guard by my bed, clearly not wanting to disturb Miles, who has started to toss and turn. I know that he is nowhere near awake, since his teenage-boy body clock is set to an afternoon wake-up time.

"Come here, you," I say and point to Miles still sleeping deeply.

I pull her to me and nuzzle into her neck to elicit a chuckle, but she doesn't make a sound as she wriggles in my arms.

Anticipating my need, she gets up quickly and brings me my tote bag, where my travel-size toiletries are packed in their Ziploc bag. She pulls my small suitcase from under the bed and unzips it to reveal what she thinks I should wear today. I packed nothing special: some plain tops, a pair of jeans, and a wash-and-wear dress that is passable for church, since Ateya will want to show us off there on Sunday. Ti'Louse looks slightly disappointed. She was looking forward to dressing me up, but she quickly rebounds, as if coming to the realization that I am enough. I leave her sitting on the bed as I go to the bathroom to bathe.

I squat over the toilet because the scent of strong detergent mixed with urine reminds me of a public bathroom. I will have to pour half a bucket of water into the bowl to flush. I know that no water flows through the plumbing that was built into the house's infrastructure. It would be a sin to use so much water for one house when it can be shared among the entire yard. Instead, the water is fetched from one of the communal spigots.

In the bathtub, I use the remaining water in the bucket, knowing that Miles, who has never showered like this before, will use more than I will. I pour water over my head and feel it mix with last night's sweat. That one cup is just enough to moisten my body so I can lather up every crease where dust has collected. I roll the soapy washcloth over my hips that arch on either side like a bow and then run my bare hands down my legs. I can say that I am in love with my body. I have only recently learned this, only after observing First Lady Michelle Obama, whose shape is like mine—arms as long and taut as my legs, birthing hips that I sometimes feel Bright holding on to in waking dreams. My maker has been neither generous nor stingy in the allocation of breasts. "More than a mouthful is a waste," Bright used to whisper. I wish I'd loved my figure more when I was younger, at least as much as he did.

I carefully step out of the tub and listen as the drain slowly slurps the faint clay water. I throw on the clothes that Ti'Louse has selected. I know that she has done so as meticulously as a bride selecting her wedding gown.

As Ti'Louse and I leave the room, I holler over my shoulder: "Your turn, Miles!" But as expected, he does not respond. I know that he has been dreading this unfamiliar and therefore uncomfortable manner of bathing. He will have to bend down to scoop the water that he is unaccustomed to rationing. There is no strong spray conveniently coming down from above nor taps that can be turned to his preferred temperature. This is the easiest of the annoyances he will experience over the course of this trip. I laugh at the thought of him attempting to dodge soggy trash in the streets to keep clean the sneakers I told him not to bring. As if reading my thoughts, Ti'Louse chuckles in solidarity.

Ti'Louse and I hold hands as we make our way to the kitchen. Not wanting to draw her mother's criticism as a greedy child, Ti'Louse stays out of the kitchen. She will not come in unless and until she is called. I am so hungry and can't wait to eat the smell-good that has surrounded my taste buds all morning. I join Ateya in the kitchen, where my breakfast is already plated—hard-boiled eggs, beets, watercress, and avocado take up half of the plate. Boiled plantains topped with calf's liver and onions smothered in tomato gravy occupy the other half. I already know that Miles won't eat this. So does Ateya, who grudgingly turns the knob on the gas cylinder to light the stove.

"Come here and help me," I say to Ti'Louse, who has been peeking into the room. She attempts to whisk the eggs, then fails, so I take over. She is more accustomed to using a fork for this work, but she wants to impress me by doing it the "American way." I lose myself in the beating, staring at the flames that bloom like a lotus around the small pan. Ateya has added too much oil but I don't dare pour any of it out. Miles will just have to eat *fried* scrambled eggs.

I can hear him splashing water and imagine the mess on the bathroom floor that Ateya will make Ti'Louse wipe up. I don't want to argue about this since I plan to take Ti'Louse with me to Port-au-Prince to enjoy the tour of the capital with Miles and Mimi. When I finish making the eggs, I distract Ateya by running my fingers along the wood-paneled wall, which sags with the weight of photos in ill-hung frames. Ateya smiles proudly, knowing that she has things I don't.

"Wait. I'll get the albums," Ateya says. "I bet you don't even have any of these photos of yourself when you were little."

I let her have this moment to boast. She nearly drops one of the five photo albums she is carrying as she pulls up a chair to sit next to me. I know these photographs. They are the same ones I have seen every summer since Ma and Ol'Lady started sending me to Haiti so I could learn to speak proper Kreyòl and *vive kilti*. Now I am doing the same and sharing it with my son. I reach over to help Ateya with the treasured books, and one falls. I can feel her scowling over my head as I bend down to pick it up. She does not allow me to touch anything anymore. But I hold her wrist gently to ask her to stop at a page here and there, begging for forgiveness by allowing her to gloat. She enjoys the fact that she recognizes people and places

I don't. I feel her heart beating in her wrist, on which she is wearing a thin, gold-plated Seiko watch Ma sent to her long ago. A heartbeat displaced, not a pulse, but a whole heart in her wrist, an oval cyst pounding, not pulsing, through smooth skin. I wonder to myself what anatomical anomaly could have produced something so abnormally normal. She pulls her arm away and flips the pages, some of which are stuck to the yellowed glue that holds the pictures in place. She goes on pointing out the various relatives I don't remember or never met.

I keep expecting to see smiles. The upturned corners of mouths reaching for raised cheeks, the remnants of a chuckle. I keep expecting to see, at the very least, the thin lines of neutral grins awaiting a piece of good news to tip the lips toward joyful eyes. I keep expecting an explanation for the blank stares, for the frowns practiced so long they have become more than habit; they are permanent traits. I keep expecting to see coffins, evidence of the tragedies mourned by morose looks mirrored in camera lenses that replicate the sorrow. I keep expecting to see kneeling. Over open graves, women poised to throw themselves in after too-soon-gone children. I keep expecting to see children, at the very least children, caught mid-laugh in an unplanned snapshot taken during chases around sparse trees. But all I see are drooping looks of suffering, terror, and terrible pain. Still, I keep hoping for smiles, against all odds triumphant. At least, at the very least, on the faces of the children, living, breathing littles, lost in play and captured by the grown-up snapping joy. Left alone, the children, who haven't yet acquired the habits of their elders, can erase the imprints of twisted lips fearful of the thrill of joy.

I see the young ones clasping hands over mouths ready to burst into laughter. Afraid of the tap on the shoulder, a pinch of the baby fat on the back of an arm, or a slap on the back of the head, they straighten up, eyes forward, mouths closed, chuckles chained in chests. They are raised and age that way. Despite having a husband, Madame, Ateya's grandmother, scowls. Young, shapely, and envied, Ateya's mother, Guit, frowns. Affluent and attractive, Ateya couldn't keep her bitterness at bay long enough for a camera to click and record the moment worthy of memorializing.

With lowered eyes close to closing, long faces slouch over ill-fitting formal suits and dresses. The women wear no makeup, just a dusting of face powder to keep away the shine on their foreheads. Maybe if they wore lipstick, they might find a reason to let their mouths loosen in the mirror, their eyes might light up a little at the sight of a pretty face. Not that their faces required painting—a smile goes a long way to improving the looks of an otherwise unattractive woman. And the men, smooth- or wrinkled-skinned, auburn, bark-brown, or char, might show the pleasure of stealing glances at the lovely and loving women they desire. But none of this was allowed. They certainly would not show their contentment with what they had or what had been sent from that other place, that golden road lined with tall money trees and even taller buildings. It's not that they never smiled. Laughter was allowed, especially in the dark during sex. But that was the crime—flaunting what should only be performed in private. Especially for women, an open mouth signaled lust for a tongue or something more to fill it feloniously.

I wonder at what point smiling became a sin. It must have been generations for Ateya, Guit, and Madame. But Ma and Ol'Lady broke the curse upon arrival in New York. My mother and grandmother sent open-mouthed pictures for months or years and then . . . And then what? Were they received with anger or disappointment during their first visits home? Or were they reminded by relatives whose faces condemned the foreign joy of lucky loved ones? Maybe it was the money. It is always the money. Brought home in secret sachets, various size rolls for each eager hand or sent via Atresco, CAM, Western Union, or a traveling friend. Ma and Ol'Lady were in the habit of sending photos in the envelopes, pocket- and locket-size pictures for their closest cousins, but were told that their smiles were insulting and the pictures inedible and, therefore, wasteful as well as boastful. So they sent them sparingly, if at all. Headshots only, so their well-fed bodies would not show. Downcast eyes to hide their hopeful, beaming eyes, no longer the vestiges of offensive laughter on their lips.

They counseled the just-come braggarts in their small circle of immigrants to stop showing off shiny cars they did not own, borrowed necklaces they could not afford, decorous dresses just taken off of layaway. They preached to their community to close their mouths as tightly as their purses, lest back-home kin reach into wallets for assumed but absent riches. Otherwise, "don't get mad when the insistent calls come." Not the requests but demands that money be sent home for school fees, the funerals of distant relatives, and baptisms of godchildren they had never met. When the money slowed to a trickle rather than a free flow, family on both sides of the tossed coin, judgingly and begrudgingly, ceased the sending of pictures back and forth entirely. Even the wallet-size souvenirs of school-age children in crisply ironed uniforms remained in their respective countries until a visitor announced while reminiscing over albums, *"Mwen pran ti foto sa."* "I'm taking this little picture."

I try not to show Ateya that I am critiquing these photographs, even though I know that she is doing the same. She is waiting for me to decide which ones I will take.

"Vini. Gade," Ateya calls to Miles. Miles jumps at the chance to leave the uneaten greasy eggs on the plate. I am embarrassed and try to signal to him to finish his food, but he pretends not to understand what I am telling him to do.

"Are you finished?" I say in a whisper as he walks over.

He nods and makes a face.

"Pass it to me," I say, reaching for his plate. Although my stomach is full, I force myself to eat the rest of the eggs. I dip the bread crust into my café au lait, which is still warm.

"We're leaving soon. Mimi is here," I say before I hear the beeping of the pickup truck as it backs up.

"We'll finish looking at these later, Ateya." I touch her wrist again. The smooth stone is still there, as if the skin around it might spit it out like a peach pit through puckered lips. She withdraws with a forced, apologetic grin.

"You know, Gen, when we were little, I always wanted to go to America with you. And you always wanted to stay here, but now, I can tell that you can't wait to leave," Ateya says as she sadly stacks the photo albums on top of one another. She leaves one album open to side-by-side pictures—one with her, her mother Guit, and her grandmother Madame; the other is a picture of me, Ma, and Ol'Lady, smiling without showing any teeth.

Ateya flips to the last page of the album before closing it. There is a picture that I have back home. It is one of Ti'Louse's school pictures. Her mouth is upturned in a smile. She looks as if she is trying to restrain herself, to keep from bursting out in laughter. I don't know how the photographer let Ti'Louse get away with it or why Ateya didn't demand that the picture be retaken.

It is sad but that was the extent of Ateya's generosity—to give her daughter the gift of a commemorated smile. Everything else came at a price.

9

There must have been a famished family
too wary of foreign and familiar givers
to accept hard-earned needful things

Ateya always made sure that her neighbors, all of whom were debtors, knew what and how much they owed her. She preferred not to be repaid, so she could own them. Supremacy meant more to her than money. She basked in the way they relinquished their pride with lowered eyes, bowed heads, mouths forced into disingenuous grins. She had *moun Nou Yòk,* so she always had or could always get more things. She crowned herself ruler over the yard, sat on her throne, using her neighbors' dignity as her footstool.

Ateya, Guit, and Madame were concerned about the debt their daughters would incur for their passages to America if permitted, one that could never be repaid. What was worth more than a life? For that is what was being offered.

Ateya's grandmother had given her husband six sons and a daughter in exchange for respectability. Madame had opted for a stretched and stitched vagina and an irrepressible, permanent paunch to obtain and then retain her title of Madame. Her husband had given her the right to change her given name for the married title "Madame," which is what everyone in the yard called her. She and Monsieur, whose first and last names no one remembered, lived like husband and wife, although they'd never sealed their union by signing their names on a certificate in a church. Even if the formalities had been the established custom in that community of poor people, what name would Monsieur have used? How would they have signed their names, given their illiteracy? But none of that mattered as long as the *lakou* recognized their bond.

Everyone acknowledged the fact that Madame had a man who was singularly hers, who kept his name clean and had no outside children. No woman dared doubt or violate the couple's enviable union, for they all hoped that they or their daughters would someday secure the same—a newly constructed cinder-block house and enough food to feed the entire household. Monsieur commanded more respect than other men, thereby elevating his wife's status even higher.

Just in case a newcomer to the yard had not been informed of Madame's standing, she had a photograph to flaunt as proof of their happily sealed bond. In it stood the happy couple, Madame holding their newly christened firstborn son in her arms, Monsieur standing next to a wedding cake topped with neither icing nor the plastic rendering of a well-dressed white couple.

As final confirmation, and although it sounded ridiculous, she'd been called Madame Monsieur while her husband was alive. After his death, Madame told everyone that she would retain her title out of respect for the respectful and respected man. However, it was a boastful move, like the foil-thin ring she wore on the fourth finger of her left hand.

Having worked so hard to name herself, Madame resented the moniker her youngest child and only daughter got stuck with. As the girl's preadolescent figure curved into breasts and hips held together by a small waist, the men in the yard started calling her "Guitar." Since the tongues of her neighbors refused to relinquish the name, Madame shortened it to Guit, so she wouldn't be reminded of the fact that her daughter was destined to trade her prized figure to become a wife, if she was lucky, or a mistress, if she was not. But it was Madame who'd doomed her daughter to a hard life in their township. Although she wanted more for Guit, Madame wrongfully repurposed the tuition money that her sister Ola sent from New York. In lieu of schooling, Madame built a table and placed a paucity of dried goods for Guit to sell on the side of the road in the hot sun every day.

During every annual visit, Ol'Lady begged her sister Madame to let her take Guit to New York. Out of jealousy of her well-to-do sister and the outdated belief that girls are meant to care for their mothers until the day the old women died and bury them, Madame refused to let her take Guit. By the time she was ready to let the girl go, Madame was tiptoeing toward her deathbed and Guit was pregnant with another son. Even in the afterlife, Madame's powers were too feeble to keep Guit from repeating the same mistakes. The dead woman's spirit could not rest as it watched her daughter miss out on the opportunity to trade a hopeless life in La Tranblè for the ability to boast about a promising *la vie Nou Yòk*.

~⁂~

Ateya never understood how Genevieve could love Ti'Louse. She thought that Genevieve should have been repulsed by the face of the little girl whose pictures she would send to America regularly. She was puzzled that Genevieve would send such beautiful, expensive-looking clothes for the child and convinced herself that Genevieve was just as greedy as her predecessors in New York, who, despite having girls of their own, were so enamored of little girls that they begged to take their nieces and girl cousins to New York with them.

Ma and Ol'Lady had each had a girl the first time around. So why did they need anyone else's daughters? Were they that selfish? Ateya let herself believe that that was the answer— that her aunt and great-aunt wanted all the girls in the family to themselves. She reasoned that they hadn't just wanted the girls out of a hoarding sort of love, but to turn them into *rest-avec*, little indentured servants to cook and clean in exchange for the privilege of living in a nice home, eating regularly, and being educated in the U.S. What a debt these aunties would be owed!

Ateya, like her mother, Guit (before she died), and her grandmother Madame (before she died), never believed in unencumbered generosity. She imagined the worst of her relatives in New York who wanted to take her only daughter away. Why did they only want the girls? Were they coalescing a coven, a brothel, or a convent? Convening *ounsi*, acolytes for the chief *manbo* worshiping Ezili, or a school of swimmers in the service of *La Sirène?* A legion of *lougawou?* Or some other nefarious, clandestine women's collective? It was easier to believe those things than to believe that Genevieve, Yanique, and Ol'Lady were altruistic saviors.

Ateya's miserly imagination was the legacy of simple-minded, stranded women who believed everything had to be paid for. The god they worshiped had given his life on a cross to wipe away their sins, and in return, required absolute devotion, an entire day dedicated to laborious rest, a tithe of ten percent of their earnings and remittances received, and other acts of submission. There were always and only trades and, with nothing to barter with, there was always debt. And again, Ateya, like her mother and grandmother, preferred it that way. It was a system they understood, having been indoctrinated into the national cult of both deprivation and depravity. This conditioning was in their blood, in their generational genes. The lives of their ancestors had been sold to slavers in exchange for things. If they were fortunate to have a captor who allowed them to buy their freedom, the captives paid with around-the-clock labor with no rest, went hungry to repay the cost of food, or forfeited their bodies to men and women alike.

Over the years, Ateya continued to wish that her mother had sent her away, if just to be a servant, a witch, or a hooker, because even the Haitian maids who had gone to the U.S. returned home with lighter skin (from brutal, sunless winters and the wrong color makeup), smoother feet (calluses from factory shifts scraped off at shitty storefront spas), smelling downright edible (knockoff fragrances bought on street corners), with designer handbags (same source as the fragrances), looking richer than the ladies from Port-au-Prince's exclusive enclave, Pétionville. How could she know that these maids were frauds, who gave their impoverished countrywomen false impressions of what life in America could yield?

What she knew and also did not want to know was that she would be able to hear out of both ears today if she had been sent away. Or died. When she was younger, she'd alternated between the two options that would have saved her the pain and embarrassment of her infirmity. If she'd been taken to America early enough, she would have never lost her hearing at all. Even if she had been taken after injury, her hearing might have been saved. And had she died on the spot where she'd fallen on the occasion of her first Holy Communion, she would have gone to heaven—all of her ten-year-old sins, for which she was clearly being punished, forgiven.

10

There must have been a woman
holding up a house,
bracing herself in a doorway,
arms spread, Christ-like, afraid to let go,
lest her world fall apart

I smile at Ateya, a wide and toothy smile that shows all of my teeth. "Let me go and see if Mimi is ready."

"Don't go out now. Too much dirt in the air. They've just finished picking for the day," Ateya says as Miles and I stand up to join Mimi.

We go outside anyway. It is hotter than it should be for an overcast day, but, despite the heaviness of the humid air, I know that it won't rain. I reach for Miles's hand as we walk toward the truck, which is backed up against the boundary between the grove's soft floor and solid, rocky ground. Mimi is directing three laborers in baseball caps to load sacks of plantains into the truck. We will drop the men and the plantains off on our way to the city. Ti'Louse picks up any plantains that fall on the ground. When the men finish, they will squeeze their bodies in between the sacks in the back of the truck.

"My clothes are dirty," Ti'Louse tells me while trying not to touch me, although she very much wants to.

"Your mother won't let you go with me unless you change," I tell her. "Wait for me and I'll help you pick out one of the outfits I brought you."

As she runs off, dust trails her and clings to her thin legs like cinnamon powder.

I turn around to stare at the plantain grove with Mimi and Miles beside me. We are enchanted by the dewy scent of the gut-wrenchingly gorgeous green before us. Mimi and I know what we look like to the neighbors, who always wonder how plantains are harvested from an empty, barren parcel of land.

"I'm forgetting my phone!" Miles shouts as he pats himself down. "I'll be right back." I know that he will also grab his notebook.

As he turns away from me and walks quickly toward the house, I am reminded of the man in his sketches.

"I forgot to unplug the fan!" I call after him.

Ateya has likely already unplugged it or has directed Ti'Louse to do so. She has probably ordered the girl to make the beds and sweep. Possibly knuckle-knocked the child on the forehead for my sloppiness. An ache passes through me for not having done the chores myself. "I'll be back, Mimi." I turn and walk quickly toward the house, hoping to reach Ti'Louse before her mother has a chance to harm her.

I want to help Ti'Louse get dressed quickly before Ateya changes her mind about letting the child go to town with me. Ateya looks at me askance, as if I have asked to take Ti'Louse to the moon, as if I might kidnap her daughter. Hers, hers,

hers. I don't hear her words because there are none. We never talk about it until it is time for me to leave, which on this trip will be in a week. We have seven days of not talking about what we know we must eventually discuss. Her daughter. Hers, hers, hers.

My feet are light on the ground. My sneakers make me bounce as if the earth is made of playground paving. If I let myself go, my body will soar like I'm on a trampoline. I am giddy running to Ti'Louse. This time, I will take her home with me. I can feel it. This time Ateya will let her go.

I stand in the doorway and see that Ti'Louse is already dressed. She has chosen the outfit I was going to have her wear. It is a soft, light-blue, denim two-piece jumper with bright embroidered flowers along the boat neckline. It is made of traditional Haitian carabella fabric and looks like new, although it isn't. I am hoping that Ateya doesn't have a picture of me wearing it in her albums.

For some reason I cannot explain, I am suddenly aware of where everyone is and what they are doing. I am alert with a sense of foreboding. I want to run to everyone at once, to hold them steady, to know they are safe. I want to love them as never before, even Ateya, who hates me and the one whom I love, who is hers. Hers. Hers.

Ateya is sitting on the back steps abusing a cock she has already killed. After plucking its feathers, she singes the remaining plumes off, then carves the carcass. She scalds it, a second death with boiling water, before seasoning and placing the pot on the oil-drum stove out back.

Miles is searching for his cell phone, which he hopes is

properly charged and receiving a signal it hasn't had since we arrived. He is homesick just a day into our stay because he hasn't heard the familiar voices of the family we left behind.

Mimi is dragging two heavy plantain tree stalks. She is aware, as she always is, that the workers wish she would be less of a man who helps them with the labor and more of a woman who fucks them after a hard day's work.

Ti'Louse is twirling in her newly inherited outfit, waiting for my adoring eyes to compliment the fit of the pants that cling to her lean, model-like legs. She cannot contain her excitement over this second outing, accompanied by her favorite members of her family—me, Mimi, and now Miles, whom she has only stared at nervously since we arrived.

I am standing in the doorway with arms outstretched like Christ on the cross. I am smiling at Ti'Louse as she spins, listening for Miles as he searches, hearing Mimi's directives, smelling the seasoning on clean, raw chicken. I am staring at the smile my presence has brought to Ti'Louse's face. I have elevated her from hated to precious, from laughed at to loved. She is the only one I have made happy by being here, and it is because she believes that I am here for her and her only.

But I have come to lick the little wounds inflicted on the well-fed body of my privileged self. I have added the weight of my own fear to a frightening place and a frightened people. If I had remembered the misery, I would not have carried my suffering here. Selfishly, I have added my own sorrow to the grief of a perpetually grieving people. I have brought tears, but no water, a stomach, but no food, loftiness, but no ladder. I have nothing good to offer. A few dollars, a few dresses, a few Black dolls that look like the little girl I love. But what have I gifted to this place? In this land, the pain of poverty contorts souls that are so easily misjudged as resilient by the culpable seeking to ease guilt. Neo-colonial culprits pretend that the people struggling under these circumstances have transmuted their troubles into a special brand of jubilant survival.

I have brought them an abundance of what they already have. I have brought a child who wants to die to a country that is nearly dead. I have carried myself to compete with a mother who just wants to keep her girl child near, who wants to provide rather than rely on remittances, who wants to shake off judgment for the letdown of lustful men. I have brought *things* when what my people need is to feel valued.

I have hauled my hurt to Haiti, expecting to find healing, oblivious to the contagion of my pain. I am an incurable curse on an afflicted land. I have insulted my people, implored the impoverished for pity they must save for themselves. My presence is the weight around their necks. My wealth is the restraint around their wrists. I am a perversion of their will to live because I am dissatisfied with my life. I am the needy come to beg bread from the hungry.

I have added one more stone to my country's load. I have piled my shortcomings on a nation that keeps coming up short and so must borrow from colonialist gluttons, schemers, and siphons. I am a scavenger come to peck at what little remains after unnatural disasters. I have laid my troubles at the feet of the tormented. I am the hurricane and the drought, the flood and the famine, the sickness and its spread. I am the god-sent savior come to destroy so I can congratulate myself on the rescue.

How much worse can I give? How much more can my country take before it breaks open and swallows itself to sate its hunger?

I look at Ti'Louse through the slanted doorway. I know she is looking to me for a way out. I see myself reflected in her eyes. I am running from the danger my people cannot escape. It is the danger of broken things.

~~⁓~~

I hear a strange moaning that turns to a growl that turns to a roar. The trembling beneath my feet turns into a shake that turns everything upside down. The earth is on the attack, raining down blows from angry slabs of stone that knock us down and crush us to death. The shaking does not stop. It opens up the ground beneath our feet and flings us into crumbling houses and one another. Sharp stones come from out of nowhere and fly toward us at speeds we've never known. We are an overlap of confused screams. We don't know where we are, let alone where to be. The ground continues to convulse. We are overwhelmed by the explosion of the things crashing down around us and the boom of our own shouting. The sounds that come from us ask how it is possible that we are being struck from above and below. We are in between large, heavy, and imposing things. We have no way to escape. The quake follows those of us who try to run and trips us into open pits filling up with broken bodies and shattered cinder block. Those of us who stand still are taken down by boulders, tree limbs, and furniture flung about. We are in the mouth of a monster, who pounds us from above and grinds us from below.

Three

〜

11

There must have been
cracked patterns on pretty plates
reflections sliced by blinded mirrors
a one-way window banishing light
sharp bones under thin skin,
falling apart, falling away

Something I cannot run from has knocked me backward down the steps. I am tripping, falling, and frightened in ways I should not be on steady ground. My body vibrates while everything else around me crumbles. My senses shatter and go dangerously dark.

When I come to, I am lost in the ruins of a world that looks nothing like itself. I am awake, trying to find myself. I am seeing and looking for my eyes at the same time.

And all around me I see, I hear, I feel the weight of broken things.

Glass is crashing and someone will be faulted for its falling. I have to get to Ti'Louse before Ateya does. If she reaches the girl first, I will never forgive myself. There will be too many broken things, pieces that I can't pick up and put back together.

I try to rise from under the things that keep falling on top of me, falling away from me. But there is no floor beneath my feet. I would feel if it were there, since I am barefoot. My shoes are gone, somewhere I cannot see because I can't see through the dust. I am on my back, flat, fallen. I pass my hands over my face to bring light to my overcast eyes. The sun is out where it was not. The sky floating above me is cracked by the mocking light of the smiling sun.

I try again to stand but the ground will not let me. It only allows falling and then surrender. It owns me. I belong to the earth. I am hers, hers, hers. Everything gives. Everything falls on their knees and bows. I am on my back where the cement-block stairs to the house used to be. Whole hunks of home fall away and toward me. I close my eyes and raise my hands to protect myself from the downpour of rock, cinder block, and glass.

I know there is screaming, although I hear nothing. There must be screaming. There must be Ateya standing somewhere. Inside, scolding Ti'Louse for all of the broken things around her.

"Mom! Mom! Mom!" Miles must be calling. From somewhere beneath the ceiling cracked by the laughing sun, the light of it coming in through the jagged gaps. There must be noise. After lightning there is always a clap, the delayed echo of the strike. There is always thunder after the crack, the clap, the gap between clouds. But this time the rumbling that I do not hear has come from below, from the core of the hard ground under my body. A spread of stony fingers, as crooked as tree branches, claws from below like a beast rising from its grave.

All I hear are broken sounds.

My hearing goes in and out as if my ears are afraid of noise, as if they cannot withstand the calls, the cries, the screams, the scolding, the clamor of broken people with newly crooked bones. I hear what I cannot see and see what I cannot hear. I see the sound of Miles crying for me to come. It is the bellow of something breaking. "Mom! Mom! Mom!" I know that I must go to him, but I must also get to Ti'Louse before Ateya breaks her for all of the shattered things, even the in-and-out sounds, the racket of rocks, the uproar of stone against glass against bone.

All I feel are broken things.

Beneath my feet. There is nothing at all on my hands as I try to hold on to invisible walls. My heart stumbles off kilter in panic as I try to crawl into the house. There is no passage through the front, so I crawl backward to return to where I came from. I try one more time to stand up and once more the ground knocks me to my knees, shocking my already distorted senses, crippling my attempts to restore my balance. I am down, but I am not praying. I am willing myself to get around back to the other door. I am relieved to see Ateya on her back, caged in by piles of impenetrable debris.

Since the earth cannot cave in on itself, it protrudes convex. It builds small pyramids of dirt and stone, blocks broken down to gravel. I am standing now on my own over the shingles that have formed a protective peak over Ateya. She frees one of her pinned arms and reaches for me, but all I hear are Miles's cries and Ti'Louse's quiet. I rush as much as the rubble allows. I have to get to Miles. First. Ti'Louse is safe because Ateya is down. Miles first. I hear him calling in between my clogged hearing. In my mind I can hear Bright blaming me for breaking Miles. I have not only spoiled him; I have ruined him. I brought our son here intact and destroyed him with my insistent attempt to fix him.

Miles doesn't want to die, not like this, not here.

I find a single foot poking out of a crack just inside our bedroom door. It moves, so I know that it is not broken; neither is the leg to which it is attached; neither is the boy to whom it belongs. Deafness goes in and out and in between the cracks in my hearing. Miles is calling. The sun at my back breaks into the room and I can see his face. A foot and a face. No hands, a leg is missing, no torso, no thighs. But hopeful eyes covered in dust but not blinded. His lips form an O as he moans.

I borrow sound from somewhere. "I'm coming, baby. I'm here. I'm here."

His eyes are watering, lips trembling. I imagine he is wet under the fragments pressing him down.

All I feel are broken things.

Beneath my fingernails as I dig through the wreckage to free my son. I can see more of his body now. There is no blood, nothing broken that I can see. He extends a hand to me and I grab it with both of mine. My bare feet grip bits of earth to steady myself as the ground keeps shifting. Miles's pushing balances my pulling until he is finally free, and we tumble to the ground outside the ruined room. I drag him behind me by his right arm, not wanting to turn around to see his left dangling like a Christmas tree ornament.

I hear Ateya. Whatever is still standing succumbs to

another shorter, weaker tremor. She is buried deeper. She will have to free herself. I am searching for Ti'Louse, who is hers. Hers. Hers.

Miles and I step in between flat, open cracks and make a loop into the other back door, where I think Ti'Louse's silence is coming from. I hear it. Her quiet is hers. I hear Ateya's groans too as she crunches behind us, trying to catch up, trying to catch us before we can reach Ti'Louse.

Somehow the three of us arrive at the door at almost the same time. I lead with bloodied feet, releasing Miles's healthy arm as I move forward. I can hear what Ti'Louse is not saying. I can hear mute stones on top of fragile bones. As I start to pull debris from the spot where Ti'Louse is buried, I can hear Ateya picking up loose but broken things. I turn to see her holding something square, dust-covered, and flat to her chest. She has found what she was looking for. She cannot see over Miles's shoulder to see me digging to find what is hers. Hers. Hers. Before I can spot Ti'Louse's face, I hear Ateya scream, "Look at what they have done to me!" When I turn to look, she is holding some new dusty thing. Torn plastic over a torn white dress, a crooked crystal crown reflecting the small shards of light poking through the doorway—the communion gown I sent for Ti'Louse a year ago. This is what Ateya holds to her chest as she cries. I turn away from her and dig, passing pieces of unrecognizable things to Miles, who grabs and tosses them with one hand. He hasn't let out a single sob, although tears flow down his face. The wet streaks are rivers between the banks of grayish-brown dirt.

All I see are broken things.

All around Ti'Louse, who is free from the chunks of ceiling that collapsed on top of her, there are shattered things.

There is no blood as I lift her up and over my shoulder with a strength I should not have. It is the same strength I used for Miles, like those superhuman mothers who make the news for lifting cars off of their trapped children. "I'm not your super-woman, Bright. I am theirs." I hear in my head what I have said so many times out loud.

Miles backs out of the house and extends his good arm, which I do not grab, lest I break it like the other one. Ateya is on the ground in the crack she had just freed herself from, still holding the dress against her chest with one hand, flipping through the dusty, square, flat thing with the other. She never looks up or over. She never asks for anything or anyone, nor do I ask her to help me with what is hers. As Ti'Louse starts to slip off of my shoulder, I hold her with both hands and cradle her close so I can see where I am stepping. I feel no breath against my chest, no rise and fall of a rib cage responding to lifted lungs. I see no open eyes or trembling lips. I feel no sweat. I hear no whimper. There is no attempt to raise a finger or tilt a head.

"Ateya!" I call, hoping to rouse her from her stupor. I hear her coming, cracking loose cement every time she takes a step. She is still holding the dress and an intact photo album. She stands facing me and I extend the limp body in a trade for the inanimate objects she is clasping. She holds the things closer and closes her eyes. She stumbles away from the lifeless one that is hers. Hers. Hers.

I find a surprisingly empty spot between a jumbled pile of indecipherable things and lay Ti'Louse there. On top of a nearby pile, I see one of my sneakers, shockingly clean, and I reach for it. My other shoe is perched on another pile out of my grasp. My feet falter forward as I latch on to the first shoe

and I fall trying to grab the other. Miles finally groans as if
he can feel the pain of my fall, the pieces of things piercing
my bloody feet. My shoes are on now, making it easier to get
back to where Ti'Louse's body is not moving. I lift her again,
searching for a different spot to lay her down.

In the distance that seems closer than it should, the proud
trees in the plantain grove persist upright, rigid, and safe.

Ti'Louse's legs, as thin as wishes, dangle over my arm.
I hold her head to my chest as if I can love her back to life. I
want to know where the bruise is, the wound, the blood, the
break, the place I can fix. I want to blow breath into her, to
pump her heart into beating, to shake her awake, to whisper,
Stay with me. Stay with me, baby girl, over and over until I can
reach a place where I can heal her. "It's not like you're a real
doctor," I hear Ma say, and for once, I regret not becoming a
surgeon or something useful. There is nothing I can do for
Ti'Louse here, so I reason that I must take her with us—to
where? A collapsed clinic, a hospital heeling like a dog on hind
legs? Wherever I will find help for Miles is where I will take
Ti'Louse too. I must do what Ateya cannot in this moment.

I squeeze Ti'Louse's body, bringing her head so close I
can smell the pomade in her neatly combed hair. I am tempted
to lift her eyelids, to look deep into her eyes to make her see
me. I want to be the reason she wakes up and lives. I am standing on the border between reality and dream, between death
and life, between cracked earth and an unbroken softness. I
wish for water to soak her skin, to free her from this pall, to
wash her back into this world. But the best I can do is lay her
down somewhere safe.

Mimi walks toward me, her arms outstretched to relieve me of what she believes is a burden. But the weight in my arms is a flyaway life, as light and elusive as air. I am prepared to fight Mimi if she insists on reaching for the love in my arms. I want to give baby girl my heartbeat so she can escape what I have convinced myself is only unconsciousness. My mind takes pity on my heart and lets me wander as I think of ways to resurrect Ti'Louse. With my chin I gesture for Mimi to open the bed of the pickup. She orders the men out so I can lay Ti'Louse down. The men, like Mimi, are uninjured, since they were outside with nothing but the sky to fall on top of them. Still, they are reluctant to move, afraid of losing the only possibility of getting out of the ruins of the *lakou* around them. Their eyes question the need for a dead girl to take the place of the living. But I know that what is now mine is not dead yet.

I believe with all of my being that I will take Ti'Louse with us to America, where she will get the proper medical attention to revive her. She will get the same care as Miles, who is leaning against the cab of the truck. He is waiting for me to come care for him. He is my own and he is alive. As I come closer, he starts to cry. The tears swell like waves and crash as I pull his head toward me. Soaked with his and my own tears and sweat, I bring him even closer so we can float together in what must be a bad dream.

I am awakened by the wail of someone who has just discovered the crushed body of a loved one, the sharp cough of a nearby body fighting not to die.

There is help to be rendered to the injured and the dying, the SOS of the wounded to respond to. I call on my memory of things learned long ago to do what I know how. How long has it been? With the world around me transformed into endless wreckage, med school seems like centuries ago.

"Mimi, let's go!" I yell louder than necessary.

"Go? Go where?" she answers, annoyed by my inane command.

"We have to find the supplies."

"The supplies we brought to the clinic yesterday?"

"I'm sure that Ateya kept a stash somewhere."

"We can't go back into the house. What's left of it is falling. Can't you see?"

"We have to try."

"Try to die?"

"There has to be something we can do for them." I look around, trying to find them, but they cannot be seen, only heard from beneath the rubble.

"The best thing is to get out of here before anything else falls or rises to block the road."

I hobble away from Mimi through the maze of rebar poking out of chunks of cement. I need to reach the screams. There has to be a way. I can't just leave.

Mimi grabs me by the shoulders to shake me out of whatever reverie has me in its grasp.

"And what about Ateya? We have to take her with us," I say to Mimi.

"She is not here. Can't you see? Look at her! She is not with us. She cannot help us." Mimi raises and deepens her voice for emphasis. She has learned how hard it is for people to take words spoken through her soft squeals seriously.

"Get in the truck! Get in the goddamned truck!" I yell at Ateya.

Whether she is pretending not to hear me or really cannot, I do not know. How can she not hear? I am close enough to kiss her. I shake her. Hard. Mimi grabs her arm. Ateya fights both of us. She doesn't even acknowledge Ti'Louse in the truck. We are all confused, afraid, grieving.

We need to get out of here. All of us.

"Drag her, Mimi!"

She tries but Ateya bites her hand.

Mimi gives up too easily. We both do. I because of Miles. Mimi because she remembers what I do not. The grove, the graves, the land. All of the things crushed under the collapsed house. Ateya wasn't going to be separated from any of it.

Mimi softens toward me. "You have to leave Ti'Louse here," she says in a tortured voice. She caresses my shoulders.

"No, no, no, I can heal her. I can bring her back."

"Heal her how? Bring her where?"

"Let me try, Mimi. Don't make me do this. Don't."

"Mom? Mom?" Miles interrupts, knowing that his voice can pull me out of the unknown place where my senses are trapped. I take stock of his body again, and his pants pockets are bulging outward. I am afraid that other parts of him are injured. When I look more closely, I see the outline of his cell phone on one side and his rolled-up notebook sticking out of the other.

"I need you!" he shouts.

My heart releases what is not mine and holds on to the cries of the one who is.

"I'll get her out," Mimi says, already just a leap away from the truck bed.

"No! I'll get her. Please, let me get her." The words stick in my throat awash in tears.

Ateya doesn't follow me as I carry Ti'Louse.

There is nowhere to bring my charge except into the green. Maybe the mist will be enough. I know that this is not true, but I want to believe so badly that she can be resuscitated. I should have taken her with me when I had the chance. So many times. I could have just kidnapped her and brought her back to the States. Some forger could have produced a birth certificate listing me as the mother, provided DNA documentation as further proof. I should have ignored Ateya and all of the laws that are broken every minute in this country. I had more than enough to offer bribes in the right amounts to the right people. If I had taken her, she would be alive right now.

Instead, I am left to enter the grove with her lifeless body cradled against my breasts. I must lay her down on the silt under the plantain trees, hoping hopelessly that the broad, melancholy leaves can breathe back into her the life that has left. I want to believe that the fronds can perform miracles, that if I stay with her, the grove might wake her up, turn me into a little girl again, and we would play. And, if not that, I would lie down with her, let my life leave my body, and make myself at home.

As my final act, as my lone good-bye, I kiss her hand and cover her with a verdant shroud.

"Good-bye, baby girl."

There is no time to dig a grave.

12

There must have been
a cacophony of primal yells from dying human animals
bodies flattened by dense slabs of invincible concrete
in closed caves with only space for flies to feed

They had come to expect disasters descending from the sky. They had survived the commonplace deluge from named hurricanes and anonymous storms before. Shrugged shoulders signaled their resignation to their mundane fate—if people died, they died, and it was God's will. They yielded to destruction long known and even expected eventualities. Unceasing lightning strikes might knife the sky and break thunder over their heads, bringing no rain. The improbability of a tornado made sense in a country that had been battered by the fury of their god targeting them and only them for a catastrophic apocalypse. It was quite plausible that their savior's crushing footsteps could come down on them to announce his second coming. Maybe missiles meant for America would miss their target and unintentionally slam into their little plot of land as the start of a third world war. Any calamity could come from the heavens. But the earth had never arbitrarily betrayed them, no matter how much they had harmed it. That it could vengefully and audaciously open from underneath to swallow and crush, cripple and kill, and, worse, give them final confirmation that the universe was indeed determined to wipe them off the face of the earth, had been unimaginable. But a people accustomed to living their worst nightmares, who had seen monsters manifest in all shades of skin, quickly accepted yet another cruelty. As in the past, they shook off their shock and quickly awakened to the reality that there was work to be done.

Around her, the air was thick with screams Ateya did not hear. Fractured arms and battered backs found strength from out of nowhere to reach tortured voices and lift slabs of concrete off of crushed bodies.

A man pulled his wife's raised skirt down over her legs to cover the only visible parts of her body severed at the waist. There was no sense lifting the chunk of rock off of her torso to confirm that it was her. He knew her body by heart. It was best to reserve his strength to find and hopefully save his children. Another man threw his shirt over the shoulders of the mother of his two youngest children as she sat shivering in the humidity, hoping that her compressed legs could be saved. The two men had one whole wife between them.

There were no instruments besides bare hands to reach the bodies that were closest to the surface of the concrete piles. A few neighbors hollered for Ateya to lend tools, to no avail. If they were waiting for her help, the dying would die, and the wounded would succumb to the inevitable. Sitting in a round of rubble in her front yard, Ateya was upright but barely conscious. She could not even raise her head to see Genevieve, Miles, and Mimi drive away in search of safety. Unacknowledged, the pickup truck's brake lights blinked their red eyes as it rolled over mounds of debris that had crashed down on the road.

Blinded by the residue of cement layered thick over her eyelids, a teenage girl knelt over the hole from which the cries of her newborn son came clearly to a mother's ear. She distinguished her own baby's screams from all the others, her silence comingling with the tangled screeches of sorrowful women who had already found their own perished babies. There was no sense adding her hollers to the discordant tousle of confused calls. There was no sense pleading with the people around her to save her days-old son, interred in a cave of rebar and rock. No one was coming to save her, her baby, or anyone else.

Ateya started to stir from her stupor to take stock of the devastation around her. She walked her eyes up her smashed front steps, over the pile of blocks that was the only evidence that her house had once existed. Her eyes squinted into the castoff from the sky's blue light to see what, not who, could be found. She did not look for people, living or dead. She could hear no one even in her hearing ear, which was now shocked deaf. This was the second time she had been felled and deafened by a blow. Now she had a matching pair of useless ears.

Even though, once again, rescue had not come; Ateya hopelessly whispered a prayer to her dead mother, wishing for the protection never proffered. Maybe in spirit form, Guit would come to her rescue. Maybe Guit would spread her body between Ateya and the remaining concrete tumbling in the aftershocks. Out of desperation, Ateya cried for what would not come, what had not come decades ago. Guit could have, should have, stood between Ateya and the oncoming blow from a grown man's balled hand all those years before. She could have, should have, pushed the girl out of the way and taken the hit or stopped it entirely. At the very least, Guit could have added a shout of "No!" to an onslaught of curse words to freeze the father where he'd stood—his raised arm armed with a ready fist. And now, she could have, should have, spread her shadow as a shield against the pummeling pieces raining down from what was left of her daughter's roof. But Guit did not come, leaving Ateya to take a beating alone once again.

As Ateya tried to pull herself out of memory and wishful thinking, she found her fists gripping the torn, soiled communion dress and toothless tiara and the dusty, square photo album. With broken nails, she traced the holes where crystals once nested in the crown. She got the idea that, if she looked hard enough, she could find the jewels under the splintered shingles at her feet. All she wanted was to find what was precious to her under the heaps of debris.

Of all of her ruined things, Ateya was most distressed by the damaged gowns she knew were buried under the Sheetrock, splinters of wood, and mangled steel. She could not puzzle out to whom the dress in her lap and the others belonged. She only knew that they had to be connected to her somehow. No matter who once wore the dresses, they were in her hands, in her mind, in her house, and, therefore, the bearer, like the dresses, belonged to her. Since she saw only herself—her bloodied knuckles, her dust-covered knees, ashen arms and legs, heard only her voice reverberating between her choked ears, Ateya reasoned that she was the only person who existed and so everything was hers. But that did not keep her from wanting more, even believing that she deserved more.

Still groggy and shaken, propelled by ill-conceived

thoughts of proprietorship, Ateya pulled herself to standing to search for the rest of her things. She knew that she did not have the strength to lift anything to search for everything. Instead of looking down, she looked up and decided that the sky, the stars, and the moon belonged to her. She turned toward the plantain grove and decided that it was hers too because she was the only one there to see it. The breeze that shook droplets from the trees was also hers, as was the sprinkle of mist blowing toward her. She claimed the fronds extending fingers, beckoning her to come. She seized the cracked earth birthing itself from inside itself. Every hunk of rough and solid stuff blocking her path to the grove, and the smaller pieces—gravel, rocks, glass in shards and splinters, slivers of sticks digging into her soles as she walked forward—all of it belonged to her.

When she finally stumbled to the border between yard and grove, she became disoriented. She heard a voice calling her from the green and it was hers. Hers. Hers.

Not knowing where she was, who she was, or whose she was, Ateya was lost because there was no one looking for her. She only had herself.

Exhausted and sweaty from hiking over obstinate debris, Ateya carefully crawled over the boundary. She held her two halves together. Requiring the strength of both of her selves, she threw her body in and ran. Her two halves took turns chasing each other playfully through the rows of trees until they collapsed from fatigue and sadness. They only had each other, and no one knew that the one was actually two and those two were one. There was no one in the world to find them/her, no one to claim them/her. Ateya reabsorbed her shadowy second self and wept.

She wiped her face with fists full of soil and slathered it on the skin of her bare arms. She rubbed more over her face, and the silt mixed with tears and sweat and stuck, making a mask. If she'd had a mirror, she would have seen a face that she both recognized and despised staring back at her. That was the first time she remembered that there was someone who existed besides her other half. She did not recall exactly but had a sense that that other was as much a part of her as her soft self. That someone was as slight as string, as black as the loam between her fingers, with glittering eyes lighter than her skin, and lips unaccustomed to closeness. Ateya had no clue how this someone was related to her. She only knew that she should be searching the soil.

As she lifted the wide leaves at the base of the plantain trees, the wet earth cradled her knees. The deeper she dug, the more desperate she became to find what she knew was there, although she did not know what she might find. Her face? The one darkened by mud? Black pupils in pools of shining whites? Would it, whatever it was, be small, slender, fragile? Would its skin be bruised with raised welts or smooth and flat as a copper coin? Would it scream once uncovered? Or would it remain as silent as a death? Would it be dead? Was this thing, this someone, dead? Was she, Ateya, the owner of a dead thing?

The chorus of screams from the mouths of other mothers kneeling in ripping rocks soared above the canopy of the grove and dragged Ateya a bit closer to consciousness. She finally accepted what she had been denying—that she was not the only person in the world. Worse yet, the knowledge that she was a mother, like all of the other wailing women outside of the grove, felled her like a heavy branch, pressed her into the earth, and threatened to bury her with the truth of who she was. She was the mother of a smooth-skinned someone who had died.

In a frenzy Ateya searched for that someone she now knew was hers. Hers. Hers.

Ateya knew that she had to widen her search. She dug along the jagged seam where the earth had opened from below, running the length of the grove. The cracked path parted before her as she crawled, digging shallow graves with hands curved like spoons as she went. Before she knew it, she had arrived at the boundary with hands empty and grimy, her face caked with mud, looking like the girl she had been taught to hate. As she went along, Ateya unearthed more guilt than love. Guilt that she did not know what foods had been her daughter's favorites (browned chicken gizzards and hearts, fried and boiled plantains, and black coffee). She didn't know that Ti'Louse didn't like sweets, that her favorite color was the indigo blue of washing balls, and that she relished the crunch of the undissolved chips of ironing starch. Ateya now regretted not knowing the things that she might use to tempt the child into showing herself in the moonlight peeking through the canopy. Although she had never paid attention to her daughter's preferences, focusing more on the bare necessities, she knew that girl was hers, and she now understood that she had always loved Ti'Louse and loved her still. She wanted to stay, to continue excavating to find love. But she needed to stand, to shake herself sober, to make her way to the shed for tools and to come back properly armed to resume her search. Her legs shaky, Ateya faltered as she tried to stand.

Now fully upright, she felt a child's palm, cool and damp, push her out of the grove.

Ateya dragged herself over the mounds of rubble into a darkness as sinister as the monster that had opened up the earth beneath her. While she had been sitting in the grove, the sun had set reluctantly, struggling against the dusk, fighting the night to give rescuers and mourners a little more light to dig out the dying and the dead. As she lifted her heavy limbs, she became aware of the inertia of insects. The silenced lights of fireflies. The stilled limbs of cicadas. The hunger of mosquitoes resigned to fasting for the night. Only the flies were active, making their way into crevices where the trapped lay crushed under mounds of debris.

Trying to find her way around the yard by sound alone, Ateya squeezed her nose with her thumb and pointer and blew to make her ear pop. It opened up to growls, deep and loud, like continuous thunder. But the accompanying falsetto wails she heard produced no sterling cracks of lightning to make sense of the pounding sounds. She stumbled between houses until she saw the stuttering sparks of flickering lighters on the tips of cigarettes. A circle of smokers crowded around a make-do pile of sticks, chunks of wood, and man-made charcoal, trying to coax forth fire. Once it was lit, they made crude torches out of sawed-off pipes and kerosene-soaked rags.

In the lambent light, she could see her battered arms. Her heart had broken itself apart and the pieces had lodged themselves in the flesh just beneath the raised contusions. It could not remain whole. Intact it would throb, typically arrhythmically, and explode, killing itself and taking her with it. This was no time to die. She had to find the ones who were not looking for her, just as she'd sought out the one she could feel at her heels but could not see. Every time she turned around to find the owner of the rough, bare toes digging into her Achilles tendons, she saw no one. Hounded and pounded, Ateya made her way up the hill to the road. In her confusion, she turned south and west, toward the capital, rather than north and east, away from the catastrophe.

Slabs of concrete stopped just short of the center of the road, leaving a wide, passable lane. Multistory buildings with sagging storefronts had either buckled in on themselves or crashed backward away from the street, leaving spaces wide enough for cars to crawl and jagged lines of punch-drunk people to pass. A truck crept behind her; she turned to see an overloaded *camionette* manned by an unflinching driver who had long been used to bumping along streets of cracked pavement. Even if the vehicle had had space for her, Ateya would not have tried to flag it down for a ride. At that moment, she distrusted anything that shook. She was fearful of and for the frail metal frame of the cut-out vans she had regularly ridden to Port-au-Prince. The wobbly people trying to prop one another up leaned but did not fall, despite their sprains, fractures, and oozing gashes. The quake seemed deliberate in its selection of things and people to lay waste to. It had spared rickety kiosks but split the ground beneath sturdy dwellings, swallowing them down a gravelly throat.

She searched for the shaky stand where she'd sold her mother's goods as a child. She saw what she wanted to see, her mind constructing visions of known, comforting things. A row of small tins of evaporated milk, one-pound bags of rice, strings of dried smoked herring, salted cod, sachets of assorted grains—barley, millet, wheat, ground corn of varying coarseness: quarter kernel for smoked pork and kidney-bean stew, a mealy texture for polenta, and powdery for sweet porridge. An assortment of hair products—relaxers, dyes, and straighteners, oils to grease the scalp, and the multiuse petroleum jelly as a primer for a hot press, a cure for ashy skin, a gloss for cracked lips.

Ateya remembered how her mother used to scold, pull her ears, or swat her with a slipper for extending credit to already-indebted customers. The severity of the reprimand had matched the amount of money owed and the humility of the debtor. One thing worse than awarding undeserved credit was telling people where you were going or where you had gone. You did not tell, like you did not smile. Open mouths were not allowed under any circumstances except when doing the thing that Ateya had been too young to know about.

Although she was not alert enough to be sure of anything in that moment, Ateya's body remembered the eight-mile journey to Port-au-Prince that she had frequently taken with her mother until she was old enough to go alone. Mother and daughter would walk to the capital and take a *tap-tap* back home with their parcels of goods, if there was money left. On the days when they went to pick up remittances, her mother would insist on the repayment of a loan from a borrower in the yard for carfare to the city. When she returned, she would lend more to that debtor, who served as a bank from which she could make withdrawals at will. Ateya's subconscious led her through memories of her mother just as it directed her mind along the memorized path to the city. She knew exactly where she wanted to go and how to get there, but she couldn't remember the name of the place. She knew whom she was looking for but could not find the voice for the syllables required for a shout. She knew everything and nothing at the same time, and the everything she knew was as imprecise and mysterious as a dream.

Shaken awake by the tortured voices of people calling for missing loved ones, Ateya's jealousy bullied her into remembering. It pained her to hear the hollering of silly nicknames bestowed by a clever community, twisted syllables that sounded serious as they reverberated through a night heavy with grief and shock. Every moniker, ranging from the endearing to the absurd, had a story.

"Jezila!" "Jesus is here" to protect the home from robbers scared away by a screaming child.

"Pakole!" "Don't get stuck" in the womb or too attached to a mother for a child born past its due date.

"Tet Pilon!" "The head of a pestle" for a girl with a long neck and a talent for grinding spices in a mortar.

"Ti'France!"

"Ti'Pierre!"

"Ti'frè!"

"Ti'soeur!"

And all of the other *Ti*'s that evidenced a people's proclivity for the diminutive—the legacy of subordination and enslavement.

Despite all of the screaming *Ti*'s echoing along the road, Ateya still could not remember the name of the child she had never deserved. Unlike those around her, Ateya called out for no one, nor did she stop to help others dig for their charges. Not the woman attempting to drag her mumbling husband away from the smashed face of a destroyed chop shop, nor the small boy sucking on the finger he'd singed on the tip of a candle's lit wick. She only paused once to observe a dying man as he tapped his rum-bottle-brown fingers on the dusty ground, as if typing out Morse code.

She squinted to catch the light of small fires sprouting like seedlings every few yards. Weary flashlights with jaundiced bulbs sputtered every few seconds. She lifted her legs over a downed electrical pole, the only one for at least a mile. Rescuers would resort to hacking it for wood once the charcoal ran out and already-anemic batteries succumbed.

The driver of an overloaded van blinked low beams, beckoning weary pedestrians. He did not honk his horn; the moment demanded silence. Only searching voices had the right to sound. Those on foot lumbered to the side to let the van pass. On hands and knees, they slowly clambered up haphazard pyramids of rock and tripped over bricks to get out of the way. Just as the vehicle started to pick up speed, an intact slab of cement crashed down on it like the new knowledge of a husband's affair on an unsuspecting wife.

A stranger grabbed Ateya's wrist as she started to lose her balance. But there were no strangers now. Survivors would forever be bound by calamity. Unbeknown to her, neighbors would become roommates under vulnerable tents in the days, weeks, months, and even years to come. The man released her once she found her footing, but she was not ready to let go. She reached behind her with one hand and clasped the fingers of a child who was not there. She extended her other hand forward and held the hem of the dress of an invisible woman. In her mind, she had formed a line of her women kin, holding hands like the velvet ropes that barred the entry of the unworthy, the unwanted, and the uninvited. Her steps were sure, even as she scaled mounds of crushed cinder blocks and toed dislodged tin roofs.

As she stood on top of the ruins of the collapsed clinic, she surveyed the extent of the devastation. The leveled building, slanted and half sagging, entombed its lone doctor, a handful of barely trained house-girls passing for nurses, and doomed patients. For the living, there was nowhere to go to be bandaged, stitched, or splinted.

Led by the ghosts of her grandmother and mother, dragging her daughter behind her, Ateya tried to find her way out of and away from her hometown. She halted when she saw that the rickety curved bridge over Rivière Grise had collapsed into the water beneath. It was the only way to the capital. She had never learned to swim. Although the ocean was just a few miles from Port-au-Prince, the beaches had been privatized and charged entry fees that few parents could afford. Reluctantly, Ateya stepped into the water, where she found the waist of another stranger who was willing to drag her along.

They moved awkwardly through the river, which was as still as death with the toxic stink of chemicals and human swill. As the man paddled, Ateya unconsciously slipped one hand downward below his navel, then lower to his pelvis, left bare by his soaked and sagging pants. She was practiced at repaying men for even the smallest kindness and didn't even have to think about what she was doing now to and for the man who was saving her life. She motivated him forward, giving him the hope of restitution with more than just spoken thank-yous when they got to the other side. She matched him stroke for stroke as he lifted one arm after another, clearly careful not to kick her as he struggled through the muddy water that was as thick as flour-fattened sauce.

To her left and right were leaky canoes rowed by flapping sandals on the hands of occupants desperate to stay afloat just long enough to make it across the less than quarter-mile distance to the shore. They could have walked across the shallow river, had they been brave enough to let their feet touch bottom. But, having felt the earth crack open beneath them, they had no reason to trust the riverbed below equally unreliable water.

Lanky man-boys with tightly laced-up sneakers took their chances jumping the gap between the two sides of the split bridge. They practiced running starts to clear the invisible track hurdle, barely making it across. The ones who missed received deep slashes from splintered wood and steel and cried over the pain of failure just as much as over their wounds.

Those escaping Croix-des-Bouquets to make it to what they believed would be the safety of the city on the other side ignored the swimmers going in the opposite direction in search of the same.

As soon as she reached dry land, Ateya walked as fast as she could, leaving her exhausted savior without even a nod of gratitude. As far as she was concerned, she was done with her willing exchange of sexual acts for small favors. On the ground of Croix-des-Missions, she promised herself that she was done with appreciative hand jobs, grateful fellatio, and comforting quickies.

Feeling a tug at the hem of her dress, she slowed her pace but did not turn around. She wanted to spare herself the disappointment of seeing that the one she searched for was not there.

13

There must have been unplanned places
formed by fortune, found by chance
by lost people fleeing the peril
of repeated history

We speed out of La Tranblè as if we can outrun the long road that tears a crooked line of stitching north to Cap-Haïtien. I take stock of the traffic along the crude highway that climbs into the mountains and realize that this trip that normally takes six hours will likely take us twice that. If we are lucky, we will make it to safety by dawn.

Aftershocks follow us as we make our way. A strong one rocks us, and we stop cold for twelve seconds that feel like as many minutes. Our jittery instincts misdirect us to stand still, as if that would be better than forging ahead on proven steady wheels. Those on foot beside the line of vehicles have also come to a halt, dropping down on all fours as if they can hold the ground together with their hands. The pedestrians and cars in front of and behind us follow suit, and for those seconds we are all frozen in our tracks, waiting for the world to whisper its calm into our ears, letting us know that it is safe to move again. All of us creep tentatively, waiting for the jolt that will surprise us when we least expect it.

We form a caravan of lost souls, tiptoeing so as not to wake up the subterranean beast that has fallen asleep for the time being. But every time the thing wakes up, yawns, or stretches, we stiffen until it goes dormant again. As we go, shocks wave beneath our feet, the tremors surging into bursts that get shorter and shorter each time. Our fear begins to subside as we grow accustomed to the movement the way we have acclimated to all other disasters in our country. We reckon that this too shall pass, and that it will come again, when nature pleases, until it is done with us. We anticipate but cannot plan for our own extinction, which we know is inevitable. Eventually there will be none of us left to recount the catastrophes. Maybe the earth will come to the realization that the history of its fury requires narrators, victims to tell of the misery it has wrought. Maybe it will decide to spare a few of us for this purpose, and we will procreate again, repopulating the country like masochistic griots bent on a survival that extends the life of true tales from the past.

As we scale the path into the hills toward Mirebalais, the crowd alongside and behind us thins until our headlights are the only eyes that can be seen. We feel ripples beneath us every few miles as the tremors tail us. Mimi and I are both shocked at the ground's insistent pursuit. There is no way to escape the earth's extended tantrum.

I will later learn that the quake boldly extended across waters as far as Cuba. Measuring 7.0 on the Richter scale, the first earthquake to hit Haiti in nearly a hundred years was followed by 5.0 aftershocks. Unlike previous upheavals in other parts of the world, this leviathan grumbled to life only eight feet below the surface, with few obstacles in its path upward. Although Haiti is at the epicenter, it is not the only country courted by this abusive suitor. However, we are at the heart of its sadistic affections. We are a pillowcase of kidnapped kittens shaken and then dropped by a cruel child entertained by our vertiginous stumbling.

Our truck presses forward faster and faster and we fly past sporadic sightings of lean-tos, murmuring to passersby the existence of a town.

"Slow down, Mimi." I see a woman with a child on her hip flagging us down.

"*Lougawou!*" Mimi exclaims as she whisks us away from the trap of a seductive beldame bent on our capture.

"Don't forget where you are," baby girl whispers in my ear.

"The open earth has released all manner of fiends, believe me, Gen." Mimi grips the wheel tightly as if she couldn't let go if she tried.

"Don't forget where you're from." Another spirit whisper shimmies down my neck.

"He'll make it, Gen. On my life and my ancestors' graves." Mimi drives so fast the truck feels like it's gliding just above the surface of the road.

Similarly, I stroke Miles's hair so gently I barely touch it.

Fever floats from his forehead upward, warming my tear-dampened palms.

It reminds me. It reminds me.

"Mommy?"

"Yes, love."

"I don't want to die."

"I know, son."

"Am I?"

"Not by their hand, if I can help it."

We are both choked up. I don't want to think about car keys and sirens. Four colored boys laughing, joking around. Until they had to remember the lesson that starts with hands visible at all times. On the dash. Reach for nothing. Remember to say "sir" or "ma'am" even though you are not down south. Even though you are in New York. Especially because you are in New York and were born on the same day an unarmed thirteen-year-old Black boy was shot by police in the stairwell of an apartment building. You never forget his name, Nicholas Heyward, Jr., and you cannot forget that date: September 27, 1994.

"I'm scared."

"So am I, son. But I'm here for you. Always. Always, son." Or what we'll find there. If there will be stillness and order. If there will be help before Miles bleeds out from the wounds I can and cannot see.

I tear the sheets Mimi keeps for the nights when she sleeps in the truck bed. The makeshift bandages I tie around Miles's arm are soaked by the time I wrap the wound. He does not scream. I know the difference between his trembling and the shaking of the truck the way I can distinguish between the wetness of blood and tears. My clothes are soaked through with both.

I don't know where the strength comes from, but I hear a scratchy whisper emanate from him.

"Mommy?"

"Shhhhh."

"I don't want to die."

"You won't, baby."

"Am I dying now?"

"No, son."

But I don't really know, do I? Because I am not a real doctor. I know the right words to say, but not the right things to do. I know just enough—bandage and apply pressure; don't let him fall asleep; try not to move him, there may be internal injuries. There may be things you do not, cannot know. Like the answers to those "ifs." Except one: if he dies, I will take the wheel and plunge the truck over the edge of the narrow road that winds upward into the mountains. And kill us all.

Mimi applies the brakes at a crossroads. We must decide east or west. There is no option to continue north. There are no signs or markers to direct travelers away from danger. No wooden arrows with chipped reflective paint outlining the names of nearby towns. Mimi rolls down my window and hers. From the east comes the smell of smoking gunpowder. The scent of trees bleeding sap sticks to the insides of my nostrils. The air is shrouded in the wet, mossy roots of wilted flowers. The breeze shifts, lifting the odor of uncooked meat, dead and rotting things covered over by the perfumed powder of a lady's boudoir. Above the smells rises the sound of melancholy melodies against the contretemps of cannon fire.

Wafting from the west, the syrupy sweetness of honeysuckle and sweating women breathes over burning wax and spiced rum. And, although it is pitch-dark, I smell the color blue. We drive west, obeying the siren song of fresh water crashing against stones as old as the earth itself. I hear unfamiliar notes coiling around drums beating. As we drive, the scents and sounds entangle the serpentine roots of colossal, ancient trees.

The truck's tires glide over the leaf-carpeted path that leads upward. From the backseat, I cannot see what Mimi sees as she slams on the brakes. The wheels spin in place and the truck dies. She's frozen in her place behind the wheel. She is afraid of the darkness of night, lit by the blinking of stars through the canopy of towering trees. She fears the grandeur of this forest that smells and feels like the plantain grove, only wider and wilder. She does not want to move, to get out and check why the truck has stopped with her foot on the gas pedal. The lever is pulled to the parked position. The dashboard lights have gone dark, the headlights dim. I want to do something, to jump into the front seat or out of the truck to figure out what is wrong, but I do not want to move Miles, to lift his head from my lap, to lay it on the seat warm with the heat of me.

"Mimi!" I whisper a shout. "Mimi!"

My call gets someone else's attention. I feel small hands, damp and cool, over my eyes. She lifts me out of myself and I leave my body behind for Miles to rest his head on. When I open my eyes, I am with her, sitting on a stone ledge overlooking a waterfall and the pool below. They say these falls were created by another quake over a century ago. I say nothing because, at this moment, all knowledge is beyond me except for what she conveys.

She shows me the women in white, head-ties matching their virgin dresses, first time worn, only time worn, like baptismal, communion, or wedding gowns. Their gowns balloon upward and float around them in circles. Their wet bodies reveal brassiered and braless breasts. There is a wedding tonight but no groom. The women have made this pilgrimage to honor a jealous and vengeful goddess. It is she who makes the moon throb its light over the falls. It is she who blesses the worshipers waist-deep in water. They look up at us with no eyes. Their kerchiefs frame the blank space where their faces should be. Instead of fearing them, I am soothed by these women who want nothing more than to be seen.

This is what my little girl wants as well. But she cannot show me her full self. I see her bare legs dangling, carabella capris that stop just above her skinny calves. Her arms shine with lotion, nails pristine and clear. Her hair is wet but the rest of her is dry. Baby hair borders the face that I am not permitted to see. It is a blur, as if it has been erased. It is a placid place, with the stillness of a pond and the allure of a secret. It is a mirror that reflects nothing but sees all. Although it would make sense to be frightened, my body does not respond that way. My breathing is an uninterrupted hum. My heartbeat a whispered rhythmic thump, like small fists pounding soft dough.

I turn away from the absence that is also a presence and she leads my eyes back to the serene, dark pool where her face should be. She wants me to see what is not there. I feel her hands over my eyes once again. When I return to my body, Miles's is sweating and shivering. In my lap his head feels hot. The windows are fogged with his fever. Mimi's fearful, frustrated panting keeps me from making out the curses she mumbles at the stalled car.

"Do you want me to get out and take a look?" I extend my arm and my fingers reach her shoulder.

"No. Who knows what things are out there? Snakes?"

"Let me try."

"Don't move Miles," she tells me, holding back curses that want to come. "I'll try one last time."

The key clicks as she turns it and the engine grunts back to life. The steering wheel turns, barely noticeably, giving us permission to leave. We double back down the path, which now widens like a yawn as we go forward. Before we know it, we are at the crossroads once again. This time, the choice is to go north or south. Without waiting for our senses to register the atmosphere of either direction, we turn to the north and climb higher into the mountains. For an immeasurable stretch, the road is smooth-packed clay that would burn rust red if there were sunlight. The dirt road flows into tarred pavement for a short stint before the tires crunch over gravel, the chips of which ping sharply against the metal wheel well. A few bumps and we are back on a paved surface.

The terrain changes every few miles, minutes, or hours. Time and distance elude me. They tell lies, entice me with hope I should not hold on to. I am a captive who does not know that she won't live to experience liberation. Nonetheless, I persist, if just for Miles. We are in the mountains of the Maroons, after all.

14

There must have been a woman
walking the road of a girl
standing still atop a pile
of dying lives screaming
for freedom

Still wet from the river, Ateya's dress hung heavily, weighing her body down. She stopped to wring out the excess water, twisting the fabric with both hands the way she had been taught to wash her panties by hand when she was only five years old. The water that fell on the broken ground below was a murky mixture of rust and silt. This was no place to be, no state to be in. Not at this stage in life. She should not be running from and through ruin, looking for stable ground, struggling to find her sanity. She should be where she had always imagined she would be by now, but she'd taken a wrong turn somewhere, back when she'd been able to make choices.

She'd only been able to choose which man to be with. Everything else had been chosen for her—where she would live, where she would work and go to school, if she would go to school, what she would learn, what she would do with what she learned. It had not even been a question of destiny. It had to do with where she had been born, and to whom. Her sex, race, complexion, class, country, family. These had been predetermined. But she should have had a say in those other things. She would have chosen to live in America, go to a big university, become whatever she would have dreamed. But she had not been given the choice, so she did not know what she would have wanted to be. Even now, she could not think of anything different; she only knew that she wanted something better. Something more.

Ateya looked around her to get her bearings. She didn't recognize the place she had been to each day for three years to learn to grow everything, especially plantains. Boulevard Jean-Jacques Dessalines resembled nothing she had seen back then. Every stone, slab, and plank, everything that had been held together by cement or screws, was now cracked and scattered, as if all of the broken bones in all of the graves throughout all of the country had breached their tombs and thrown themselves wildly over the land. There was nothing secure to hold on to as she walked. No willing hand or generous body to grasp as she stumbled over jagged mounds of earth. She had no idea where she was headed, since all of the landmarks she had known and the block-letter signs she had read were now illegible chips of paint. All she could do was follow the other dumbfounded people, who she later learned had been headed to Tabarre via Boulevard du 15 Octobre.

She should have realized that she was in Tabarre—or Taba in Kreyòl—standing on the spot where the Université d'Agriculture d'Haiti had once stood. It had been less of a college and more of a vocational school, erected by an agribusiness NGO that, having failed at restoring the country to its glory days of exporting abundant telluric goods, had reinvented itself as a school for the fortunate few children of subsistence farmers.

Ateya had been the beneficiary of a scholarship from the Banc de Yanique, her mother used to quip with a snide twist of her bottom lip. When Guit had found out just how bountiful Yanique's coffers and connections were, the requests for richer remittances had overwhelmed the telephone in New York so much that Ol'Lady had kept the phone off the hook. *Tab ba*—a low table. Gold- or silver-plated, Guit had imagined, piled high with big-bill greenbacks, enough to run irrigation lines from Rivière Grise to the budding plantain grove in La Tranblè. Ateya had imagined none of this. She had simply been grateful that she'd no longer had to stand behind a kiosk of canned goods in the punishing sun. That place was gone now. A minute-long tremble had brought it to its knees, and her with it. But she could still make out the outlines of her old school in ruins.

Here is where Ateya had learned to dance. Rocking and winding. His front to her back, pressed pelvis to pelvis, holding with no hands. This is where she'd learned to kiss. Slow dancing. Rough hands on Coke-bottle waist, smooth as glass. This is where she'd laid it down. Her first time in the garden while grafting to make hybrids. Bastard offspring, like many of the people on this half island. This is where she'd learned to fuck. Flat back. In the soil. Standing up against a wall. On the chemistry lab counter. Legs wrapped around his waist. This is where she'd learned to cry. That first time. And the next. And the next. This is where she'd learned to fight. To keep bad things from happening again. And again. And again. This is where she'd learned to breathe, to rock, to kiss, to fuck. And stand on her own.

From the wreckage of the university Ateya could see light. A few stubborn lampposts persisted, which should not have surprised anyone, as there was almost always electricity in Taba. It was the site of some of the most important places in the country—the Barbancourt rum factory and the U.S. Embassy compound, which is where Ateya assumed the hordes of people in front of her were trying to get to. Following the crowds, she passed the ruins of the NPH hospital. A hopeful few attempted to dig through the wreckage to find supplies—bandages, splints, alcohol, anything to piece themselves back together. They were scared off by the death rattles of buried patients and doctors.

She wanted to turn back and retrace her steps. Taba was in worse condition than the yard she'd left. To find what? To find whom? She had left a bad place and dragged herself into hell itself. She could not even remember whom she'd been searching for, or why. She had chosen and landed here, in a place that did not look like a place where people once lived, but like a war zone. While looking for something better, she had arrived at a place as unrecognizable as she was to herself.

She walked backward to where she'd started. Against the current of lost people, she sought out the blocks and metal that had been the façade of her school. That was where she would find the site of her first lone decision. A boy, a man, really, who'd had a wife, a fact she had not known at the time. He had had children, a home, some land. He had come to school to learn how to take command of all he had. If he could master the earth beneath his feet from his farm to Taba, then he could control everything else in his life. She had been his respite from the burden of the heavy crown (a straw hat) and his iron sword (a steel machete) that he had donned to rule his world.

Ateya could see so much more clearly now. All of her choices. Beyond the piles of rubble, the greenhouse stood, daring any- and everything to crack its glass. She knew that she was only imagining things, because how could the quake have left that intact? She made her way to it and stood inside, examining the exposed roots of a sapling that had already grown too big for the shallow flowerpot in which it had been planted. From where she stood, she could see the garden where she'd learned how to till and tame recalcitrant topsoil. She was ankle-deep in the dirt with budding dark-green lives begging for sips of water.

Beyond the garden lay the grove and she was there too, at the same time. Premature plantain trees strained their torsos and spread their leaves upward like arms that only reached her waist, desperate children wanting to be lifted and loved. Just as she extended a hand to touch, she spotted the graves from which the bones of broken homes protruded. She followed the crack in the ground and was in her yard.

Lost and turned around, she doubled back and followed the crooked line up the gravel hill and into the road, where a line of lost people lumbered along, while others battled heavy blocks to bring loved ones back to life. As crumbling storefronts gave way, she reached the street named after the brave man who had been torn apart, limb from limb, by an angry horde of suffering people, eager for the liberation he had promised. At a crossroads, she followed Boulevard du 15 Octobre, named for the anniversary of the return of another man, who had also promised freedom. He had been ripped out of the country and replanted in foreign and shallow lands, where his roots had breached the pot and found passage back to his native home. Ateya wanted to find her way back home too. Not this carcass of a tortured land but a place full of life. Not a resurrected country but one that had never died at all. She wanted to stand firmly on ground that would not give and plunge her into a premature grave.

Ateya walked until she was too tired to go any farther, only to realize that she had been standing still the entire time.

Without warning, a backhand knocked her to the ground, and when she looked up, she locked eyes with her long-dead mother.

"Where is your blood?" Ateya recoiled at the sight of her mother's raised hand. "Where is it?"

Reeling from the blow, Ateya rose to her feet with one hand extended, as if she were waiting for someone to help her up. She placed her other hand protectively over her stomach.

"After all I've done for you. I killed that man! And you come here with a bruise on your face. You let some man hit you? You come crying, bringing me a belly? After all I did to keep you from ever getting knocked about again by a man?"

Ateya recoiled as her mother raised her hand again. She would not allow another blow to land. The slap had been the third and would be the last.

"Listen to me real good. You're listening? You're going to do to that man what I did to your father." Guit leaned in closer to Ateya. "Make sure the two of you are in bed. Bring him here, if you have to. Give him the best you have ever given him. Wait until he falls asleep. You're listening? A nice deep sleep. A sleep so deep, he doesn't even dream. Get up and go to the kitchen. Put some oil in a pot. Clean oil, so he doesn't smell anything and wake up. Boil the oil. Make it so hot, it would burn anything you put in it to *chabon* in seconds. Grab a glove and a ladle. Walk carefully, so he doesn't wake up and so you don't spill anything on yourself. Save it all for him. Once you're standing over him, pour the oil into his ear." Guit took a deep breath and extended her hands for Ateya to examine. "You see these scars? I burned myself when I did the same thing to your father after he hit you and made you deaf."

More afraid of her mother than ever, Ateya took a few steps backward. "I didn't know. How could I have known?"

"You thought I would let him get away with what he did? Then you really don't know me. Do you?" Guit ran her hand over her head and removed her wrap. "You see this?" She pointed at an X-shaped keloid scar. "He did this to me. Cracked a bottle of cane liquor over my head. If not for my mother, he would have blinded me. That's a story for another time."

There were tears in Ateya's eyes as she remembered her mother's edict:

"If any man ever raises his hand to you again—he doesn't even have to hit you—you have my permission to kill him. I will deal with the fallout."

~⁓~

Going backward when she needed to move forward, Ateya felt stuck, as if she were standing in a basin of thick mud into which an invisible hand kept pouring resin. It almost didn't matter; there was nowhere to go to escape the devastation around her. The only option was trailing the hopeless crowds that moved as if they were bound together. She pretended that it was a market day, when clumps of women marched to sell and to buy in a cyclical trade that kept both merchant and buyer in debt. In fact, what seemed like the forward movement of a line was actually a circle. Those walking toward the capital to find help, safety, or some make-believe port of departure doubled back and joined those who were headed away from Port-au-Prince seeking relief.

Umbrellas that had once formed a colorful canopy of shade over the heads of traders lay on top of and underneath uneven sections of rough rock, forming an almost beautiful, unintentionally constructed abstract sculpture. She carefully scaled the crude monuments under which unclaimed carcasses were stiffening and decaying simultaneously. As she looked down from a particularly steady peak, she saw where the lines in front of her were going. America. That perfect land of safety, abundance, and possibility. Where there were more than just meals. There were ways of making money, so that there would always be food. The weak survivors, bent but not broken, curled their bodies in a fetal position at the gates of the U.S. Embassy like Black children hoping to be adopted by strangers who passed them over in favor of lighter-skinned infants. Desperate American citizens with throaty voices waved their passports as proof of their worthiness of being whisked away.

The strong ones in the crowd, the determined ones with no papers, tried to storm the gates of the embassy compound. Ateya knew that these people, her people, had rarely been told the truth about the place of plenty or had rejected the harsh realities that had been described to them.

They ignored the debris of Sheetrock blowing toward them and the smell of melting paint that spoke of fire, and held on to the embassy compound's obstinate metal bars, which remained fixed in the ground. They pleaded for entry into a place that was no more intact than where they had come from. Although the main building was still standing, its interior had collapsed, leaving an alluring façade, giving false hope to those desperate for a reprieve from their own broken country. If only they could see what was inside—the corrupted, smoldering guts of an imploding place. Just then, a deteriorated cluster of cinder blocks gave way under the crush of bodies trying to breach the gates of heaven.

Some of the crowd started to make their way to a real place of escape—the airport. As they got closer to the flimsy chain-link fence, they saw the raised serrated edges of ripped tarmac on which kneeling airplanes seemed to be praying for restoration.

As the men and women beside her elbowed one another as if to see why their newly made companions were moaning, Ateya silently backed away from the crowd. She had stopped longing to get out of Haiti when she had gotten pregnant the first time. Since then, Ateya had not hoped, dreamed, or even wished for more or better than what she was or what she had. She had as much power to choose her present and future as she did her past. Up until hours ago, the only control she had had was over those who needed the scraps that she extended stingily. They would need her more in the aftermath and she would have even less to lend.

But who cared, anyway? Since the one who belonged to her, the way she had belonged to her mother and her mother to her grandmother, was hiding. Her someone only peeked between the curtains of this world and the other to tease Ateya, pulling her puppet strings to make her long for, hope for, want to die for. To show her who was truly in control.

15

There must have been blood, so much blood
greedy gods with open mouths
each awaiting a turn
for the red to flow over their lips

The truck bounces over a bump and then dips. I jump with it in a way that reminds me how easy I am to startle, how weak I am. I try to hold on to Miles so he doesn't feel the shock.

I am *not* brave. I am not strong. Life is like water in my hands. I cannot hold on to it. It slips through my fingers. My hands are empty but wet. A taunt to let me know that it is there. But it will not be held or incarcerated in the leaky vessel of palm joined to palm. It does what it wants, goes where it dreams of being. But even when it appears to vanish, it is there. In the air as mist. On the ground, where it feeds gardens. Gives its life to bring life. And there is still enough to keep my hands wet.

I cannot protect this thing that has been left in my care. A life. That I cannot keep alive. His tears are a life slipping through my fingers. I have been lied to. I did not create this life. I only birthed what was sent through me. I was led to believe that he was mine. I have no courage, no strength, nothing required to care for the life that only slips through my fingers. When he is gone, I will be left with my own soaked skin, leaky palms clasped in prayer. But I do not trust. I believe in nothing.

I can't say this to Miles, who would not hear me anyway. I stop trying to keep him awake and let him fall asleep, so he won't cry himself into a headache. I have been there before. With him in my lap, soaking wet, weeping for someone who was not there. Should I tell him what happened? What made his father run, run, run?

I want to tell him everything. But everything would leave him drenched. His life, like water, would slip through his fingers and leave him damp, hurting, hateful, wanting to die.

I have never had anyone to tell everything to. I have no therapist. I could never tell Ma or Ol'Lady much that they had not already deduced from my moods, as I tried to hide my crying in their presence. They know what it is to mourn a man, although Ma has never admitted it, will never do so. Loss of a romantic lover gone looks different from all other types of longing. It leaves you speechless, not wanting to, not able to recount the good parts of him and a life together. You can't reminisce, lest you fall deeper in love, in that hole where you can never again be whole.

Ol'Lady mourned the man who gave her Ma. Ma mourned not knowing who my father could be. Even at this age, I have seen her looking for traces of several men in me. I imagine that she has reduced her guesses to two, one more than the other. I imagine that she remembers more than her stares convey. I look more like her than anyone else, which makes her grateful, so she can look at herself reflected back at her. But our resemblance forces her to go deeper and deeper. Topsoil easily gives way to dark earth, while the layers lighten until she reaches ivory bone. Her heart breaking to the core, she digs until she finds him. In the shape of my nose. The way I tilt my head in all of my pictures. Thank goodness for pictures—otherwise she might go further into me and find out that I have nothing left after: after I give to her, Ol'Lady, Miles, and Yves. Instead, my hands are empty but wet with every life except my own.

Even with nothing left or perhaps in the hope of getting something back, I hold on to Bright. Leave but don't let go. I could never tell anyone how we sometimes dance in the hotel rooms to music we listened to when we were together. I can't even tell him what the music feels like, how my head feels pressed against his chest as we rock in place. Not even he knows how far my love for him reaches. We make love when our longing gets to be too much. We schedule it and meet in secret; we cheat on each other with each other. I love knowing that he is betraying himself by holding me. I am doing the same. It is worse for me. I am the victim. I am the one reliving the before, the during, and the after. I am breaking my own heart every time I let him make me feel good. The wedding, the honeymoon, the infidelity, the make-up sex, and the cheating on ourselves. Ours is a dangerous pleasure that we never discuss. I don't want to hear his sorry, his promises not to, his talk of what could still be. If I would just open up and let him in beyond my body's arched back. Beneath the cool sheets on top of too many pillows. I never speak of it. As if my open mouth would mean an open heart. I keep my lips sealed except to kiss so no words slip out.

Even the things I want to say I keep to myself. How I found her wallet in my car. His was at the shop. There were pictures of the two of them in plastic sheaths. Even though "She means nothing" and "It's over with her." Despite him kneeling before me, telling me that I can call her to confirm, because he knew that she would lie for him. She did. She told me what I wanted to hear. I felt ashamed for having called her, for not believing him enough not to. I believed his "Never, never again," his "Our family is the most important thing." To me it was. I wanted to believe him so much that I trembled when I screamed, my mouth pressed against his chest.

We have been having make-up sex for years now. He does not say but I still hear him wanting to go back to the before. I am too embarrassed to tell anyone that I have let him back in, to my body, at least, which is why we go to hotels. At least I haven't let him lie on top of me on what used to be our bed. I kept the mattress not for spite but to sleep with his smell deep in the foam. It has been years, and his scent is gone. I try not to strip myself to the bone for him to see that, if not for the boys and what the tumult of the ups and downs, the breakups to make-ups would do to our sons, I would tell him the secret that Ma and Ol'Lady knew the first time they guessed that we'd been sleeping together again.

I open my mouth to tell Mimi to drive, drive, drive faster into and over the mountains, into the forest. Farther and farther along the winding road between the stone walls not meant to be scaled and the ravine that calls us to crash.

Somewhere between Mirebalais and Hinche, we take a wrong turn and go east, far, far east. Deep into a forest that looks like a jungle, giving way to a grove of sweet fruit trees and then fields of hateful cane. Somewhere between my Maroon ancestors fleeing re-enslavement and the lashings with cane strips and bullwhips. Somewhere between conch shell calls, steel against steel, and fingers against drum skins, is the battle to survive once again, the threat of an arm mistaken for a stalk and a bleeding machete.

From Pignon to Dajabón are the mountains where our people hid and then sprang down on enemies wanting to put them back in bondage. Somewhere east to the river, where my people were massacred, where they became sacred en masse, baptized in their own blood. Where were the ancestors then? The Taino? The Arawak? Ibo? Nago? Dahomey? The Africans from the west coast? From where? No one can say for sure. Did they come down in '36 the way they had in '04, the way they had in '42? The centuries are all mixed up, like the people. The topsoil turned over again and again until time is measured only in periods between enslavement and occupation. Between a fear that never leaves, and a bravery birthed from confusion. There is no name for the illnesses of the head and heart because there is no such thing as post-trauma for my people. The shocking pain is a pendulum that swings from hurt to suffering, wounded to dead.

Just miles from the bank of the Rivière du Massacre, two tires go flat, landing us in a ditch. The radio turns on without a touch. The static starts an unintelligible, scratchy monologue. We imagine that it is broadcasting what we just fled from. Mimi turns up the volume, which wakes Miles, who is delirious from fever. Or is he just confused from the pain and the jolt of the truck? Mimi feels brave enough to get out of the truck, which tips a bit more toward the ground as she shifts her weight.

"*Merrrrrddddddde!*" She draws out the word "shit."

We're not going anywhere with two flat tires and no spares. With no one around to push us to a road or tow us to a place with more light. To load us into a truck bed and take us away to the safety we have been seeking but still have not found.

I do not dare get out of the truck. My body is what is keeping Miles alive. His head might fall off if I move, and he would only have one hand to hold it together. I do not have to move. Baby girl strokes my cheek with a flower-petal touch. She lifts me out of myself again—this time she leaves me at the riverbank.

I am sitting on the ground, which is moist and cool beneath me. The water is high enough to touch the tips of my toes. I am thirsty but am held back from drinking the liquid that would be pink if I could see it with light stronger than the eyes on the front bumper of the truck.

There is no one in the river. Not a whisper. Not even the sound of ripples. No calls from ancestors, who fled as far away from Dajabón as they could get. Not a word from those who were brave and insane enough to pitch sticks and lay bricks and tiles under tin to make their homes on the bank of this river. Those so desperate to keep close to their long-deceased loved ones that they honored the lineage and legacy of agony. They found what they were seeking by feeding from the river, where their reflections did not come back to them whole. I do not hear them, but I know they are there. I do not hear her tell me out loud, but I remember things I did not know before.

These are not my memories but for a moment, they push aside what's in my heart and head: My fear for Miles. My fear of Bright, if and when we make it out of here. The threats he will make about taking the boys or, worse, about coming back to the family he broke apart with promises unkept. He did not stay, so he cannot come back and then leave again. Take back our hearts only to throw them away. *Again* is a scary thing.

For a moment, I can be afraid of something I have not experienced before, something distant and unknown, something so far back before my time that I know I will leave it behind the way we left the raised rocks in La Tranblè. Like the cracks that crept far enough north that we raced to outrun them, these things will never catch up with me.

Baby girl's small hands push me into the water. She holds my head under, pushing me deeper and deeper until my feet nearly touch bottom. What am I doing here? What does she want me to know? I am not strong enough to fight for knowledge or life. So she shows me the story that is really the sound, that is really a word, *perejil,* that my people drowned and died trying to pronounce.

She releases me but I still hold my breath, although I am no longer under or in the water. I stand and walk. I drip all the way to the truck. I wring my shirt, and the water runs pink from the river. From Miles.

I am too heavy with the water on my body, so I kneel beside Mimi, who is mumbling curses and prayers at the same time. Here I am again. This place has brought me to my knees. All the while I have been sitting with Miles's head in my lap, my hands stroking his burgeoning beard. He is so still, I am afraid to try to wake him; if he does not stir, I will die.

I see the fingers that are attached to the hand and the broken arm move and I finally let out the breath that I have been holding since I rose from the river. Mimi jumps into the truck, and it shifts a little under her weight. It regains its balance. The steering wheel turns itself without her help. I exhale and the tires reverse. We lurch forward with only a tap from the small finger on a tiny hand attached to a strong arm that wants me to stay.

She does not want me to leave just as much as she wants to come with me. If she doesn't let go, what reason will I have to come back?

Somewhere between Ouanaminthe and Dondon, the static of the radio lets a word slip through like water between fingers that are desperate to hold on.

16

There must have been a grove
that would always and only
grow ghosts and graves

As she wound her way around the capital, Ateya could hear the conversation that would decide her fate.

"You have your own daughter. Why do you need mine?" Ateya heard her mother raise her voice so she could hear. That was unnecessary, since Ateya had been standing outside the bedroom door waiting to learn her fate.

"Let me take her with me when I'm going," Yanique pleaded.

"Take, take, take."

"I give too, Guit."

"I was waiting for the day that you would throw that in my face."

At this, Ateya crouched down and peeked through the doorjamb to see on the faces of the two women what was *not* being said.

Guit let go of the skirt gathered in her lap and clapped her hands for emphasis. "You think you can buy my child? Slavery is over. You couldn't pay me enough. You don't see me as a mother, do you, Yanique? You think I just breed. I have too many children, some would say. Even I will admit that. But I was waiting for a girl. And if I had to have five boys before I got this girl, born on this dirty ground right here, then it was well worth it." Guit pointed her finger at the floor between her legs, unembarrassed by the discolored tiles.

Ateya saw Yanique's eyes go dark. She waited to hear Yanique's response. But it was her mother who continued.

"This girl you see here, she is the only one who will be there when I die. The boys have already gone on their way to live their own lives. Everything they have is for another woman and her family. They don't belong to me anymore. They were on loan to me. But this one, I didn't borrow her. I own her outright."

Ateya waited. She knew her mother well. She could feel Guit building up to the slap she had been waiting to dole out to Yanique for a long time.

"*She* will bury me. No one else. Not even you. I don't even want you at my funeral. Don't even bother to send money. Or Ol'Lady." With these words Guit had gone too far. She had done the most hateful thing a person could do—banish someone from their funeral.

"My plot is ready. Right back there with my own mother." Guit gestured toward her future burial spot with her chin. The beginnings of the plantain grove were sprouting over Madame's grave.

Ateya felt her hopeful spirit drop and then collapse entirely. If she wasn't taken to America now, she wouldn't get another chance. Yanique was unaware that Ateya was pregnant and, for now, it seemed that Guit would keep it that way. But Ateya knew that her mother was leaving the best barb for last to win the war.

"Ateya could finally get her ear fixed. Don't you want that? I know you do."

"It's too late for that. I'm used to it and so is she."

"How do you know that? Do you even speak to your daughter? You know she'd rather be with me in America. There's so much she could do."

"I always knew you wanted a little maid to serve you and your mother. When she was small you would have bought her as a gift for Genevieve. Isn't that why you sent Genevieve here every summer? You wanted me to see them playing together and think what? That they were sisters? That they needed a playmate? Why didn't you leave Genevieve here? You wouldn't give her away or sell her. Well, Yanique, I bleed when I'm cut too. Just like you."

Ateya could hear defeat in Yanique's voice. "Fine. I don't have it in me to argue with you anymore. At least she's in school." Yanique dropped her head in her hands. "At least she doesn't have a baby on her hip. That's why you should send her with me. Before she has a child and places an additional burden on you."

"Breasts are never too heavy for their owner. No matter how big they get."

"Don't you ever wish that your mother had let you come to America with Ol'Lady?"

"Not to be your doll baby."

"Your life would have been so much better."

"Who said my life was bad? You people come home and

all of a sudden what you grew up with is no longer good enough for you. No one is good enough for you."

"Guit, I just meant that life would have been a little easier. You could have gone to school. You would have been spared—"

"A-te-ya." Guit enunciated every syllable.

Ateya jumped when she heard her name.

"Is not going anywhere. I let her go past the gate, she ended up on the road, so I set her up to sell there. She ended up on her way to the river, so I moved the kiosk farther ahead. She crossed the bridge, so I sent her to Mache Taba. Each time she went a little farther, I gave her a little more rope. Then you made me send her to that school. You cut that rope. You did that, Yanique."

Ateya waited for the words to come crashing down. Positioned awkwardly, her legs started to cramp. She ignored the pins and needles as she pushed her hearing ear closer. She held her breath so she could hear without the interruption of breathing.

"You made me send her. Did you think that getting her closer to the airport would make me give in? Well, I have news for you. Ateya and her baby are not going to America with you now or ever."

Ateya pulled her head away from the door. She straightened out her legs and pressed her back against the wall. She knew that it was done now. She didn't have to look at Yanique to see her defeat.

"That's it then, Guit." She heard the hurt in Yanique's voice.

"Yes, that's the end of it. *Pointe final.*" Guit stood up, waiting for Yanique to do the same.

"I'll take her and the baby!" Yanique suddenly proclaimed.

Ateya gasped and immediately placed her hand over her mouth to hold back a scream. She could almost see the words spill out of Yanique's mouth like the body's water waste held too long.

"I know you're bluffing. What are you going to do with a baby? A head cannot carry more than one load at a time." Guit grinned spitefully. "Go ahead and take them, then. The only thing is, once you take them, they are yours for good. There is no sending them back." She extended a palm out to Yanique. "*Kale'm lanjan'm!* Give me my money!"

Ateya knew it. She knew that there was a catch. Her mother wanted payment.

"How much?" Yanique retorted.

"I don't think you'll be able to afford it even if there are money trees in America."

"How fucking much?!"

"Oh-oh. You came here to curse me out. To steal my child and tell me off."

"Enough, Guit. How? Much?"

"I want it in cash. Lump-sum. No monthly crumbs, like you and your mother send now. I'll even give you a discount since she's ruined. With a baby it will be harder for her to keep a job or find a man."

"Stop playing games, Guit."

Ateya reluctantly poked her head in the cracked door again. She didn't let herself get too excited. She would not. Not until she saw herself on the airplane and felt it take off. Her heart was beating so fast her chest could no longer hold it. It started searching for another place to be, a larger place that could accommodate its swell. It moved down to her stomach but found no room there with a baby and all. It skipped and split itself into halves. One went toward her throat. The other squeezed itself into a corner between her abdomen and pelvis. The halves broke into fourths, then into eighths. Before she could catch up to count the pieces, before she could figure out where each one had lodged itself, she heard the word she dreaded.

"No, Yanique. No. This is not a game. I do not have an auction block."

"And you have nothing to offer them. A pregnant teenager and a fatherless child."

"Watch yourself, Yanique. Let's not talk about being fatherless. Do you even know who Genevieve's father is?"

"We're all fatherless in this family, Guit. Don't you get it? There are no men. Only boys, your sons, your brothers. I don't even have boys. I wouldn't know what to do with them."

"You would love them, Yanique. You would love them the way I love all of my children."

Ateya didn't know what to do with herself. She had never heard her mother say the word *love*, let alone that she loved her. Never mind her brothers. They were gone. She was the only one there to be loved. How could she leave the one who loved her?

Ateya stood up and tiptoed to the back stoop. She reached for the beans that had started to burn. She had forgotten them on the fire. She heard Guit coming up behind her but now her mother's footsteps no longer inspired fear, not even when she heard her yelling about wasting food.

"There isn't enough money coming from America for you to be ruining the few beans I've grown."

Ateya waited for and then jumped when Guit slapped her on her back. At least Guit's hand wasn't wet. At least she never hit her in the face again. At least she didn't kick her. At least there was love in the beatings.

"I only hit you to correct you. I want you to learn. I want a good girl."

She was wanted. Ateya's torn-apart heart tried to pull itself back together to feel her mother's love. But it could not and would never again become one. Hers was a patchwork heart that sometimes sewed itself together haphazardly, pretending to be whole.

~~❦~~

Ateya didn't understand how she had gotten to this place. She didn't know which one of her selves was where. It didn't matter much, since nowhere was safe, nowhere was without pain.

One of her was sitting on the concrete slab on the hill above Port-au-Prince remembering the someone she'd been seeking along the eight-mile trek her mind had made from Croix-des-Bouquets to the capital. She also remembered the shards of Haiti's history that she'd been forced to memorize in school. Haiti had had two capitals for a time—one in the north and one in the south—with a palace in each. She sat in the destroyed south and wondered if the new palace would be built with the labor of a new generation of enslaved, dispossessed women and men who would never inherit the fruit of their toil. Would they ever spend a night in a well-lit room with its private electrical grid? Would they ever know a place that would never go dark, never lose power? Would they ever again set foot on the soil after lining the green hedges with flamboyant flowers? Or fly over the grounds as birds, leaving a segregated paradise of the worst wealth flourishing side by side with the greatest poverty?

She rose to her feet and clapped her hands to release grains of glass and chipped rocks. All around her lay the expansive grave of inexpensive lives disposed of in the landfill of the Western Hemisphere's waste.

It didn't matter where she was since she hurt everywhere.

Ateya had never experienced what it was like to live without heartache. The closest she had come had been the first and only time her mother said that she loved her. Her mother hadn't said the words *to* her. She had said them *about* her. She had not said the words lovingly, but to injure someone while making a point during an argument. Having heard Guit refuse to let Yanique take her to America, Ateya believed that she had finally learned and experienced what love was. However, she did not know the half of it and would not until she had her own girl child to argue over and defend. What was love?

Love was the passing down of a small plot of land that would first become a graveyard, the restful place of the dormant dreams of a long line of women who'd secretly buried their men there to maintain ownership of a matrilineal inheritance. Love was the line of humble tombs with markers memorializing only one occupant, although two, sometimes three inhabitants were housed there. Love was the secret raising of dead men to prepare the soil that would become the home of fat-fingered leaves and arm-length fruit owned by Ateya and her mother, Guit, before her, and her grandmother Madame before Guit, and the mothers and grandmothers before them. It was laying claim to the few dry, rocky acres of deceptively intractable land that only required a few generations of brave and patient women to bring forth fruit.

It was the first of these women laying claim to this small plot in the time of Dessalines and taking up arms against Henri Christophe, their second slaver and self-proclaimed king-for-life. It was the slaying of greedy traditionalists, men, who, mistakenly believing that their sons deserved what their daughters did not, died at the hands of their unmarried wives, who were determined to prove them wrong.

Love was the slaying of men who dared raise their plantain-length arms against the rebel mothers of their girl children, or against the girls themselves. Love was the enslavement of generations of dead men raised from their graves to till a sometimes visible, often disappearing plot of irrigated earth, where the enviable arms of sometimes yellow but most often green limbs were grown by the hands of one woman named for the ground itself. And love was the land, and the land was hers.

Ateya lived long enough to execute Guit's mandate to bury her no more than six feet deep in the grave. She'd dug the crude pit herself, planting a tree over it to mark her mother's resting place. It was a fresh, uninhabited grave, unlike the ones occupied by her women ancestors. Both of her parents should have been in the same grave, but Guit had done what had never been done before. She had killed a father and then a son, buried one on top of the other, leaving no room for herself when the time came. Father and son rested one over the other and rose together at night to work and wander the land that had never been theirs.

Guit had not meant to kill Ateya's father. She had only meant to deafen him the way he had maimed their daughter. She had not meant for him to awaken and find her standing over him with a pan of boiling smoking oil. She had only planned to pour the oil into one ear, not to splash it all over his face and her own hands. She certainly had not meant to punish herself but reasoned that she too was culpable for Ateya's deafening since she'd failed to protect her daughter from the blow that left the child with one hearing ear. Guit had not expected the father to kill himself after seeing his pretty caramel face drip skin and flesh from the bone. But she proudly took credit for his death and buried him twelve feet deep in the grave where she was supposed to be buried in the tradition of her mothers, grandmothers, and the great and grand women before them.

Guit had intentionally killed her son. She knew that you were never supposed to kill your own children. But she hadn't had a choice. The boy, whom she'd sent to school before Ateya, using money earmarked for the girl, had dared to suggest that Guit sell a piece of the land, her land, to pay his way through medical school. For as much as she would have liked to boast about a doctor in the family, what her son had suggested was blasphemy. Furthermore, his request, that came out more like a demand, had forced her hand.

She had known of no son in prior generations who had assumed that the blank, untilled parcel was theirs. Husbands, lovers, and fathers had dared do so to their demise, but never a son. He had to be put down before he contaminated her other boy children with the same assumptions. Thus, she became the first to lower one of her own into the ground. The pain of doing so had nearly killed her, but not quite. It certainly did not hurt as much as the thought of a daughter losing even part of the inheritance meant only for women. Guit would have fallen into the open grave alive if she'd even entertained the unthinkable—not having a daughter to pass the land on to at all.

The thought that a daughter could die before a mother, that a mother could have no daughter to be buried by, that there would be no grave for either, that these possibilities even existed, would have shattered the earth in jagged halves, cracked open long-sealed graves, scattered bones about like curses without carefully identified targets.

Guit had not slit her son's throat or beaten him to death. She wasn't strong enough to strangle him, hold his head under water to drown him, press a pillow into his face to smother him. She had waited until he had a cold and then a fever. She'd boiled bitter *asosi* tea that was a known cure-all, added chamomile to put him to sleep, crushed water hemlock to kill him, and stirred in rat poison to make sure. The neighbors assumed that he had died from typhoid. They didn't question his burial in one of the graves that lined the empty square of land, since that was where the family buried all of their dead.

More than two decades later, Ateya could not have imagined but nonetheless repeated the ritual of burying a stingy, greedy, and violent man. He had withheld from their daughter, Ti'Louse, the light complexion that would have meant a much easier life. Like the women before her, Ateya had marked the spot for his grave and gone to bed. Only the dead could dig a pit twelve feet deep without the fear of being buried alive. She had made the dead man dig his own grave, twelve feet down, place himself in it, and fill it with dirt again. That had been his first chore as one who was doomed to work for the rest of his dead, restless life.

But she had killed the man for something frivolous, for his inability to do what was out of his control, for his failure to pass down an inheritance less valuable than soil. Light skin was not altogether worthless, not in a country where it often determined one's quality of life. However, it certainly was not as precious as property. Not to a people who had once been owned, who had killed to own themselves. The soil they'd been enslaved to till was worth the life's blood that had nourished it. To them the land was as sacred as life. By killing for color Ateya had committed a curse-worthy crime. She had entombed and thereby enslaved a man for something less valuable than proprietorship. She deserved whatever she would reap.

At that time, Ateya could not have predicted that she would not have a daughter to bury her on top of the tight-fisted man or anywhere else ever at all because of a random quake. She would have no girl child to inherit the land that had belonged to the only daughters of generations of women who'd murdered men to ensure the fertility and viability of the few acres passed along the maternal line before Christophe, Dessalines, and even Louverture before them. Although she would eventually blame herself for withholding love from her daughter, she would never piece together enough of her own history to understand why she and her entire country had been damned.

All she knew was that she was reaping the worst—a daughter who had died before her mother, a mother with no one to bury her, and no prepped grave for either.

17

There must have been blame laid
at the feet of a hated nation
by presumed innocent people
who always find fault
in everyone and everything
except themselves

Between the static on the radio come frantic fragments
that Mimi and I take turns deciphering and repeating to each
other. News of the earthquake has made its way north faster
than we have. Undoubtedly, word has reached outside of the
country.

We hear of the Enriquillo Plantain Garden Fault, which
runs just south of Port-au-Prince, the capital of Haiti, a small
country that shares the island of Hispaniola with the Dominican Republic. They report that Haiti is the poorest country in
the Western Hemisphere. That it has been plagued by natural
disasters for centuries. That it has suffered under brutal dic-
tatorships for hundreds of years. We hear nothing of its fight
for independence from French slavers in the eighteenth and
nineteenth centuries, nothing of its history as the world's first

free Black republic, of its role in liberating other countries in the Caribbean and Latin America, of the richness of its natural and agricultural resources, nothing of the grandeur of its landscape, the faithfulness of its people. Our people, my people, my country.

I hear myself think "my" and am ashamed for ever having been embarrassed by my heritage, for having associated Haiti with the television depiction of dusty children with flies in their eyes, the ashen hands of barefoot beggars, women with dirt-stained buckets of polluted water on their heads. I used to think only of the stereotypes spat from the lips of classmates who did not even know where Haiti is. "It's in Africa. In the jungle. They do voodoo there—dolls with pins stuck in them, disembodied skulls, zombies with arms out coming to get you." Although I told them that those things weren't true about the people of Haiti, I never said "my" people, "my" country. I explained that not everybody practiced vodou. I pronounced it correctly, although I was too ashamed to say that vodou was a belief system like and unlike any other, that it was the religion originally practiced covertly by the courageous people who freed themselves from bondage. I didn't dare speak of how magical and, yes, how dangerous it was, that my mother and grandmother, my aunts and cousins, could cast spells, that my ancestors could haunt, could fight on my behalf if I was wronged. I didn't tell them that the people honored deities the way saints were worshiped. I still wouldn't say "my" people. I argued on its behalf, for which I would pat myself on the back, but I didn't claim the incredible history of my country, my people. Although I have been raised by women who would have been devastated if they knew of my omission of the "my," I could not bring myself to extend my hands, open my arms, my mouth to say, "I am Haitian. They are my people. Haiti is my country."

Even when I got to college, I pretended to be a tourist on trips to volunteer in "that" country. I still argued on "its" behalf, but I just couldn't say the word, even though my last name was Ducasse and some of my professors recognized it as French, and because I was Black, they guessed that I was Haitian. I had no accent. I'd extracted any trace of Ma's and Ol'Lady's ways of speaking and turns of phrase that might have led to the conclusion that I was not from "here." When I finally admitted that I was Haitian, it was because we were there and I could show off the fact that I spoke Kreyòl—"and French," I never failed to add. I told my classmates that I was from Pétionville or Delmas rather than La Tranblè. I didn't claim the rural place where I had spent so many summer months when I was a kid, and then just weeks as a teenager.

When I finished medical school, I tried to join Doctors Without Borders and was rejected. I was appalled that they didn't want me. I recognized this as karma but also prejudice. I was a psychiatrist, and the assumption was that people in the places where DWB operated, like Haiti, did not require help processing their trauma. They were survivors, happy; look at them. "My" people did not need mental or emotional healing. Not from their rejection by the world that had first abducted them, then enslaved, owned, counted, and treated them like chattel, looted sugar, rum, produce, then robbed them of francs to buy themselves from their colonizers, occupied, occupied again, occupied again, denigrated how many times? Too often and forever.

I had not studied enough and, therefore, had not known enough to recount these abuses to those who blamed Haiti for its own problems. Those who talked about my people as oppressing one another, of nature punishing devil worshipers, of stripping their own land of nutrients and greenery, of being happy with the state of the place because otherwise, why would anybody remain in these conditions? Isn't it such a shame? Yes, it is.

It is a shame that I was so ashamed. I am ashamed still of ever having been.

Now another thing has happened that will bring attention to my country. The stereotypes will be reconfirmed and reported as truth. There will be tours of the devastation; among the places brave journalists risk their lives to capture will be a collapsed *ounfor*, where priests, priestesses, and acolytes are trapped. There will be a close-up shot of the decapitated statue of Saint somebody or other; pan over to a "This might be disturbing to some viewers. Discretion is advised" crushed body with a severed head. Zoom out to the pillar at the center of the space that miraculously is still standing. There is a saying in Kreyòl: *"Fanm se poto mitan."* "Women are the pillars." Ma and Ol'Lady always add, "We women are the ones holding up a collapsed country."

If I am the *poto mitan*, why am I running away at this time when my people need me most? I have to get Miles to safety. I'll come back. I'll remember my medical school training. I will bandage the wounded while I listen to them tell me about their other hurts. I will counsel them as best as I can. I will dig deeper, but I'll keep to myself what I know about generational trauma. "Post Traumatic Slave Syndrome." The "nervous tension" with which all colonized and formerly enslaved people around the world suffer, knowingly or subconsciously. I will keep to myself my own trauma as I treat my people in my country. I'll be back. If I can't, if I don't, I will send . . . Send what? To whom? How? "Text 9999 to make a donation"?

Miles whimpers in my lap. I hurt everywhere he hurts, which is how I confirm that he has internal injuries, other broken bones, a headache. I experience a mother's empathy pains. Then something else, someone else's. I feel pain in my right foot, but it is not his. It is Mimi's. I realize now that her foot is fractured. That she has not had the strength or pain tolerance to press on the gas or brake pedals. She knows it but has been too afraid to admit to herself that she has not been driving all this time. Turning the wheel sometimes but not determining how fast or far we go or if we go at all.

Pain radiates throughout my entire body, inside and out. Some are fresh wounds—scrapes from falling debris, fractures from Miles and Mimi, missing Yves, fear that this circumstance might shatter Ma and kill Ol'Lady. Heartbreak over the possibility of Bright coming back. The thought of him trying to take the boys away from me claws down my back. I want to tell Ma and Ol'Lady to take action now. This is the time to lay hands on him, to quash any wicked plans he might be conniving. The hole in Miles where Bright should be growls its hunger for rescue. Since Yves has only ever known the family that he has now, he does not know that anyone is missing. Bright is not just gone. To Yves, he was never there. He nearly missed Yves's birth, wasn't there to name him, didn't even attend the christening. He didn't come back until the following fall and then left in the spring.

This decade-old hurt is manageable except when my body is racked by the remembrance of broken families, men sold away from women, children from mothers, hope from hearts.

This is where it all started, and it is still here and all around. Love could not bloom; yanked from the roots, it never stood a chance. This is the thing that has been there for centuries. Hurts with no time to heal before the next season. Soil with no opportunity to rest, turn over, recover before the next harvest. It is a miracle that anything grows here, inside us. The womb of this place is broken; it keeps reproducing dysfunction. All of this boils in my body. Even my blood hurts, the marrow. Even the dead parts of me—nails, hair. The pain is almost intolerable.

A few yards ahead, I feel another thing. Not pain. Longing. It's her. Baby girl. I can't carry her now. The thought of having laid her body in the grove is too big a burden at this moment. I know that she didn't die but followed me here, that she has been pushing the truck and pulling it back, stopping it at will—a tug-of-war. I cannot haul her longing right now, although it is as light as the last strands of masticated cane. She insists on my attention.

A headache that is not mine sharpens when all three of our phones ring at the same time. Miles's is in his pocket, which I can't reach. Mimi won't let go of the steering wheel. I am sitting on mine, but I get it out in time to hear Ma say, "Are you okay? Are you okay?" I don't get a chance to answer her. At least she heard me say hello. The line goes dead. Hopeful, I touch the screen to ring Ma under "favorites." No signal. A bit farther ahead, the phone rings again. "Gen? Gen? Where's Miles? Are you o . . ." Bright this time. I clutch the phone so tightly, my knuckles crack. I try to call again. I need them to figure out a way to get us out of here.

The truck falters.

"Shit! I can't do this with you now!" I scream, making my head hurt more.

Baby girl whispers into my ear, something I do not hear.

"Please, let us go."

She tells me that it is not her.

Something, someone is stopping me from moving forward. Telling me that there is no help there. I did not dare go to Dajabón. Too much pain there. Nonetheless, I feel that hurt. Treacherous machetes gut me, hack off my hands, twist my insides.

Baby girl strokes my hand. "Wait here," her touch says.

The smell of burning wood and cooked food floats into the truck. I recognize it—guinea fowl. There are no farms around. This must be some other bird, something wild, or something stolen. She brings me to them.

They know how to free me the same way they freed themselves. Their movements promise release and healing. The grass burning, the herbs boiling, speak of a return to medicine practiced and stolen like everything else taken from this land. A red-hot steel spoon gingerly handled is brought close to me. I hold the wooden handle as my hand is guided to Miles's bandaged arm. I unwrap the bloody cloth with one set of fingers. When I hesitate, my hand is pushed, then pressed downward. I turn my head. I hear the sizzle, his scream, and his breath fading, which tells me that he has fainted. The blood has stopped its oozing. The smell of burning flesh makes Mimi retch. I can stand it only because Miles is mine. But also because of the pain from before, so long before, when these people, my people, were branded. They fled here, to the hills, to join the ones who had been there since time was counted by the sun's movement. Together they proved that they were human. Cattle do not fight back, do not run, do not speak, handle arms, swing sickles, set fires. In the hills my people were not marooned, they were sovereign.

After the healing, they pull us out of the mud and push us on our way.

18

There must have been
a Black girl come
from the seed
of a Black man come
to give a gift
to a Black earth come
to kill a place
for the sin
of coming out Black

The earth shuddered wildly, tossing debris about like a wet dog shaking water off its body. The aftershock knocked Ateya down on all fours, where she remained, without raising her head or making a sound. She leaned her ear into the sounds around her—the tolling of the bell of the partially collapsed Cathédrale de Notre Dame, the screamed prayers of incredulous believers begging their god to wake them from what must be a nightmare, the intermittent crash of loose cinder blocks. When she finally felt stable enough to stand, she fixated on the toppled statue of Neg Mawon bathing in the floodlights that fell from the split façade of the Palais National. The

Maroon lay on its side, its conch shell silenced. There was no call to the mountains for reinforcements because there was no visible or conquerable enemy, only tempestuous nature more violent than any slaver felling people at will, forcing them into submission. If this exquisite effigy of a rebel could be laid low, she knew that she had no chance of standing up against whatever this monster was. If this grumbling beast could swallow and spit out simultaneously, its feral patterns could never be predicted or prepared for, then there was no hope.

Neg Mawon was resting and would awaken in its own time. It would be made new, shedding the spell of the father who had ordered its construction. The people would lift its bronze body to its proper position. The roar of its seashell horn would silence their hopeless bawling.

The lifelike sculpture held Ateya's gaze like a worshipworthy god. Although she craved him now, she never would have lusted after a *mandengue*. He had the height and the strength, but he was far too dark for her. She had always taken in-between lovers with hues that ranged from vanilla-tinged milk to smooth brown egg. Neg Mawon was attractive in this moment because he was the strongest man in the midst of the ruins around her. He promised not only protection but escape. Although he had inhabited the capital for more than forty years, he could flee to his home in the hills at will. She imagined his promise to take her with him.

Ateya wanted to climb him, believing that, perched above Port-au-Prince, she would be able to see the someone for whom she searched. What she saw was the burning carcasses of foreign buildings that had colonized plots of Haitian soil in the name of philanthropy. Médecins Sans Frontières spewed fire out of its front doors. The smoke emanating from the

United Nations building was so dark that flames could barely be seen. The blaze from both structures brought slivers of much-needed light to persistent seekers following sounds to the places where the determined dying clung to life. In the morning, the foreigners would bring help from around the world, but not the sort that Ateya needed.

No one would send sanity, or healers who could restore the fragmented minds of a repeatedly battered people. They would not send those who would heed the calls of shattered spirits, who could at least try to reassemble hurting hearts into something resembling a whole. They would bring their corrupt souls, their own twisted shouts echoing their own narratives about the needs of a people they could never understand because they had never suffered repeated losses, had never heard the silent cry from an open mouth. They had never and could never hear the dog-whistle shrieks from the guts of gutted mothers filling tiny graves with huge losses.

Although the yells were hers, Ateya could not hear herself hollering. Her scream wound itself around the night air and hung there until others joined it. She had been told about broken sounds like these, but she had never heard them. There were those who'd been privy to the wails of mourning mothers carrying their dead or dying babies. They'd spied women walking to the sequestered priestess beyond the yard. They could recognize the pain that was more than pain. There was blood in the howls. Sounds so powerful they blackened moonglow. The cries shook the ground so hard, they split it down the middle in two perfect halves, open just wide enough for a child to fit. Ateya's cry was so sharp, it sealed her hearing ear. She felt only the vibrations of another aftershock, which made her cough up a cry: "I have always loved you!"

Ateya looked around for the shoulders of something high and sturdy on which she could climb. She needed to be heard, and if her calls could not claim an ear, she would look for a clear path through which she could run. She did not want to stand still or stay on the ground. She wanted to move, to go somewhere she had never been or back to the place where she had last seen her someone. If she couldn't win against inertia, she reasoned that she might as well be dead. She wanted to throw herself off the mound on which she'd been kneeling and tumble downward to her death. She wanted to land under the body of the fallen Neg Mawon, protected by the bronze bend of his elbow. She wanted to be carried off with him to wherever wild men went. She wanted to be taken to the forested hills, keep his company far from all that was familiar. She wanted to sever herself from tradition, expectations, and proscriptions. No, she did not need or want forgiveness. She would lift the curses herself if she still believed in such. She would shed shame like the skin of a benevolent succubus mislabeled as a violent captor of men's dreams.

She craved flight, an effortless escape far above the world she had known all her life. She wanted to be gone, to disappear like her someone. Maybe in the vanishing she would find the one she'd been looking for all along. She wanted to set herself free without judgment or assistance. She wanted not to want anything so much ever again. She wanted to be alone with others seeking the same solitude. She wanted to have choices. Only the self-liberated can decide for each of their selves who, what, where, and how to be. Ateya wanted to get up off the ground, stand, run, climb, fly, and be as loose as she could be. To make peace if she wanted to. To wield arms, if she wanted to. To lie down or rise up. If. She. Wanted.

Out of her right mind (who's to say if a mind is right or not?) she chose the respite of the unburdened insane. She believed that she wanted to be a willful warrior atop a liberating mountain. She thought she would become a Maroon—the female but unattached version of Neg Mawon. In truth, what was happening was the complete breakdown of an already unstable mind. But who's to say?

If she could have, Ateya would have admitted that her madness had first manifested as meanness. She had been the first target of the cruelty of the people in her yard. After Ti'Louse's birth, their malice metastasized itself within her, resulting in a twisted thing that resembled but was not absolute hatred. Her community denied knowing the thing. Surely it was something she'd eaten. Maternal milk gone bad, poisoning both mother and child. Making the mother callous and the daughter unworthy of the thing that was every child's due. Had crazy come calling to collect its debt for the mother's belief in a nonexistent garden? They faulted everything except themselves, ducking blame for corrupting the best thing a mother could give, depriving a child of love before she could even walk.

The night before Ti'Louse was born, Ateya had thought that she was going crazy. She saw a naked woman curled tightly around the base of the lone papaya tree, like an infant's hand around an adult's finger. Seduced, she sat under the low-hanging branches and ate unripe green fruit.

"Since you didn't eat the ripe ones, the baby will have a teardrop birthmark. It will be on her bottom because you were sitting down when you ate," the midwife said, standing in a corner of the room, waiting indifferently as Ateya paced.

"I wasn't craving sweets."

"You'll have a bitter child."

"My baby will be sweet to me."

"You really don't need me here, Ateya. You've had so much practice giving birth, you could teach me."

"Who would keep the baby from dropping to the ground?"

"The same one who put it there should be here now to grab it." The midwife chuckled.

Ateya had laughed until she'd coughed. A line of mucous had stretched downward from between her legs.

"Keep laughing like that and the baby will come faster."

"This one better be a girl." Ateya groaned into the words.

"She would be pretty. Her father is light-skinned. Good grain of hair too."

Ateya was squatting with her back against a wall when she spat out an infant girl who came out as dark as tobacco juice. The baby would only get darker, since Black children are always born shades lighter than they will eventually be.

"Too much eggplant. You're not supposed to eat the skin."

Ateya held the baby against her chest. "I'm going to plant a blackberry bush on top of the afterbirth. Her curls look like the bumps."

"You know better than to think that soft hair will stay like that. It's going to turn into peppercorns before sunrise."

"Doesn't matter. I finally have a girl."

"You know how it goes. Ten days inside. If you step outside before then, God only knows."

"See, if I had had daughters to begin with, one of them

would take care of me, bring me everything I need. These boys . . . what's the point?"

"I'll send Mimi in." The midwife turned and left the house without blessing the afterbirth. The baby was as black as the blood congealing in the bucket. As she opened the door, the dog crept in like a nosy neighbor who knew its visit was unwanted. "*Soti la, chien!*" The midwife shooed the dog away, but it did not move.

"Ti'Louse, Ti'Louse, Ti'Louse," Ateya called to the dog. "She belongs to you and me," she said to the dog. "Protect her."

The dog ended up serving Ateya as much as Mimi did.

"I didn't think I had any love left," Ateya whispered into the baby's face.

For ten days, she loved the girl. In the morning and at night, Ateya dressed her beautiful daughter in the frilly, doll-size clothes the women in New York had sent. The light-colored clothing glowed against the baby's skin like glitter against the inky side of carbon paper. For ten days, Ateya hummed into her daughter's face until she found the tune that soothed the baby most easily.

"Mimi, what do you think of the name Hosanna?"

"Do you know what it means?"

"Does it matter?"

"You will make an idol out of that child. God is a jealous god."

"What do you know about God, Mimi? Weren't you an *ounsi*?" Ateya reminded Mimi of her days serving the priestess who lived along the hem of the *lakou*. "You could have done whatever you wanted then." Another reminder, nearly accusatory. Ateya did not have to say the word *madivine* out loud for Mimi to understand.

"Do you need anything else tonight?" Mimi said begrudgingly.

"Are you mad at me? Come here, Mimose Ducasse." Ateya used Mimi's full name. Ateya knew how to hurt a person's feelings.

Mimi's last name was a pinprick on a fingertip. Her chance to go to America under a forged passport, under Yanique's last name, had slipped away like a wet bar of eroded soap. No one really wanted her. She was family but not family. She was different, and everyone knew it even back then. She might corrupt Genevieve. The gathering of Mimi's documents had merely been a ruse to make Guit jealous so she would let Ateya go.

"Don't be mad. You know I was just playing. You know I'm always joking." Ateya remembered her confinement and how much she needed Mimi's help. "I'll see you tomorrow, right? If not for me, for her."

"Let's go, Ti'Louse," Mimi called to the dog. The baby released Ateya's nipple when she heard the name.

Ateya learned that her daughter was ugly while leaning her ear against her front door. The women of the yard had gathered there, waiting for her to come for the baby's first outing.

Black as coffee grinds. Dark as molasses. Burnt-sugar black. Dog-shit dark. Dark as soil in the grave. Nwa kou chabon. *Black as a mourning woman's dress. Black as* djion-djion *water. Darker than a Doberman. Blacker than a* lougawou's *skin.* Nwa kou baka. *As black as the men in the mountains. Dark as Danto. Shut up. Don't curse Ezili like that. Didn't the midwife say Ateya had seen Danto naked wrapped around a tree? If that were true, the baby would be beautiful. That's not so-and-so's baby. All of his other children are as yellow as the sun, with syrupy hair. He is going to die when he sees this baby. You've heard of Dark and Lovely? This one is Dark and Ugly.*

Ateya did not dare open the door. She stayed inside for days after the required period of confinement, hoping that the yard would change its mind, but that only made things worse.

She knows how ugly that child is. That's why she hasn't come out. Better for us. My eyes couldn't stand to see it. Give the food to Mimi. I can't go in there and see that. My skin might turn black too. Color is contagious. But can't be inherited, if that woman is to be believed. What's going to happen when that child goes out in the sun? She'll get so black, she'll turn white. God help us all when she finally gets teeth. Black-bean sauce over rice. Devil's child. She'd better take the girl to see an houngan. *There's no cure for ugly, priest or hospital doctor. I hope this child has a thick skin. She'd better be as sweet as candy—otherwise nothing can save her.*

Ateya brought the child out into the fresh air for the first time at night. She brought her daughter out earlier and earlier, until the baby finally saw daylight. She'd gotten so used to hearing that her child was ugly that she came to believe it herself. Soon Ateya was treating the toddler with such disdain that the dog started barking anytime the mother approached. Mimi would come running when she heard the dog to make sure the baby was okay.

Ateya was only alone with the baby at sundown, which is when she was most gentle, most maternal. The darkness gave her permission to love her once desperately desired daughter. Away from the circle of storytellers and gossips, far from the tortuous tongues of a hateful, self-hating people, she could lean against the papaya tree and cradle the infant that had become a toddler, despite the stunting talk. That was the only time she would utter the child's name, Hosanna, because she could not afford to go against her community and adore her daughter to the point of praise. Not hearing her name often or loudly enough to own it, the baby had shrugged it off and chosen her own. In actuality, the dog had given her its name, along with its protection, until her death.

~~~

In the hours after the earthquake, Ateya never heard the dog bark because it had not. She never saw it again because it could not be seen. Ti'Louse the dog was the only one who knew where Ti'Louse the child was hiding in the plantain grove. Together they had disappeared into a darkness as black as nighttime love.

19

There must have been a grief so real
that it was hard to say
that nothing had ever lived
that no one was ever loved
that no one was ever there

I would give anything to have Ol'Lady here now. Miles's legs would be in her lap while his head still rested in mine. She would help me bear the weight of all this.

I never had to care for the boys alone when they were sick. Without me having to ask, she would take over the nursing, holding my hand as well as the boys'. I would have to sit through her assumptions and advice, but the comfort was worth it.

She would take care of me too if she saw that I was not feeling well—whether body or heartache. I would never tell her, but she would know, or sometimes guess. Even when she guessed wrong, she'd come close. I would try not to give myself away.

~⁂~

"Only the sun and moon get back together after fighting each other for dusk and dawn." Ol'Lady couldn't help but show me that she knew that Bright and I were still sleeping together. I wondered who was the sun and who was the moon.

She served me boiled coffee strained through cloth. Combined with full-fat evaporated milk and white sugar, it warmed and comforted me. Her hands were dead still as she laid the cup and saucer down on the table—no trembling whatsoever, like one might expect of a woman her age. Her fingers looked like the rest of her—as old or as young as she had always been. Her face was the same, with a ready smile for me and downturned lips whenever she said Bright's name. On this particular morning, her mouth could not settle on a shape. She wanted to be both serious and soothing.

"Think about what you're doing, Genevieve. It might be a girl."

I didn't want to answer her. I couldn't, with my stomach rising into my throat, nauseating me. She knew everything. She could smell him on me even weeks after an encounter. But what she was smelling at the moment was the aftermath of my decision. What she thought was morning sickness was the sallow and gray pall of a termination. After looking at my face more closely, she finally guessed. She had seen the results of what she'd thought of as mistakes in the skin of many back home. The color of regret and relief smeared all over exposed flesh. The mournful hues that could not be seen in the darkness when generators ran out of gas. Better to do these things in the dark to give the visage a few hours to heal before morning made the deed obvious to those with discernment.

Although he never said a word about it, I suspected that she had told Bright. When would she have done it? While

Miles and Yves were in school? And why? What did she think Bright would do five years after Yves was born?

The thing with Bright, this thing of ours, wasn't meant to be seen in daylight. I would do this other thing alone under the cover of night, when none of my colleagues would see me leaving the hospital with that distinct tint staining the surface of my countenance. One of them took care of this thing of mine and never spoke of it again. We were co-conspirators under the bright lights of the hospital lobby as we walked into the darkness of the garage and went our separate ways.

Bright insisted on seeing me days after. I begged him to let me be. I made excuses for why I couldn't meet him. Despite my angry protestations, calling him the names I usually reserved for our public encounters, he would not leave me alone. He must have known that I didn't really want to be alone. I just couldn't face him and was in no condition to be intimate. I ended up giving in. Whether it was my silence, my frail walk, the careful way I sat on the bed, or my refusal to get under the covers, he knew something was wrong. I convinced myself that he didn't know about the thing that was mine alone to know. I lied to myself that Ol'Lady had just been guessing to see my reaction. She couldn't have told him. Even before the divorce she would only grunt at him when he greeted her with a customary kiss on the cheek.

He kissed me that way too while I lay on the bed, shivering in the heat of the hotel room. Of course, it was winter. February turning into March. Too close to Valentine's Day, but with spring approaching, he must have known that this might be the last time we would be together until the following fall. He knew better than to speak or to make me get under the covers with him. He covered me with a blanket and threw his arm over my waist as we spooned. He patted my stomach as he had never done, even when I was pregnant with the boys.

I figured that this was how he must have held his girlfriend when their baby died.

I had never, would never have, wished that on anyone. Nonetheless, I had felt guilty when I found out that SIDS had stolen a life from him. I had even thought of her. Sympathetically, compassionately, with pity over the loss. Before then, I had only longed for Bright and the patches of hair I'd lost after he'd brought the baby over unannounced.

I hadn't seen the car seat in his hand at first. In the seconds it took me to register what was happening, the boys had run to see who was at the door, hoping that I was surprising them with pizza for dinner. They stepped aside to let Bright into the apartment while I tried to hide the look on my face.

"This is your baby brother, boys," Bright had said with a hopeful tone to encourage Miles's and Yves's acceptance of the gift they hadn't asked for or wanted. "Bradley Wright," he said to break the silence.

"Junior?" I said, staring straight ahead, trying not to look at the baby.

"The Second."

"Typical." I could only think of his arrogance at naming the child after himself and his pretentiousness adding "II" as the suffix.

Miles didn't even try to force a smile at the infant. He only reacted after Yves said: "I wanted a brother my age," as any four-year-old would. Miles put his hand on Yves's shoulder and pulled him away. He led his brother, the only brother he would ever have or claim, out of the living room and slammed his door.

I stood up to let Bright out. I closed the door behind him as quickly as I could so my breath could escape in a panting rhythm that signaled a panic attack. I tried to calm myself down in case the boys came running after hearing Bright leave. I needed to put my mind back together. I sucked in my tears and called the pizzeria.

Since there had been nowhere for my suppressed pain and stress to go, the emotions escaped through the invisible follicles on either side of my head. I never saw the hair fall. I never saw the hair anywhere at all. It was just gone. Like Bright.

I dragged my mind back to Bright's hand on my abdomen, him turning me over onto my back, placing his head below my breasts. He cried. I was too numb. We didn't wake up until morning and made no attempt to get out of bed. Maybe he had guessed, like Ol'Lady.

Ol'Lady blurted out, "*Mové san.*" Bad blood. "I'll make you some leafy greens so you can get back your strength. You need iron."

I bravely downed the rest of my coffee, which she'd reheated.

"The coffee is okay, but you should drink it black. It would help more."

Ol'Lady changed the subject. Gossiping about Ma was one of her favorite things to do. Listening was mine.

"Don't let your mother fool you, Genevieve." Ol'Lady always started her one-way conversations at an odd point. "She's still out there, you know what I mean? She does her things in secret. That's where you get it from. The only thing she ever succeeded at hiding was where your father vanished to."

"Why are you telling me this?"

"Maybe having a father around would have kept you from Bright. And all those things you think you're hiding from us."

"Bright and I have been divorced for how long now?"

"Keep it that way. I didn't say you shouldn't indulge. You're still so young. So am I," she laughed. "But you know about the sun and the moon."

"You never told me which one I was."

"Both at the same time, like an eclipse."

Ol'Lady didn't just think that she was still young. She believed wholeheartedly that she was. When she was just going to the store, she would throw a wig of synthetic hair on over her cornrows like a hat. But when she was really stepping out, she would put on a stocking cap to flatten her braids and then fix her favorite Brazilian hairpiece, the one with the bangs, above her eyebrows like a crown.

She would smile a coy smile that may as well have been a wink. That was the most I would get from her. She saved the flirtatious cutting glances for the pastor at church, the short guy who minded the fruit and vegetable stand downstairs, the manager of the supermarket, the bus driver who drove her downtown to Fifty-ninth Street to sample Lancôme fragrances and variations of eggplant-colored lipstick at Bloomingdale's.

She was too much of a snob to go to Macy's. Even at her age, she still wore push-up bras that showed a little cleavage. Her skin was still smooth. Neither her exposed bosom nor her neck bore any of the pleats of old age.

"Talk to me, Genevieve. I am an open flower. I'll tell you anything you ask."

"Why should I have to ask you, Ol'Lady?"

"So I can tell you lies." Another sly grin and then she would launch into a distracting story. "Did I ever tell you about my boy?"

I thought she was talking about a son that I had never known about—one who hadn't survived. I should have known better.

"In a way it's because of him I could come to America."

I perked up. I had never heard this part of Ol'Lady's origin story, since life had always begun with her and Ma in America.

"I didn't bother with the boy again, not after I met Yanique's father." I couldn't imagine a young Ola more coquettish than the *ti-granmoun* I grew up with.

"Sure, he had taught me how to read and write, to speak French. But he wasn't going anywhere and, therefore, couldn't take me anywhere. I was twenty years old. If I can mesmerize men now, imagine how I turned their heads, almost broke their necks, back then."

I smiled but, not wanting to interrupt her, I didn't laugh.

"Back in La Tranblè, in those days, our elders didn't want to send children to school. Educated kids, especially girls, would only lead to ruin in the community. The sons and daughters would conspire to take away their families' land and sell it. Every young person wanted money for passage to

America. That's how I ended up learning from a market boy who thought he was my boyfriend. I broke his heart when I told him I was pregnant. He thought I should have gone back to the village instead of staying in Port-au-Prince with a married man who would keep me as a concubine until I started to show. No one would want me then. They would see the belly first.

"I did not go back. I stayed in Port-au-Prince, gave birth, and stayed as long as I could in the room the man had rented for me. And I could only stay there as long as he didn't try to hit me or my child. He understood not hitting a grown woman like me, but not being allowed to discipline a child with smacks on the backside or a tug of the ears was an insult to him.

"Your mother was going on eight? . . . I don't remember exactly how old, but she hadn't yet shown signs of puberty by the time we left.

"I don't think I ever told you about how lucky we were. The woman at the embassy, a white American woman, spoke to me in Kreyòl. I was so glad that she hadn't tried to test my French because I wasn't quite confident enough in my proficiency to speak to a *blan* who made me nervous. I'm not saying that the woman was kind or even nice. But she approved the two visas for me and your mother. The woman didn't think I understood when she said under her breath in French: 'She'll make somebody a good maid.' Who cared about the insult? I was going to America!"

Ol'Lady said nothing about love. To hear her tell it, she'd had no affection for the boy tutor, her daughter's father, or any other admirer. Her lies to me were lies of omission. Everything that had come out of her mouth was true.

"And when it was all over, they gave me a little kick that

landed me here to tell you this story." She ended her incomplete tale with the words and flourish of born storytellers.

"Your mother won't even tell you this much. Yanique is my tightly closed rose. But every once in a while, she allows a bee in to suckle pollen."

"All right, Ol'Lady, I have to go now," I said.

She rolled her eyes. "I won't ask you where, so you won't have to lie to me. As if you ever could."

∼⸱⸱⸱⸱⸱⸱⸱⸱

I need a story now. A distraction from the pain of watching my son's strength wane. I need Ol'Lady's healing for Miles's body and my soul. I would tell her everything I have ever kept from her. I would let her see me cry over Bright. I would tell her anything she wanted to know about our marriage and our breakup.

I hate to say that a part of me wishes that she were no longer living so her spirit could come and help me here and now. I feel guilty for feeling burdened. I am needed and in need. Ol'Lady has the kind of might that can lift cars or concrete off of loved ones. I am too weak.

20

There must have been music
pulling the strings of a dancing and deceived people
There must have been a cord cut
to free the limbs of a woman
moving only to the sounds in her head

Long-treasured songs gifted themselves to Ateya, bring-ing solace to her failing body. Although she wanted to col-lapse, the music in her mind held her upright, making her sway to sounds only she could hear. In the grip of the possessive rhythm, she clasped her hands behind the neck of an invisible man, her waist rolling between his strong hands. She tilted her head back, chin forward, lips parted for a much-needed kiss. Her fingers spread themselves in his hair as she brought his head forward for an embrace. The boleros of her youth flowed through her until she trembled against the body of the type of lover she had never known. She would remember this night because of the song pulsating in the breaking beat of another aftershock. She would remember the song because of the third—or was it the fourth—quake vibrating through her, while the rest of the world fell apart and away around her.

With rubble beneath her feet, she released the man to dance alone. The slow song gave way to a medley of boisterous tunes from her adolescence. The violent yet pleasure-filled tremor commandeered her movements. She did not want the feeling to end. She wanted to capture the pleasure the way she'd held orgasms inside of her to make them last a little longer. When the savage trembling stopped, it left her longing and frightened of what appeasing sound might follow.

Ateya had been pregnant with her second—or was it her third—boy when Baby Doc's advisers had planted the idea of hosting a series of concerts. They plotted to appease the emboldened masses shouting for his abdication from the presidency. She'd missed the performances of the self-exiled bands who had gained notoriety playing for the voluntary diaspora in New York, Miami, Montreal, and, in fact, most of the Black francophone world. While the music of Tabou Combo, Skah-Sha, and the Martinique group Kassav' banged out exhilarating kompa and zouk, she'd sat at home with one, maybe two terrible toddlers running wild and an equally rowdy baby wreaking havoc in utero. Her relief had come from the vinyl albums repeating themselves on the record player Yanique had sent from the States.

On swollen feet, Ateya would swing her hips to try to dance, at times holding her two-year-old's hands to amuse him as they swirled around the room. Year after year, as ensembles came and went from abroad, she had satisfied herself with LPs and 45s allowed by Duvalier up until his ousting, which had coincided with the birth of her third son. She'd lost count. Her boys had shot up like the plantain trees in the grove until they were old enough to assist the living and the raised-from-the-dead laborers with the harvests.

The boys would sit with neighbors on the doorstep to listen to the new hits in the language of home, penned and tested in foreign places and filtered through the dictator's sieves. Some daring youngsters had managed to stow away under the benches closest to *futbol* field gates. They peered from their hiding places consuming and memorizing the sound of every instrument, the movements of swaying backup singers and dancers, the reverberation of the lead singers' solos, and held the feeling of all these in their bodies. Those fortunate few would carry tunes home on their tongues, like memorable first kisses, and rhythms on their waists, like the bells and beads of vodou celebrants. They would lay what they had witnessed and absorbed at Ateya's stoop for the privilege of listening to the songs emanating from her stereo system.

A new sound had evolved in those years after the despot's ousting and the vodou Rara had roared in celebration, condemning a regime and its enablers, inviting home the exiled and the musical revolutionaries, who descended on their homeland like Maroons from the mountains seizing conquered plantations. Carnivals turned into long-suppressed, syncopated revolts by revelers who let loose in the streets. They performed the unchained gestures of a liberated people, redefining what it meant to be wild, reinventing restrained waltzes into waist-winding *banda*.

While her people had become malleable clay under their own hands as both creators and creations, she had hardened into a brittle effigy imitating strength, fearing the fragility under the threat of romantic and even maternal love. She'd stiffened into celibacy after her fifth and final son, who was born under Aristide.

As revenue from the plantains supplemented and then nearly supplanted remittances, her condescension had toughened into something approximating disdain for the neighbors who'd come to rely on her the way she relied on her women kin in New York. Her dependency on imports from America had started to simmer a small pot of resentment but had not stopped her from wanting and enjoying more new things. These gifts had lit aflame her loathing for her own people as she'd exploded in rants that would make the yard sizzle. Boastfully proffered loans had singed the fingers of borrowers while she'd flaunted the bounty of the most recent haul from overseas.

Inside her body, her traveling heart had stoned her like a sinner and kept greedy suitors at bay. However, longing and arousal had forced her to seek out frequent upright encounters with a string of one-night-stand paramours, who never actually spent the night. She'd never had to increase the frequency of sun-drying her sheets, which was how her neighbors had known that the men had heeded their warnings about the trapping Venus who could make a man disappear into the mirage of her plantain grove. These lucky ones had left her like the long line of corrupt fleeting occupants of the Palais National.

Only one man had made the mistake of and paid the price for lying in her bed for hours after sex. A year into the new millennium, Ateya had found herself in love with and pregnant by a coveted mulatto-looking stranger from the north. She'd believed that she had finally been sent an equally affluent mate who might make her a rightful mistress, which was good enough for her and more than she'd ever expected. She'd still had to kill him, twisting the family ritual to suit her vengeance for hoarding his high-yellow hue.

Having survived the men who'd come and gone through the swinging back door of Haiti's presidency, Ateya felt that her daytime trysts with other women's husbands made sense, as did her assassination of her daughter's father. Asking Ateya to name any of the men who'd bent her backward to satisfy themselves would have left her as stumped as asking her to recall her country's leaders in the years between Aristide's presidencies. He had been president for the third and last time when Ateya had given birth to Ti'Louse.

She'd been able to remember the songs that had been popular in those years, but not the men. The music was more important: arousing, satisfying, wanting nothing from her but giving her everything on command via the ever-evolving conveyers of sound—record, cassette tape, CD, and then an iPod Genevieve had brought for Ti'Louse's fifth birthday. The generosity of the tunes had nearly been eclipsed by the unnatural calamities that had regularly robbed Ateya of peace.

In addition to the music, she had marked the years by nature's near annihilation of her country. Storms fought songs for space in her memory. She would feel rain streaming down her face, pooling in the cradle of her collarbones, where she might have allowed a lover to kiss her. Sweat and tears the flavor of broth would flow over her lips. The stream would become a flood as rain pelted her body, collecting around her bare feet, where her toes clutched the creamy mud.

She could remember the names of hurricanes and tropical storms, and the anonymous cyclones, torrential rains, floods, and the lone tornado. The storms were easy to recall because she'd been glad that none of her children bore the names: Gordon, Georges, Ivan, Jeanne, Dennis, Wilma, Alpha, Fay, Gustav, Hanna. The floods had also forced her to learn the names of places she had never visited and about whose history she had been and remained oblivious: Camp Perrin, Jacmel, Les Cayes, Jérémie, Kenscoff, Isle de la Gonave, Ounaminthe, Mapou, Latortue.

Port-de-*Paix*. Where was her peaceful harbor? There had been no semblance of calm for her until she was finally able to forget everything except the town she had never visited and the song that had been playing when she'd first learned that one of her sons and his father had made a successful car journey north. Months later, a neighbor had interrupted a beautiful ballad with word that their flimsy motorboat had not made it to America or even the Bahamas.

Port-de-Paix. The name of the city clung to her like wet clothes. It made sense that she could not remember the storm that had remained over the ocean and swallowed the small craft straining toward Miami. The tempest had not been christened because it had only brought inland flooding and uneventful mudslides. No winds had tossed the world about, just a random gust that had carried away the names of her second son and his father. They, along with the name of their drowned vessel, had disappeared somewhere inside her resistant brain.

Port-de-Paix. Although the messenger burdened by the devastating news had grown up in the yard with her sons, Ateya could never figure out how to move her tongue to make the sounds needed to summon him for an explanation of what he had heard. She'd relied on hand gestures and facial expressions to coax information from the boy. By the time she had finally come to grips with the knowledge that the son she loved and the man she did not were lost to her for good, she had already forgotten everything except their resemblance to each other. She could not picture their specific features, just the perfectly shaped oval of their heads, which everyone had said signaled a sharp, retentive intellect.

She wondered if they remembered anything, wherever they were. Could they conjure up the texture of the staccato cough of the boat's engine? The height and weight of the waves? The prayers of their fellow passengers? Would they remember her? Maybe not the man; he wasn't important. But the one to whom she'd given birth? Would he recognize her if she appeared to him at the bottom of the ocean?

The same thought crossed Ateya's mind as she looked down and around at the city below her: Would the girl remember her? Although the dark face was slowly fading, she tried to hold on to the infant smile, which had remained the same, even after teeth had started fighting for space in her daughter's mouth. She wondered if her little girl's name would permanently vanish wherever it had buried itself inside her. She reasoned that it must be under a slab of rock, waiting to be uncovered along with the title that would be assigned to this earthquake. Another aftershock would jog her memory.

Ateya knew that earthquakes had no names, only dates she'd learned in school that had fallen out of her head as soon as exams were over. She'd retained two events that came to mind as she looked out over the splitting Palais National— the quake of 1842, because it had demolished the Palais San Souci, the home of King Henri Christophe in Haiti's north-ernmost city, and the one in 1904, because it had hit on the centennial of the country's independence. Now, she wanted to release this date from her mouth, the twelfth day of January, in the year of our Lord, Two Thousand and Ten.

She put both of her hands on her head as if she might scream. She didn't know what she would say if her hoarse voice cleared—a date or a name. It took her mind a few minutes to catch up to her open mouth. It hollered, "Hosanna," and baptized the monster that had not finished birthing itself from the angry core underground. Hosanna—the formal name she had given to her daughter—was worthy of shouting because of the church song in which it featured. The hymn promised protection from any demon attempting to invade one's home. Although Ateya believed that she was the one who had forgotten, it was her daughter's nickname, the dog's name, that had hidden itself from her.

She knew. Something was being withheld from her, like air denied the body of a suffocating soul. Gagging on her own grief, Ateya didn't want to hear the strained dirge expelled from the hoarse throats of weary mourners kneeling in the rubble around her. If she had to listen to something religious, it would be a vodou hymn or the drumming for vengeful, possessive spirits that would overwhelm her senses.

She wanted to surrender to something other than the pain of loss. With this thought, her body shook, casting her out of the cadence of predictable beats into soulful, screaming rhythms. She moved spasmodically as her head bobbed loosely forward and back. Her shoulders dropped while her hands swung at her sides. The whites of her eyes gathered the darkness around her and turned black. Her body was not her own. It belonged to the *lwa*, who allowed her to forget what had been done to her and what she had done to the detriment of others. The gods released her from the knowledge that she was alone and alive in a place of unfathomable fear. The willful monster continued to open up the ground beneath while a cruel ghost dug its rage into her heels. If not for the peace of dance and denial, she would find no relief from her agony. She would be forced out of her trance and awaken to the inescapable sight of the destruction around her.

21

There must have been a secret
unearthed and desperate for a grave

This trip was supposed to be a chance for me and Miles to connect with each other and learn our history. It was supposed to be my first time visiting Saut-d'Eau, La Citadelle, San Souci, and Cap-Haïtien. I was supposed to be pointing out sites on Miles's iPhone while driving to these places, smiles on our faces, uninterrupted by our recent history as mother and son. We were supposed to enjoy and understand each other, make promises, bond, heal.

Bright was probably right. This would have been a vacation. At least I did better than what Ma suggested: "It wouldn't hurt to stay in a hotel for a few days before going to the village. Ease him into things. Give him something sweet and then the bitter. Alternate between the two. Jacmel and then the hard road north. Maybe fly rather than drive to Cap. Don't take him to Ouanaminthe. Leave that leg out. Next time just go on the cruise that stops in Labadie." How enlightening Labadie would have been—an entire islet in Haiti leased by an American cruise line. Colonialism at its finest.

We are being chased north by ground opening under our feet. I am dragging Miles underground with me. I am exactly the mother I believe I am. The inadequate and even dangerous kind. I have given Bright every reason to take my boys away.

I wonder what it would take for me to hand them over. I considered it when his baby died—maybe loan the boys to him for a bit. It's not like he didn't beg enough, that he wasn't sufficiently contrite, in enough pain for me to take pity on him. He didn't deserve my boys. He had his chance—twice. Unfortunately, by the time he was ready, he was not wanted. I feel guilty for thinking it, but even his infant was taken away from him as retribution for what he put Miles through.

I tried. I took him back after the first time and the second. I didn't want my boys growing up without a father. I didn't want to be alone without a husband, without him, specifically. But he squandered his opportunities and took me, us, for granted, assumed that I would always forgive and take him back. But there could never be a next time. My love finally opened its eyes and saw him for who he was. Who he still is. Weak and wanting. I see me in him and him in me and I don't like either. At least I am no longer blind.

But I'm still screwing him. "*San wont,*" Ol'Lady says if she really wants to hurt me. There is never judgment in her eyes. She understands what women do. Ma is a different story. She turns her eyes outward while inwardly she is as needy as I am. At least she isn't sleeping with my father. Sometimes I think that I am a test-tube baby by a donor. It would be just like her to have been so progressive in her day and so fearful and disdainful of the opposite sex to cut the encounter out altogether. Oh, I definitely believe that she has been having sex, but for her own reasons and needs.

Only a therapist would be comfortable enough to think about her mother's and grandmother's sex lives. Has a med student ever specialized in psychiatry and gynecology? A doctor should never treat herself. I clearly haven't done a good job. Also, I already know that my children will end up on the couch. I always believed that it would be because of Bright. Fat chance. I'm the one who has fucked up.

~⁓~

Counter to my training, I am convinced that digging deep into the past to get at the source of pain to start to heal is harmful. It is better not to know. It is better to remain oblivious. To shun knowledge. To leave the bones in the grave, cover them with soil, pat it all down. Pour a layer of cement to seal it properly.

I wish I could go back and un-know what has been exposed, like how much America hates my sons and why. There's nothing worse than knowing that your children are hated. If I could have suppressed my need to know, I could have lived a peaceful life of ignorance.

I even wish I never uncovered Bright's infidelity. I wish I put my head in the sand and pretended that my suspicions about his cheating were just paranoia. We would still be together and my boys would have their father at home with them.

I should have let it go, fought my desire to know the truth. And if I couldn't let go of my need to know the *what*, I should have resisted knowledge of the *why*.

But I needed to know, to show Bright that I knew, and

even more, to prove that I understood his reasons for cheating more than he did. He couldn't accept the truth that, after growing up as the only boy among sisters and girl cousins, he was accustomed to being worshiped, and needed that adoration, felt robbed of it when he interacted with Ma and Ol'Lady. The women Bright had previously dated had brought him home to admiring mothers, aunts, and grandmothers, most of whom had known the pain of being single mothers, abandoned by or robbed of men who'd been killed, gone to prison, died of curable diseases, or run away because they were ashamed that they couldn't take care of their families. These wounded women treasured Bright, couldn't wait to be in his presence, and made him feel needed, not just wanted.

In a world in which he was hated, constantly disrespected, endured violence, tolerated fetishization, he needed Black women's true love. Even though he had mine, he needed to feel special around my family. He hated that, despite my love for him, I didn't insist that they accept him, nor did I defend his manhood, Black manhood, when they ignored him.

I tried in my own way to give him what he needed early on in our relationship. But once I had Miles, I became more concerned about Ma and Ol'Lady welcoming and loving my son. Once I got pregnant with Yves, I threw myself into ensuring that they would accept him too. I appeased my family so they wouldn't hate my boys. I sacrificed my husband on the altar of my goddesses.

Bright never wanted to hear my rationalizations. He thought that these reasons or excuses meant that he was weak, insecure, and egotistical. I thought that they just made him a Black man in America. To him, those were one and the same.

He wanted to be more than that. He wanted to be a man. Just a man—ordinary and great at the same time. Even, and maybe especially, if manhood is a fallacy.

I should have kept what I knew hidden from him and myself. But I thought that I needed to know—everything.

I have learned that the truth is more painful than the lie. Truth is an intruder. It is unwanted, inconvenient. It disrupts your peace. It comes to confirm what you suspect but refuse to admit, to excavate evidence of infidelity you'd otherwise just be guessing at. It splits open flesh. It creeps under bolted doors, a line of ants making the mind itch for more information.

The truth is never pretty and seldom helpful. We always think that we want to know. We tell ourselves that the truth is ammunition. We forget that the weapons we wield are more likely to hurt us. Like the gun in the house that is meant to be used against trespassers but ends up shooting us in the foot. It arms our impulses: "I am depressed. I don't want to live anymore. I am angry. I don't want to see you anymore. I am careless. A curious child . . ." We've heard the stories that have become our own.

The truth hates you. Like the colonizer and the slaver, it wants you to acknowledge your helplessness in its presence. It reminds you of debts you don't really owe. It is a thief. It robs you of pride and power. It cows and bows you. It feeds off of your submission. It captures you with cruelty. It bends you to the brink of breaking. But it needs you to create its reality. It can't live without you—to feed it, to till, plant, water, nurture, and harvest. It punishes you when you don't give it what it wants. When you free yourself, it tells you that you owe it your body, your breath, your labor, your life.

It is the same with the past.

History is heavy. Whether written down in stacks of books falling like bricks or carried on the honest tongues of gifted griots, the weight of it crushes. I wish I'd never learned how much the world hates my country. I wish I had not read about that in-between part of Haiti's history. I thought I wanted to know. I had asked for just enough to allow me to move about in the world safely. I did not want this other stuff—the details of damage done and perpetuated. I can accept the sight of a bruise or two, but I don't want to see the guts of a thing. I want the interior parts to remain inside. I want the crawling things to lie dormant. I want the things that have forced themselves on me to remain out of sight.

I refuse to sacrifice any more of myself on the altar of truth revealed and history uncovered.

To protect myself, I will make sure that I never uncover the biggest truth that has ever been withheld from me—the who or where or why of my father. I must ask Ma not to tell me—ever. I promise never to fantasize ever again. I prefer to see what is not there. An elusive illusion is easier than the hard and visible truth.

Having sex with Bright is a wonderful mirage. I get to pretend that everything is fine between us, that we are in love, that nothing ever happened, or at least that all is forgiven.

If I could forget my training, if it were the responsible thing to do, I would tell all of my patients to run, run, run because not knowing is merciful. Ignorance is a saving grace.

❦

"Didn't he know how crazy I was?" This is my patient. For HIPAA's sake, let's call her Mary.

"We don't use the word *crazy* here," I reminded her.

"He knows I'm bipolar."

"You are not your illness. You have bipolar disorder. You are not it and it is not you."

Mary rolled her eyes and let out a deep, frustrated, almost angry sigh. "I could have been sitting there with a gun, waiting for him. How did he know I didn't have a gun?" Mary shifted her body. She preferred to sit in the armchair instead of the couch. For someone who usually referred to herself as "insane," she tried never to sit on the therapist's couch.

"I caught him! The gas receipts. He was driving two hours to see her. Two hours. Each way. I was waiting for him to get home. How did he know I didn't have a gun? That I wouldn't shoot him? What did I have to lose? We didn't have any kids. *I* didn't have any kids. I don't have any kids. I tried to tell myself it was because of the miscarriages. He really wanted children. So did I, but I just couldn't try and fail one more time. It would have put me underground. He blamed my meds."

"Speaking of which, we might need to make some adjustments . . ." I interrupted to keep from drowning with her. It was too close to home.

"Can you believe he had the nerve to ask me if he, she, it was his? As if I were the one cheating."

"Adulterers often project their behaviors on to their faithful partners."

"When would I have cheated? Where?"

"Let's talk about how that made you feel."

"I stopped feeling after driving two hours each way to meet his mistress."

"What were you feeling when you were driving?"

"That I would kill both of them. I was angry."

"Anger is the manifestation of deep pain."

"Of course, I was hurting."

"What else? What did you hope would happen when you got there? What would seeing her solve?"

"This isn't working, Dr. Wright."

"'Genevieve,' please." I'd been insisting that patients, hospital staff, the doorman, call me by my first name. I'd been thinking about changing my last name from Bright's ever since I'd found out.

"Genevieve, I don't think this is working. I'm really struggling." Mary's fists were balled as if she wanted to hit someone. Since I was the only other person in the room, it would have been me.

Please don't stand up. Please don't, I say in my head, even though I know that she would never.

"She was fucking pregnant! She was fucking pregnant!"

Every time Mary comes in and repeats her story, I feel it all over again. That gut kick when I found the wallet. I'm still convinced that that woman had left it in the car on purpose for me to find. She wanted me to know. She had been trying to reach me on the phone to tell me about them, but I'd just assumed it was a prank.

"Where is your husband? Ask him about his friend." Hang-up.

This person must have a wrong number. I told Bright and he reassured me. "I feel sorry for the poor guy," he said and laughed it off.

It didn't matter. I was already pregnant with Yves. It was early but what was I going to do? Give her what she wanted? Kick him out? He left anyway. In the spring. At the end of the summer, he came back. Asked for forgiveness that I didn't give. I handed him a condom when he wanted to have sex. He left. He packed a bag while Miles was in the tub. He left before the boy got out.

I took him back after Yves was born.

Ma and Ol'Lady never asked. They never said a word to Bright or to me about what had happened. They never questioned his absence at the hospital when it was time for me to leave. Ma pulled Miles closer when he asked for Bright.

Ol'Lady had fixed up her bedroom for me—crib and everything. A second crib, not the one from my apartment, since she knew that Yves would be spending a lot of nights at hers while Bright and I tried to work things out.

We split up for good before Yves turned one. It was spring, of course. The cycle had begun.

"What else were you feeling, Mary?"

"I wanted to kick the bitch in the stomach."

I flinched.

"I wanted her to feel what it was like to have a miscarriage. If I had had a gun . . ."

~ ⚜ ~

"If this were Haiti, we would black out that Bright," Ma whispered conspiratorially to Ol'Lady.

"Tell me about it. He would have been buried with my mother by now," Ol'Lady chuckled. "If my sister was still alive, I would have tricked Bright into going to Haiti. She would have taken care of him. She would have shown him that the women in our family are not traditional Haitian women who take nonsense from men. Underground, *anba tè an,* is where he would be. Disappeared."

"We could at least have someone *touch* him." Ma smiled with her mouth, but her eyes said she was serious.

"Would that really be enough?"

Ma and Ol'Lady's talk did not surprise or scare me. I had heard things. On summer nights in Haiti, after the recounting of old tales in our *lakou,* the grown-ups would speak in coded language that they thought indecipherable. But I understood. Sitting under the mouths of my elders, a sign of rudeness, I had been labeled *jouda* and *sou moun.* I shrugged off the labels, went inside the house, and started eavesdropping instead.

The women's words would tumble like sorted beans transferred from plastic bowl to steel pot. Their talk had the gravity of verifiable accounts. When challenged, the women would stand up and insist on showing an unbeliever photos or locations. The men would warn their comrades around domino or card tables, cigarettes dangling from the tips of their lips, tongues savoring the last of the spicy amber liquids. Then the speaker would give an account of what had happened to a specific man—a best friend, a brother, distant cousin, traveling salesman. And everyone would laugh a scared laugh. A laugh that affirmed the tale, conveyed that the warning had been heard, advice taken, behavior modified accordingly.

I believed the stories because there were never any men around the house. Ma and Ol'Lady would have never sent me to stay in a house with men. I barely even saw my boy cousins. By the time Ateya had her first son, which was when I started staying in Haiti for only two weeks during the summers, the plantain trees were already tall enough to block any view of the leaning crosses. I was also too old to listen in on repetitive conversations peppered with fabricated details to make the old seem new and exciting to tellers and listeners alike.

The tales tucked themselves away and waited for some tidbit of Ma and Ol'Lady's chats. Then the stories would poke their heads out like spying children and fill my head with truths that eventually became relevant to me. But it had been decades since I had heard any discussion of our family back home that was not about sending money or barrels. Still, their talk of harming Bright did not bother me any more than their knowledge of things I had never told them, would never and did not need to say to them out loud.

22

There must have been one mother
arrogant enough to think
that she was the only mother

Ateya held the dead teenager's legs in her lap. The mother held the head and torso, passing her hands over her daughter's body as tenderly as if she were giving a baby a sponge bath. This should have been a private act, the final rite of ablution performed by a grieving mother not ready to release her child to the spirit world. This touching with dry hands, a palm resting on flattened hair. This loving inhale of her baby's last exhale. This kiss on fingertips. It should have all been done behind the heavy curtains of a dimly lit room. Ateya thought that she should not be witness to this farewell, the soundless cry of baptismal tears falling into dusty hair, this rocking of a body that would never come to life. This mother, any and every mother, should be grieving in her own home, with her own people, with a special someone second only to the deceased in her heart. This mother, any and every mother, deserved at least that, especially when burial in an individual grave would never be possible.

Stopping to help with the burden of another mother's pain was as much a reversal in Ateya's thinking as was her journey from Port-au-Prince back to La Tranblè. She could see that the mother was already giving up. She placed one hand over the woman's and gave it an encouraging squeeze that said: "Stay with her," "She'll come to," "She'll come back to you," "At least you can hold her." The woman pulled her hand away. Instinctively, Ateya bounced the girl's thighs in her lap while her mind wandered.

She imagined that she had the power to resuscitate this child, any child, even her own. If this one were hers, she would be carrying her on her back to lay her in the plantain grove, where the cool, misty air would erase the dust covering the body.

Why hadn't the other mother said this to her child instead of vanishing without a sound, leaving the limp neck and motionless head of her daughter on the ground? Ateya tried to gather the girl's body into her arms but could not manage the dead weight.

"What kind of mother . . . ?" she thought and then caught herself. No one had the right to judge a mother who had lost a child, not even another grieving mother. These mothers had to manage any way they could—denying, running, jumping off a cliff, hanging themselves from a tree limb, laughing until hoarse, crying until they went quiet, cursing anyone or anything or any god, burying themselves alive, banging their heads against a wall until knots swelled or they knocked themselves unconscious. They could do whatever the hell they wanted, having suffered the worst of losses. They could even hold the legs of another mother's daughter until daybreak.

In the mixed blue light, Ateya saw why the mother had

left. The daughter's face had been unmasked. Peeling skin laid bare what had once been a tender visage. Blood dried mid-drip over exposed bone. Whatever part of her that had been pretty was now an unrecognizable mash of flattened features. But couldn't the body be salvaged? It was mostly intact, at least the visible parts. Even if everything inside was broken, every organ pressed, there was something to bury, to lay in a grave that could be visited, laid upon, topsoil watered with tears. There was something there, but it wasn't hers. It wasn't hers. Hers. Hers.

Ateya lifted the dead girl's legs and stood up.

Having left a dead child behind, Ateya had no reason to hope, but she needed to believe that her child would come alive. Although she didn't deserve to even hope, she imagined herself playing the familiar game of hide-and-seek they had played away from the eyes of the unbelieving, unloving caucus of self-appointed judges of the yard. The ones who had deemed Ti'Louse ugly and, therefore, unfit to be loved would be banished so she and her beautiful child could run freely through the grove. Her love would not be confined to enactment in an invisible, unknowable place. It would be out in the open, flooding the earth and the air with the noise of celebration.

This was why Ateya was making the journey back home. Her daughter had to be waiting. Where else could she be? Every time Ateya had turned around to catch whoever had been kicking her heels, there had been no one. Something or someone else had to be pushing her home to find her missing child. Where else could she be? Where else could they be, except under the canopy of overgrown trees playing *lago cache,* mother and daughter finding each other in the dew-drenched soil.

That was where she needed to be. To run her fingers through the grains of soil between the kinky curls of baby hair. To issue warranted apologies on her knees. Soft strokes with the back of the hand over creamy, tear-stained cheeks. A nose nestled in the neck. Arms wrapped tightly around a thin body, hands pressed into the slender back.

I have always loved you.

She would breathe this repeatedly into one ear and then the other.

I have always loved you.

It was what the ones who'd left and come back home that was no longer home would say.

I will always love you.

On their knees they would crawl back; over dirt and dust-covered broken glass, they would say things to the place they'd left as youngsters and only returned to visit for a few days or weeks at a time.

It made sense that they would fall on all fours. The tallest always fell first and hardest. Sadly, they took others down with them or collapsed, crushing those beneath them. Wasn't that how it was in this country? The low high-rises coming down on top of the single stories beside them. Those with the most dropping themselves into the laps of the poor, trouncing the masses when the economy was bad, when remittances waned, when loans from richer countries dried up. The destitute falling further into penury with the impossible weight of the rich on their chests. They would be the last to rise if they were ever restored at all.

We will always love you,
the newly minted foreigners would say.
We'll be back. We'll come back for you.

Ateya pressed forward, weaving into and out of the crowd hurriedly to get to the place where she'd last sent her soft self, to find the daughter she wanted to love openly, to grieve privately. Her feet painfully picked up their pace to get her to the place where the land would absorb the bleeding, heal, and set her free to run after the daughter she'd publicly deserted. What hurt her most was knowing that her child had loved her in spite of everything—that the girl had not been able to stop herself from loving the one who had not loved her. Who mourns most? The child who loses a mother while alive? Or the mother who loses a child through death? The tree or the fruit? Who longs for whom most? The mother who births and then sends out into the world the child she's carried? Or the child who is forced to leave behind the only one she has ever known?

The lyrics to a favorite song rose in her throat: "A mother is like a plantain tree. The leaves might grow and grow. They can do what they want. Ultimately, they must come to die at her feet." That was the mantra of the far-flung diaspora, those who'd left the country of their own accord. Some, but not all, most, wanted to come back home and be buried in their own land.

That was the difference between her and Genevieve. Ateya had and would only have one home. She wasn't going anywhere, although she'd once wanted to. If she was being honest with herself, she'd never stopped longing to go "over there." At least to visit and decide whether or not she wanted to stay. She had always known that she would have wanted to stay in what she believed was that better place. Up until this earthquake, she'd wanted to go.

As she walked back to the wreckage of her house and the plantain grove she had seeded and raised, she knew that she could not leave. Her heart, more broken than ever before, had dissolved in her blood as pulverized gravel, scratching the interior of her veins. It would not let her leave. Although she no longer had anything to live for and no one to bury her when she died, she was tied to the graves of her foremothers and the hidden grave of her daughter, who, she felt, was simultaneously chasing after and running from her.

If Ateya could find the girl, uproot her from the soil, gather her up without shaking off the dirt of her interment, she would leave. She would make a home in the place of her choosing and leave behind all of the things that she had once thought were important. She would find her way to that place that made people smile in pictures. She might send her soft self ahead to that other land that lived under a different sky, leaving behind the shattered pieces of her other, hardened self. That hard self might make its home in the grove it had always been afraid to enter, and rest. Finally rest.

She heard herself whispering the words again.

I have always loved you.

Ateya looked up and saw the sun peeking through a blur of thin clouds exposing a world that had exploded around her. Gray dust lingered in the air like smoke. Nothing was whole. Even the clear parts of the road were cracked, as if a giant steel bird had run a claw down the middle from the city to its outskirts. Where structures once blocked views of the trees, open air exposed wild greenery against a low sky. Dismembered motorcycles lay on their sides, leaving no doubt about the fate of their riders. Under a solid, fully rooted tree a woman sat with legs crisscrossed and eyes closed as if willing herself to levitate and disappear.

Ateya kicked small rocks out of her way as she crossed from Taba into Croix-des-Missions. She took her chances wading through the Rivière Grise to get back to La Tranblè. On the bank, really a trash-laced gully, she stood up and wiped her face, which was covered in the dirty water she'd seen the poorest of the poor wringing wet clothes in before throwing them over rocks to dry. She shook her head, realizing that she might end up like them, washing off dirt with dirt.

Those who silently walked in the other direction bowed their heavy heads. She didn't have to see their faces to know the weight of their despair. They were her companions in having nothing. They were better off, she thought, because most of them had never had anything to lose in the first place. Can you fall any farther if you're already lying on the ground? Apparently, they could. Haiti was constantly being knocked down, falling farther and farther until it was buried. This time, even its grave had collapsed, pushing it toward the earth's scorching core into hell.

This hell was her only home. She had nowhere else to go except to the site of her birth, the place where she'd given birth to boys, now men, who were missing. Were they lost if she wasn't looking for them? They would fend for themselves. At some point they might seek her out and, unable to find her with their first pass, would quickly give up and attend to their wives, children, mistresses, maybe even one another.

She knew that, now that she had nothing to give, they would not care if she didn't come searching. Her daughters-in-law would not come either, since she could no longer house them or her grandchildren.

As she retraced her steps, passing once again chunks of concrete that had broken off from beheaded buildings, the thought crossed her mind that one or more of her sons might be dead underneath. Or, maybe, alive in some corner of the ruins awaiting rescue. Better that they were dead so they could be put to good use toiling in the still-living grove. Wherever and how they might be, she left them alone.

She could have gotten her sons out. When they were kids, foreigners had offered to take them away—to the DR, Curaçao, the Lesser Antilles, even Europe. Once, a Canadian couple had asked to take her youngest son, a toddler at the time. She should have handed him over. She had other sons, after all. She'd been . . . what? Selfish? Possessive? Protective? Prideful? She wasn't some indigent unable to care for her own. She had people in the States, money coming from them and her plantain grove, which for some reason most of the savior-strangers could not see.

Ateya stopped to rest on a mound in what had been the hospital's courtyard. The numbness of her bleeding bare feet was wearing off. She felt every prick as she picked pieces of glass and gravel from her shredded soles. She needed to rest or find bandages or shoes to continue her trek back home. The tip of a cloth whose original color could not be determined poked from between two rocks. She pulled it out, releasing an asphyxiating puff of dust. The rag sufficed to rub off the blood from one foot and then the other. Dirt upon dirt. This is what she had looked down on, what she had always feared, and now it was what she had been reduced to.

With her blistered but less bloody feet, she entered the road, which had narrowed with banks made of rock, limbs of furniture, caved-in cars, and other debris on either side. A seemingly endless line of people crowded the paved aisle. Those wanting to move more quickly took their chances teetering on loose boulders. Some used crude walking sticks made from splintered wooden pillars. Others crawled on hands and knees to keep from falling. Whether in the street or on stony embankments, the mass made their way over material and human obstacles.

To save her soles, which now bled afresh, she opted to crawl, sacrificing the palms of her hands and the skin of her knees. When these had suffered enough, she walked in the middle of the road on her heels. The slippers dangling off the feet of an otherwise buried body caught her eye. She ran as best she could to grab them before any of the other barefoot pedestrians did. She didn't wait to see if the toes wiggled or listen for a low moan. All she knew was her own pain, her own need. She moved quickly, elbowing her way through the crowd in the road, bumping shoulders, accidentally kicking the heels and ankles of slow walkers. No one fought back or spoke up. There was no noise from the limping cluster.

When an overloaded truck tried to pass, the loosely organized queue came to a standstill but the crowd refused to give way, forcing the truck to drive on an incline. Half of the passengers jumped from the leaning vehicle to keep from falling out as the wheels on one side rolled over bumpy piles of rock. A chorus of "Woy!" from the remaining riders and the walkers alike broke the silence of the morning. Beneath the unified roar, the guttural grunts of seekers mingled with the muffled moans of the buried clinging to life.

Ateya added her own mumbling to the noise. If everyone else could speak, she would too. Although she couldn't hear what was coming out of her mouth, she understood it as her attempt to say something, anything, sweet and melodious, to draw out the child playing hide-and-seek with her in the haphazard parade.

I have always loved you.

The procession thinned as marchers broke away into the paths leading to their own yards. There were no waves of farewell, no nods of see-you-around. A former comrade would simply drop out of sight behind wild, high brush, trample once neatly parted garden rows, or merge body and soul with reliable ancient trees.

Ateya, who'd missed her turnoff, had to double back to trudge her way down the hill to her *lakou*. She stopped midway to again rest her bloody feet. Her neighbors were still calling out the names of the missing.

"Rivela!" Just reaching here.

"Usa!" Can you take me to that country?

In the cacophony of meaningful names, she remembered that she had forgotten to ask the mother the name of her disfigured, faceless daughter. She wondered what the mother would have hollered or if the woman would have said anything at all.

23

There must have been
a radio playing no music
a mother playing at love

The truck crawls over the mounds of dirt to emerge from the brush of wild things, flora and fauna. The wheels gratefully and gracefully land on the smooth roadway and speed up to make their way through Dondon to Le Cap, where help and hope will be found in abundance. It is day and night at the same time.

The crunch of the radio cuts into the quiet. I want to smooth out the sound into a deep and mellow tune. A soothing voice is too much to ask for. Mimi lowers the volume, then quickly returns her hand to the steering wheel. The truck creeps along the road. At least it is moving. We are making progress. As soon as I think this, the radio rises into a drawn-out buzz that ends with a single word—*deux*. Silence. After a while, the radio resumes its annoying hum until the word *république* interrupts.

I run a dirty finger over a line of dried blood as thin as thread along the edge of Miles's face. He has been wrestling with sleep in an obvious effort to ignore the pain of his broken arm. Bordeaux strips of cloth stick to the wound, which has stopped leaking. I move only when he does, a shuddering, deep breath, a feverish tremor, an involuntary kick. He hasn't opened his eyes in more than an hour. I wish I had more flesh and fat on my legs to cushion his head. A gorgeous slice of sunlight flows through the windshield, landing on his face, which I now see has turned a familiar gray from the loss of blood. I feel the fear that he cannot express. I take it on top of my own. This is not the first time I have done this. But this time, I face it full on, take it in like a deep breath, let it flood my body like blood, all to relieve his pain, to lift his burden like a mother should.

24

There must have been
a grove of green trees craving
the lives of children shaking
on tortured ground aching
for something to hold on to

The world was off kilter. As Ateya rose from where she had been sitting, another aftershock rocked the earth beneath her and made her thighs tremble. With her arms open wide, her hands searched futilely for something to hold on to. She teetered but managed to steady herself for the few seconds it took for the tremor to pass. The old, crooked joints in the path broke off into new limbs that confounded the feet. The dirt split and peaked so that the hill whose bumps she had memorized since she could walk now tricked her into missteps that tripped her and made her slide uncontrollably down the slope. She could see her neighbors hunched over whatever lives or property lay on the ground. They dug, as if for gold, while yelling into the air already polluted with an entire night's grief.

The corpses had not yet begun to decay, so only the smell

of dying fires and sweetmeat came to her on the humid breeze. She tried to puzzle out where the syrupy moisture was coming from and quickly settled on the garden, which remained unaffected by catastrophe. It emitted the odor of abundant edible things that had taken ages to ripen and then rotted on vines that crept along choleric bushes. Only children and the elderly had ever bothered with the fruit that fell to the ground. They'd boiled the browning yield, peels and all, into viscous mixtures laced with vanilla and cinnamon. Now, shattered jars of rainy-day preserves sugared the ground under the cinder blocks. The revolting earth had turned delicious and fed the flies awaiting the appetizing putrefaction of human flesh.

When she finally made it to the yard, she crept past her preoccupied neighbors to where she knew that something fresh and pure, something precious and solely hers, was waiting. She kicked off the slippers she had stolen and ran into the plantain grove, bending her head to clear the low fronds. Drops of dew as heavy as rain rinsed off the dust that ran rusty down her legs. The leakage pooled at her feet. The soil swallowed the blood from the gashes in her soles. With pain still pricking her feet, she dropped to the ground and finally, finally rested. She had arrived at the place she had not moved from since the earth-splitting quake. Her soft self had been walking in circles, searching for the daughter, whose laughter beckoned, whose body evaded and then escaped every time Ateya got close to her.

Ateya's traveling self finally arrived to join the loving corpus with the whole, healed heart. Tears mixed with drizzle loosened her unyielding body. Like packed sand on an ocean shore, she crumbled, revealing an invisible core that carried the soul of that self that was only love. Her tender self opened its arms and soaked up its long-awaited love. Not the one she longed for, but the only one, the only self that was hers. Was it too late? Had she waited too long to become whole?

Before the grove became a grove, it had been a playground where the *lakou*'s children could play and act out without the fear of being seen. The land itself was not invisible; it only possessed the ability to make everything growing out of it disappear. What protective power! To keep from the undeserving the sight of the most precious. To hide the purest joy, unsullied unencumbered love, from those who did not, could not emote or appreciate it. Ateya had been allowed to see it for two reasons—she had once been and again became a child and she had planted and raised the plantains that had become an oasis for the innocent.

However, she would never again enjoy the sight of her daughter. Ateya had given up her child in favor of communal acceptance. She had dragged the girl around like an unwanted piece of fabric that turned into a rag. Now she wondered if she had pushed her daughter too far with her half-love and lost her forever? Or was there time to seek forgiveness?

To keep love secret is to sin against the supposed beloved. To be ashamed of one's own is an unhealable cruelty for which there can be no pardon, no redemption. To allow outsiders to dictate the value of yours, to accept their appraisal as truth, to take their truth on as your own, is to go to a loathsome place from which there can be no return. It is a finality beyond death. The mother must accept, or not, the complete vanishing of the one-sided, unconditional, perfect, and pure love of the child, especially if that child has received no love from others.

Ateya understood that now. Ti'Louse had allowed herself to die out of spite, to keep herself forever hidden, to taunt her mother with her death. This was the punishment exacted by the child whom lovelessness had broken. Without a bruise on her body, Ti'Louse had not died from a battering by the wanton earth. She had died to escape a stingy love, to be free to leave, to go where she had always wanted to be—the place where love was alive and persisted beyond death. Ateya had not understood this—that love could survive anything, but its withholding was murder.

That was it. Wasn't it? Ateya had killed love itself.

So why not commit suicide? She couldn't understand why she hadn't, since all she'd had was gone. She was as baffled by this as by her neighbors' resilience, if the human will to live and actions taken to survive could be called that. Why didn't everyone in her country kill themselves? Surely, it was not hope that things would get better. There was no evidence that they ever would. On the contrary, everything they had experienced in the past and were going through presently, everything their ancestors had suffered throughout history, told them that there was no hope and that there would never be any. Except maybe to leave the country. For those who had no choice but to stay, who had never experienced anything better, why hadn't they, why wouldn't they end their lives? They needed not fear death. She didn't. She just didn't want to be the one to do it to herself.

Ateya heard a coaxing laughter again and then a charming whisper. Somebody would bury her. Like the live-again laborers who tended to the grove, someone who had already died would dig a grave for her, throw soil over her, and maybe even say a farewell prayer, if just as a formality. She didn't realize that the laughter she heard, the whispers that seemed to emanate from the outside, had come from her. Since she did not know this, she could not know that she was the one clawing at the dirt. Although the grime under her fingernails spoke to the contrary, she assumed that the one digging had to already be dead because only the dead could dig graves without the fear of being buried alive. Therefore, the excavation of an oblong pit, deep enough for two, made sense. Refusing to believe that she was a murderer, convinced that someone would join her, Ateya lay down in the hole. She waited for her companion, whom she believed would be, could only be, hers. Hers. Hers.

It was only minutes before an aftershock forced Ateya out of the uncovered grave. The earth would not allow her to just give up, lie down and die, wallow in self-pity because of a loss. Yes, there would always be a hole in her, wider and deeper than the one she'd dug, but there was work to be done. Children to be saved.

Ateya ran out of the grove. In a frenzy, she ran to a man with a limp newborn in his hands and took the baby into her own arms. Just as quickly, she ran back to the grove and laid the infant on the ground. She returned to the yard for another, a toddler this time, and placed him in the green. She pushed a mother away from where she knelt in front of a dust-covered girl of about eight. Ateya scooped up the child and took her charge into the garden spray, which washed away the clay film from the girl's face so she could see the curved eyelids, long lashes, bowed brows. She kissed the mist-beaded forehead before laying her down. Time after time, Ateya ran to the yard and back to the grove with a silent child in her arms. When she returned with the one that made two dozen, she saw the children moving, some running, some crawling, the infants lying with open eyes and wiggling fingers. The noise of life rose from the loam and swirled around the plantain garden. There would be no graves dug for living children who would forever be invisible. Nonbelievers looking in from the outside would miss the perfection of innocence, would hear nothing, would see even less than that.

Ateya chased the children around the grove until she grew tired. She sat down to catch her breath. Someone, she didn't turn around to look for who, hugged her from behind and placed a small hand at the nape of her neck. The scattered pieces of her heart scurried to that spot. They did not come together to form a whole. They pulsated there in unison. When she closed her eyes, she heard one solid beat drumming in both of her ears, in both of her selves.

In the after, for there would forever be an after, she carried more and more children to be resurrected until every tree had its own child to love and protect.

At times, only when she needed sleep, Ateya would stop whatever she was doing to run after the hush-hush of grieving trees, believing that if she found the source of the wondrous whisper, she would find her daughter. Exhausted from the chase, she would drop to her knees, press her good ear to the ground in the hopes of hearing words never spoken. But the conversations that had never happened echoed in her more perceptive deaf ear:

Let me go

Let me go

"I should have let you take her."

"I should have stolen her from you."

Let me go
Let me go
"You should have fought me for her."
"Taking a child from her mother . . ."
"It has been done before and will be done again."
Leave me alone
Leave me alone
"I should have taken her. You are right."
"If I had known . . ."
"If I had only known . . ."
Please don't leave me
Please, please, don't leave me

Unable to answer back, Ateya would fall asleep to the lullaby of the incessant plea, wishing she had done more or nothing at all.

Four

❧

25

There must have been
four hundred years of quakes with no names
when it happened before and again and after
and many times more in unnamed centuries
ending in '52, '46, '04, '87, '42, '51, '91, '84
and now

From Dondon to Milot, we weave in and out of the elbows of the road. As our speed increases, the radio's reception comes through more clearly. Loud but low-pitched male voices shout rushed words that make the speakers vibrate. The words are not annoying interruptions to new music that listeners are trying to hear. They are the music—broken, discordant, panicked, angry.

This is an emergency. No one can believe . . . Planes have . . . Port-au-Prince airport is wrecked, the tarmac split, the runway. The runway is . . . Jacmel . . . also destroyed . . . Nowhere to land. The airport here in Cap-Haïtien . . . Rescuers are being sent from all over. Planes will land in the Dominican Republic and then smaller aircraft taken to Cap-Haïtien. The Red Cross, Médecins Sans Frontières, the U.S.

Embassy . . . their buildings in Tabarre . . . Reinforcements are being sent from abroad. No one ever expected . . . Evacuation . . . Recovery . . .

Everything is still. Mimi turns down the volume as she drives in this unfamiliar place. Even with the trash along the shore, far less than Port-au-Prince on its best day, the ocean gleams the blue reflection of the sky. It's as if nothing has happened. Nothing has. Not in Le Cap. At least not this time. In 1904, in 1842. Yes. But not this time. This time, everything is still despite everything else around—toddlers on hips, hands out, tugging at heartstrings. Tin-can cars on bald tires. Flaccid trees wobbling in the strong breeze. Lean-tos with porous roofs wincing at just the thought of rain. *In this moment, I am worse off,* I lie to myself.

I spot the hospital easily. The white building with turquoise trim, clapboard windows letting in humid ocean air, torn screens welcoming mosquitoes and flies. I don't know why I expected to find throngs of people there. There has been no one on the road with us. A few going south, passing us on our way north. Despite our detours, we have made it ahead of the rush that is sure to come. There will be those with more dire injuries. In this moment, Miles is deteriorating. We have to be first to see a doctor. All other patients must wait. Miles must be attended to now. He is the only child of the only mother in the world who matters now.

This is my chance at redemption. Save his life. I am the only mother. Mine is the only prayer. Save his life. Even if his arm is lost. I am the only mother at fault. Miles is right; it has always been about me. I have made it so. I allowed my desire to know, my anger at what I found out, my need to punish, get in the way.

I am crying so hard as Mimi and I struggle to carry Miles through the door. No nurses rush toward us. No security guard acknowledges our presence. No receptionist greets us with pity in her eyes. They've all seen so much worse. Their appraising looks run the length of our bodies, from head to toe. Miles is not special by their assessment. Everyone is someone's child.

"*S'il vous plaît,*" I say.

A woman in blue scrubs comes running from the back somewhere.

"Didn't I tell all of you to be ready? There will be many more like this today and in the days to come," she says in Kreyòl, raising her voice, scolding and imploring at the same time.

"Madame." The receptionist calls me over without raising her eyes from her ready clipboard.

"Forget about that for now," says the blue uniform, who I will learn is the doctor. She reaches out and touches Miles's face. "He has lost a lot of blood."

We follow her to a room at the back and lay him down on a low twin bed. Miles is nearly unconscious.

The doctor gingerly peels back the crude bandage on Miles's arm.

"Who did this? Who burned him?"

"It was the only way to stop the blood."

She calls out and a nurse wheels in a metal cart.

The doctor picks up a needle that is prefilled with a yellowish liquid and explains in English, "This is just a sedative. He's barely conscious now but he'll wake up once I start working on him." She injects him with this first and then a second. "Antibiotic." I know she can see the skepticism on my face. She knows that I am a foreigner and by default a doubter, with no faith in formal medicine as practiced in her country.

"You don't have to speak to me in English. I speak Kreyòl," I say. Now it is her turn at incredulity.

"Please stand back," she says in English. "I promise to do no harm." She raises her right hand to God.

"I wish I could do the same."

"Mothers carry all of the guilt, even, and maybe especially, when it's not our fault." She glances at me and then back to Miles's arm, which is bleeding again. "What did you do? Cause an earthquake?"

I am sweating and trembling, tears flooding my face. It is fear, relief, and more fear.

The nurse leaves and returns with a stack of wet towels in a plastic basin. I touch one and realize that it's drenched in cold water.

"For his fever," the doctor says, still speaking English.

The nurse rolls her eyes as she has every time the doctor has spoken. English bothers her, I assume, because she doesn't speak it. She might think that the doctor is showing off for guests.

I help to lay the dripping towels on Miles's body. I start to lift his head, so I can sit down.

"Don't move him. Don't hold him."

I reluctantly pull my hands away.

"In the days to come, force him to use his hand. He'll try to use the other one, but have him eat with this one, write, or draw, so his fine-motor skills remain on par with what they were before."

That he writes and draws is a normal assumption. But I take it as a sign that she knows something special about him, that he has a treasured notebook. I want to see what comes out of him. I hope there are tears to express inner pain, not an external break. And spoken words rather than writing.

"He'll be fine. I am a mother too. I would not lie to you," she says.

I do not believe her precisely because she is a mother. A mother would want to give another mother hope, even if it were false.

26

There must have been a son, a father, a fault

Mimi and I say nothing as we wait for Miles to wake up. We are still too afraid to speak. What is there to say? I want to thank her. Say something besides good-bye. She is the reason Miles is alive. I want to give her something. Hope, maybe. It would be disingenuous for me to leave her with something that will disappear the moment we part. I have it in abundance but not enough for her. Hope is for the privileged, for those with choices, for those who can stretch their hands out confidently and nearly touch things not seen, knowing that they are within reach. For all others, there is chance. It would be cruel for me to say, "Good luck! Good-bye!"

I hear her sigh, a release of fatigue and fear. She closes her eyes and lowers her head. She doesn't want to look at me. I represent everything she wants and does not want at the same time. I am leaving; she wishes she could. She sees my terror as I think the worst of what might happen to Miles. He is worse than it seemed. He has three compound fractures in his left arm—one that broke through the skin and bled, the others having torn through the muscle. His shoulder is dislocated.

Mimi doesn't know all of this because I haven't told her. But she knows the gravity of things. I radiate pure pain. When she lifts her head and opens her eyes, they are red and dry. They say, "I know you can't but I wish you would. I wish you could. I wish I could. Someday." She understands what we do not, cannot say and cries because she does.

I stand up and begin to pace as I try to get a phone signal in this place. My fingers move frantically as I dial and redial the numbers for Ol'Lady, Ma, and Bright. I don't know why I don't just press the one key for "favorites." For some reason it seems more effective to punch in each digit.

I stop in my tracks when I feel my phone vibrate. I don't know why it doesn't ring. I don't know why I even notice such a thing. I want the sound to break the silence and echo in the hospital hallway.

Bright is screaming into the phone. Not in anger but in panic. We are finally connected. He tells me that he has "pulled some strings." He isn't bragging, just explaining that he is getting us out of the country.

"The flight leaves in two hours, Gen."

"We need to get him to the hospital as soon as we land."

"We will. We will. I love you," he says.

I don't know if it is just reflex or if he's waiting for me to reciprocate. Before I can speak, the phone cuts off.

When the doctor finally comes out, Mimi and I both jump. Mimi raises her shoulders. I rise to my feet. There are different degrees of worry. Mine is that of a mother.

"He's starting to wake up. I've done as much as I can. Enough for him to get on the plane." She wants to reinforce that he will be fine.

"Thank you," I say with tears running over my lips.

Mimi raises her eyebrows as if I am speaking to her, as if I have just spoken words that need not be said. There are thoughts that I must push to the back of mind, things that hurt to feel and are worse to know.

I know what it is to be left.

I now know how it hurts to leave.

I know what it is to lie.

I know what it is to know.

I throw Miles's good arm over my shoulder to prop him up while Mimi stands behind him, braced to catch him if he starts to fall backward. We walk like this all the way to the car. Mimi throws the rear door open and I manage to get Miles in without hurting him. He is groggy and doesn't speak. Not even a moan. The anesthesia is still working and overlaps with the painkillers. At least he isn't in pain. At least he is, we are all alive.

$\sim$

In the land of the hungry, there will always be greed.

In the land of the greedy, there will always be hunger.

I don't know where I have heard this, but it rings true for me now as Mimi drives the length of the trash-laden shore in Cap-Haïtien to the elegant hotel in whose lobby American officials have already put up a makeshift consulate. That this hotel could exist in a country crumbling around it, that foreigners could be whisked away to safety and comfort within a matter of hours, is as painful as it is relieving.

Mimi helps us out of the truck and gets back in immediately. She doesn't stop to hug me or say good-bye to Miles. She doesn't even wave as she drives away slowly, halfheartedly, as if she wants to turn around and tell me. To beg me. Not to leave her behind.

When the truck is out of sight, I turn around to see a man with a wheelchair jogging toward Miles and me in the hotel lobby. He gently helps Miles into the chair, barely touching either since both the boy and the chair are fragile and wobbly. The man leaves Miles and me at the end of the long line of people waiting their turn to explain their circumstances and be told when or if they will be able to leave the country. My country. Why did they come here, just to run at the first sign of trouble? Why did I? Why am I leaving? I tell myself that it is because of Miles, although I know that I would want to leave even if he wasn't here with me. I am not built for this. I am not built for much.

To keep myself from collapsing, I grip the handles at the back of Miles's wheelchair so hard I feel my skin stretching over my knuckles. I enjoy how it hurts just enough to distract me. Out of the corner of my eye I see a white man in a Panama shirt. He pulls us out of the line. Even in his casual island clothes he looks official, powerful. Maybe it is because he's white. It's strange the things we notice even under the worst circumstances. These thoughts are necessary diversions.

"Dr. Ducasse?"

I respond with a nod.

"This way, please." He leads us to a table a distance away from the line of anxious people.

We are VIPs, courtesy of Bright. The man hands me the necessary documents for when we land in the U.S.

"There is a car waiting to take you to the airport. There

isn't much time, but I think I can get the plane to wait a few extra minutes."

Hold the plane? I've always known that Bright was connected but this is much more than I could have expected or hoped for.

27

There must have been a life worth loving

At the tiny airport, we are led to the front of the line because we have "connections" and papers confirming that we are American citizens. Furthermore, Miles is one of the few walking wounded.

I turn back and look at the envious faces behind us. Despair sags on the bodies of my people, whom I am leaving behind. Although unlikely, I think I see Mimi. I don't allow myself to feel my guilt over leaving her. I won't. Not until we get home. It occurs to me that she has never been on a plane. I wonder how it would feel to never experience all of the things I take for granted—flight and the power to come and go as I choose—even now.

I look at the people around me, the fortunate ones—mostly Americans. Although they are distraught, they reek of privilege. It is in the way they move their hands, turn their heads, stare impatiently at the plane on the tarmac. They are trying to suppress their anger, trying not to say: "What the hell is taking these people so long?" *These* people. My people. At least they say *people*. Like children, they press their noses to the glass pane as if that will cause the airport workers to move faster or force the flight crew to ready the plane more quickly.

This plane is one of a few that has come from the Dominican Republic to get foreigners out of Haiti. The irony of being rescued by a Dominican vessel is not lost on me. It had to fly over the Dajabón to get me and mine to safety, for the healing of severed limbs rather than that other thing done decades ago. I listen as the take-off monologue starts. In Spanish, English, and then a tortuous attempt at Kreyòl, a flight attendant welcomes, informs, and instructs. She tells us that we will deplane in Miami and other arrangements will have to be made from there.

This is the space I inhabit, the world that I live in.

Miles doesn't want the window seat this time. I figure that he doesn't want to look down at the place that has wronged him. He doesn't want to look at me either.

Groggy, he lifts his head just enough to say, "Was I so bad that you had to try to get me killed, Mom?"

He laughs first and I join in. I am thinking it is too soon to joke about what we just went through. But we laugh to keep from crying. And then he stops. He no longer wants to hide behind laughter or pretend to be strong anymore. He lets himself cry.

He leans his head against the high-backed seat in front of him.

"How does it feel?" I say.

He doesn't answer. He can't through the tears that are

coming faster than I can catch or wipe away. He doesn't have to hide his face with his hands. I am here.

I want to hold his hand or any other part that he will let me. I want to hold his six-year-old body or his manly head in my lap.

"I would never do anything intentionally to hurt you. Ever," I say. I keep my own tears in check so he knows that his are more important.

"I'm not okay, Mom." His choked-up throat allows a few words to come out. "Sometimes I just want to run away."

I say, "I know." I do not say, "Me too." I do not say, "From myself."

I think about what I will do to make him okay, to make him want to stay, when we get back. To make him want to be alive.

I will see. Him. Yves. I will ignore mirrors. I will keep myself from looking at my own reflection in their eyes. I will see them in earnest, as well as watch. For the way they hold their heads. I will look Miles straight in the face. Hold it in mine. I will listen—for changes in their voices, for sorrow, for growth, for secrets.

I will ask Miles about his writing. I will ask about the man in his drawings. Is it him? Is it Bright? Both of them? A mirror? I will stop searching for sketches of me.

I don't know what I will do about Bright—whether or not I can keep him out, keep him away, in all seasons. I hear Miles's words from weeks ago:

"You love the man who didn't love me enough to stay. You love him more."

I will try not to give Bright so much of my attention. And

if I give in, I will forgive myself. And if I slip up, I will ask my boys to forgive me too.

I want to want Bright back but I don't. I want to love him but I can't. I am infatuated with him. I lust for him, but that's not the same as the pure, immeasurable, albeit never unconditional, love. If I could decide and just settle on loving him, in earnest, I could take him back, rationalize, and defend my choice. I want him but I don't need him. I can live without him. I think. If I have to.

I'm not making sense, even to myself. Whenever I try to figure out this thing with Bright, I tie my thoughts in knots.

I imagine that Miles is as confused and conflicted as I am. Or maybe because his adolescent view is still less tainted, he might be clearer about what he wants. I'm not sure I believe that. He must feel something undefinable and elusive. He wants to love and be loved by Bright. He doesn't know what the latter would feel like since he won't let it in. It is easier to believe that Bright doesn't love him than to know that, despite his paternal love, he just can't be the man Miles needs him to be. It must be easier for Miles to resent or even hate Bright if he believes that Bright doesn't love him— enough.

Naïve as I have been, I know that love is never enough. Not a mother's love. Not a lover's. But I have always felt the completeness of a child's love. Maybe because life hasn't had a chance to chip away at it or because the child doesn't and can't know any better until it's too late. Or because that total dependency, that desperate, can't-live-without-you attachment, starts even before birth and persists as a survival mechanism. Even when that unreciprocated love is bad for the child to the point of being fatal. By the time the child is old enough to feel unloved, which is very early on, their own love is irreversible. It has already become a hungry love. And who can stop or turn back hunger? For as much as we feel and try to do otherwise, parents sometimes deliberately, more often inadvertently, starve their children. A few overfeed. A few overwater and drown their babies. The good ones know how to love their child in the right quantity and keep them alive.

"Everything hurts, Mom." Miles needs me to understand.

"I know, love." As I think about my own agony, how much I am hurting, I catch myself, then I let it all go. I do not say a word to him about my pain. I place my hand over his healthy one protectively.

By the time we're in the air, Miles is asleep.

～ᴐ～

I am convinced that I can see Mimi crying from high above. I am convinced that I can hear her begging.

I hear Ateya. Is she begging me too? Or is she telling me to go? I see her lips move like in a silent picture show. The sound of the airplane's engines is the background music to a slow-moving film. She waves from the green and mouths farewell. She is the happiest I have ever seen her. She is a true child of the earth. She is where she belongs.

Some things are out of place. From above I see the Citadelle Laferrière, the man-made peak of the mountain Bonnet à l'Evêque. The fortress puffs out its chest, displaying the fortitude of millions of bricks that represent the hundreds of thousands of freed lives re-enslaved to build this defense. It is a wasted place, as none of its 365 cannons were ever fired. The only explosion the place has ever known was nature-made—a lightning strike that ignited gunpowder, killing homegrown soldiers. God really does hate my country. Even as King Henri Christophe's army prepared for an onslaught of French wrath, a bolt from the sky, as precise as an arrow, pierced the impenetrable fort. I will never regard natural disasters as incidental or accidental. Not in my county. Not for my people.

Despite everything, my country is as brutally beautiful as my people. Like the citadel, we are a wonder of the world. We are not miracles. Freaks of nature, maybe. Cursed, for sure, if you believe in spells, dreams, and chance. Which means that you would have to trust in some sort of divine providence, a pantheon of gods, or one all-mighty. I have willed myself to believe in something greater than myself for the sake of my children. But I do not count myself as one of the faithful. How can I believe, when things from above and things from below attack me and mine at every turn?

Given the record of wrongs that is Haiti's documented and oral history, I am shocked that events like an earthquake still have the power to surprise us. It may be that we are always fighting the now to guard against the future, with the past chasing us into a hopeless nowhere. We exist in an in-between place. That is me.

I am home and almost home.

I don't know why but the pilot turns to the south. He must want to see what his passengers have run from.

As we fly low over Port-au-Prince, I see the destruction. Houses on hills topple over hovels below. From up here, the living look like scurrying ants with the same strength as the insects known to carry five thousand times their weight. The palace is split in two halves like a fruit. Seeds spill out from its center. *Nothing will grow here,* I say to myself. Then I remember the plantain garden.

～∾～

I am surprised and not that Bright is waiting for us at Miami International. Two emergency workers place Miles on a stretcher. I am expecting Bright to reach for me, but instead he bends down and takes Miles's face in both of his palms. He kisses our son on the forehead. Miles does not recoil. Miles must still be under the influence of the medications. Maybe Bright is too.

Bright takes my hand as we walk to the waiting ambulance that will fast-track us to the University of Miami Hospital's special concierge. He squeezes, and I squeeze back out of gratitude but more so out of fear. He insists that I ride in the chauffeur-driven black car while he goes with Miles.

"You have done enough. You must be exhausted," he says as he closes my door.

I have not taken a deep breath since before the first violent tremble of the earthquake. I still can't. I can only gasp and suck in short breaths as I cry with desiccated eyes wrung dry of tears.

At the hospital we wait hours for Miles to come out of surgery. Bright holds my hand the whole time, for his comfort more than mine. I still can't breathe properly.

"You aren't hurt, are you?" he asks.

It never occurred to me to check. I have only cared about and felt Miles's pain over the past twenty-four hours. Bright must be feeling Miles's and mine.

"We should be able to take him home in a day." Bright pulls me closer to him and lays my head on his shoulder. "You have to get some sleep. Eat something."

"What?" I am startled, as if he has just given me the worst news. I regain my tensely calm posture. "I'm fine."

"There's a hotel room waiting," he says softly. "If you want . . ."

What would I do there alone? One of us has to stay with Miles. What would I do there with Bright, if he came with me? No more. Not again. Not *never*, but definitely not now. Although it would feel so good, an escape, a chance to be taken care of, made love to.

"I'll stay," Bright says, running the back of his hand over my cheek. "I'll stay."

We are standing over Miles when he opens his eyes.

"Dad?" he says as if he is just realizing that Bright has been here the whole time. "You stayed?"

Should I tell him?

Should I tell him?

Should I tell him?

That I wanted to hurt his father, that I could have?

It is my fault that Bright didn't wait. My fault that he didn't stay.

———

I didn't turn around when I heard Bright come into the apartment. I had worked too hard making the perfect bacon to let it burn because of him.

"I put the rest of your stuff in the hall closet."

"I guess you're officially throwing me out."

"To the left. It's all there."

"Seriously, Genevieve?"

"I don't know where you've been spending your nights, but you sure as shit aren't going to treat my home like a storage unit."

"Can I at least see Miles before I leave?"

"And your other son? Yves?"

"Of course, I want to see Yves."

It was as if Bright would forget that Yves existed just because he was a baby. They say that fathers sometimes have a difficult time with babies, fearing they might break such a small thing.

"Yves is asleep."

"I figured. Can I at least take a peek?"

"You have to stop with this drive-by-dad bullshit."

I focused on the pan in front of me like a witch making a potion. The bacon was turning brown, the fat melting into grease. The smell permeated the air. I held the handle of the pan with one hand and I used the other to flip the strips over with the long fork.

"I'm making your favorite."

"I can smell it."

"You can stay and have breakfast with Miles, if you want."

I didn't turn around. I just pointed to the set table with the pot holder still on my hand.

"No thanks."

"What? Are you afraid I'm going to poison you?"

I turned around and faced him, holding the hot pan out in front of me with one hand while the greasy smoke rose between us. I took a step forward. I still don't know if I was holding it out as an offering or as a threat.

"What are you going to do with that? Burn me?"

"Why? Did you do something wrong? Are you afraid of me, Bright?" I didn't wait for an answer. "You should be. I wish you had been. Maybe you'd have thought twice before—"

"I didn't come here for this."

"Why did you come? Why do you keep coming?"

"Well, now I'm leaving."

I held the pan out and took another step forward. "See? It's nice and crispy." I laughed.

He backed away, then turned around.

I dropped the pan when I heard the door slam. It was a miracle that the grease didn't splatter all over me, just a couple of stinging drops on my hand. I looked down at the bacon on the floor and got down on all fours to salvage what I could with my bare hands. Ten-second rule, as the kids say.

Thinking about Bright leaving that day, sometimes, not often, not anymore, I wish I had thrown the hot grease at him. Or at least the fork.

I look at Bright and Miles now, their eyes locked and loving. Miles grips the white hospital blanket with his good hand and I place my hand over his.

Should I tell him?

Should I tell him?

Should I tell him?

That I made Daddy run. Run. Run.

28

There must have been
would forever be an after

It has been three days since we've been back in New York.

I can't explain it, but tonight I am suddenly aware of where everyone is and what they are doing.

Mimi has found a spot among the brush and trees at the base of the Citadelle, where she sleeps in the truck, waiting for the frenzy to die down in the surrounding towns. For three days, she listens to planes landing and taking off, the bellow of cruise-ship horns announcing their arrivals and departures as they deposit foreign rescuers and ferry the frightened documented ones from this place that, for them, is home and not home. Not home when it comes to getting out of the broken country to save their own lives. Mimi is not one of them, nor is she a rescuer. She is a trembling misfit, hiding in the pickup until the danger passes.

Ateya is sitting in the grave meant for two in the plantain garden with her legs spread open as she digs into the soil with earth-stained hands. She has burrowed holes at the base of every tree, searching for what is hers. Hers. Hers.

She has sent her soft self into the yard to hold the children mined from beneath hefty chunks of earth. These are the ones who have not survived. The ones whose skins bear no marks of trauma—no bumps or scrapes or blood. Her tender self cradles these ones, carries them to the grove, lays them there, and goes back for another one. For three days, Ateya's selves perform this ritual. These are acts of contrition that she knows will not bring back what is hers. But it is better than laying both of her selves in the grave dug for two and waiting. To die.

Ma and Ol'Lady are in the kitchen, gingerly maneuvering pots, plates, spoons, spices without a clank. They have lids on pans to keep from waking me with the smell of cooked food. They shush each other and gesture for forgotten things from the fridge, cabinets, and bags they brought with them. They maintain a vigil to make sure that the boys and I remain inside, where they believe my sons are safe from what they have deemed my recklessness.

The boys are in Miles's room, where Yves has slept for three nights. Out of a will derived from love, Miles forces his fingers to move so he can play video games with his brother. They have not stopped since we came back. Through their closed door and mine, I can hear the muffled sound of high-pitched cheers and low cussing as they take turns winning and losing. They grab snacks from the kitchen while Ma and Ol'Lady hold their tongues and say nothing about nutrition. When the boys tire themselves out, they fall asleep in Miles's bed. They have the luxury of leaving the lights and PlayStation on and the blessing of an unbroken bond.

Bright is parked outside of my building, where he has stayed for the past three days, coming into the apartment only to use the bathroom three times a day and twice at night. He speaks to no one when he enters, and no one speaks to him. He tracks the residue of his regret as he walks carefully down the hallway past my bedroom door. A few times I hear his footsteps stop there. He wants to knock, to come in. He wants me to let him in, to apologize, to forgive, to take him into my bed fully clothed with shoes still on. He wants to lift the covers and stare at my body through my filmy nightgown, to turn me over on my back without touching me, and without speaking, tell me what he thinks I need to hear. Each time, he leaves from in front of my closed door and returns to his car to stand guard in case I try to leave with the boys.

I am in my bed, resting in the fetal position, with my arms wrapped around myself, my eyes open. I stare at baby girl in the chair by the window. She is still in her carabella jumper, which gives shape to her dark skin over taut muscles and bird bones. Her legs are precociously crossed, a backless sandal hanging from her foot as she rocks subtly forward and back. Not a scratch or a bruise on her bare arms visible by moon-light, nor a tear of joy, nor the tight smile of displeasure on her face. Only her unblinking eyes, with their bright whites fixed on my face, as if she wants to touch me.

Drowsy from the chamomile tea Ol'Lady made and Ma forced me to drink, I close my eyes, drifting into sleep. When I open them with a gentle flutter, the girl is kneeling at my bedside, breathing an air of soil and greenery into my face. She unwraps my arms and climbs into the spoon of my body. She wiggles until her form is curved so snug that I can hear the purr of her breath. Her heartbeat is less of a sound and more of a tremor, as if it has dispersed itself throughout her body. She holds my arm, which is swung over her, and I squeeze to keep her from trembling.

Although I am holding her close, when I look over at the chair, she is sitting there watching.

IN THE MORNING, THE only morning after, ever after, in that other place, with ground still intact, there must have been slow-motion scenes of a people's unfathomable pain reaching through flatscreens northward for rescue.

THERE MUST HAVE BEEN the unseen tears of an invisible people, never again to be seen loves lost in a hopeless after.

IN THE GLOW OF intelligent telephones, there must have been a hopeful few searching for their own swallowed by the Earth that had opened beneath the feet of an entire city.

THERE MUST HAVE BEEN images in the days, weeks, and months after, not unlike the images before the quake, of crusty mouth holes, of thin skin over sharp bones, like wrinkled sheets laid over the spindly shapes of furniture frames.

THERE MUST HAVE BEEN TV commercials flashing flies feasting on the faces of living children, flies that always seemed to prefer the elusive eyes blinking, reflexively defending pupils.

THERE MUST HAVE, COULD have, would have, should have been, if the ones living in the aftermath had been lighter-skinned, louder, living, needing no help.

THERE MUST HAVE BEEN cries broken beyond recognition, like crushed bones beneath a cascade of blocks and stones. Sound wedged between cement and dry dirt, a crumbling cacophony of primal yells from dying human animals. These were the lucky ones, the ones who might be found if they could just stay alive long enough, wring a stream of tears inside of just-a-little-louder sounds.

THERE MUST HAVE BEEN the sight of bulldozers, nope, not beyond the capital, not in the randomly distributed villages sprouting from stumps like drawn and quartered limbs. There would be nothing in those places, not even a stretch of blue tents to house the remaining unseen and forever underfed.

ABOVE THE WIDE PLANTAIN leaves, there must have been the spirit skin of the only daughter of the only mother in the entire village, floating low over a canopy of green and mist.

THE PUCKERED LIPS OF the only daughter of the only mother must have blown a kiss that was never felt and would never again be.

THERE MUST HAVE BEEN enough trees, enough leaves, enough cracked Earth making unmarked mass pits for the dead in the days after.

A LONG DARK TRAIL before, leading up to the during, stretching into the after.

THERE WOULD FOREVER BE an after.

Acknowledgments

I wish I had more than just my gratitude to give to the ones who have supported, encouraged, guided, and loved me through the writing of this book.

Love and appreciation to Ife and Essen for their patience with and understanding of the focus and commitment that my craft requires. You know that my all belongs to you. Thank you for allowing me to give a piece of what is yours to the fulfillment of my life's purpose. You are not just my loves, you are love itself.

Thanks always to my sister, Marjorie Momplaisir, who has been there from the beginning of my life and everything I have ever written. It is without reservation or pretentiousness that I say: If ever there was a muse, it is you.

I would not be here without my maternal grandmother, Genia Joseph, whom I miss every day. You are forever my mirror.

I love you more is what my aunt Marie Ida Joseph always says to me and to her I say, *I love you always* for filling my empty cup to overflowing in the absence of my mother.

I have only one favorite uncle, Yvon Joseph, and I will never keep secret the fact that I am your *Fave*. You prove that to me through our special love that comes through our passion for language and literature. I hope my Kreyòl in this book does justice to our native tongue.

This book belongs to my editor, Carole Baron, who made it make sense. I learn so much from you every time we speak and laugh, through every email and mark-up, and every story you tell during our conversations. You are the true storyteller.

What can I say about my Benee? "*What give her?*" Except love to my partner in crime, who understands and believes in me, who keeps me from beating myself up when the story refuses to be written or the writing process gets frustrating and painfully slow. And how would I have gotten through the COVID period without you? You are my coach and my therapist all in one.

I am beyond thankful to Victoria Sanders and the VSA team. Victoria, you are so much more than my agent. You make me laugh and let me cuss to my heart's content as we work through the struggles of women and marginalized people in the world.

Endless thanks to the team at Knopf, in particular Abigail Endler, the most amazing publicist, and Robert Shapiro, the best assistant editor.

There will always be a special place in my heart for Kathy McLean, who honors me with her friendship, celebrates and commiserates with me, and knows that we must do the work to get through this life and be good human beings.

I will never stop thanking and loving Aunty Pamela Newkirk and Mzee Ngũgĩ wa Thiong'o.

What a blessing are bonds formed in unexpected places! My appreciation to Michelle Hicks and Sarah Loftus for safe space in a place that often feels so unsafe to me and mine. Thanks for showing and sharing with me pieces of your beautiful selves. I need not tell you to never stop reading, learning, and welcoming corporate misfits like me.

Many thanks to my hosts in my homeland, Haiti, without whom I would not have experienced the exquisite beauty, destruction, pain, and glory of the place that birthed me.

I honor my ancestors, who gave me life through centuries of torment and survival. I hope to always be the fulfillment of your hope and make you proud.

A Note About the Author

FRANCESCA MOMPLAISIR is the author of *My Mother's House*. Born in Haiti, she studied at Columbia University, the University of Oxford, and New York University. She earned a doctorate in African and African diaspora literature as an NYU MacCracken fellow under her supervisor and mentor, Ngũgĩ wa Thiong'o. She is a recipient of a Fulbright fellowship to travel to Ghana to research the cultural retention and memory of the transatlantic slave trade. She lives in the New York City metropolitan area.

A Note on the Type

The type used in this book was designed by Pierre Simon Fournier le jeune. In 1764 and 1766 he published his *Manuel typographique*, a treatise on the history of French types and printing, and on what many consider his most important contribution to typography—the measurement of type by the point system.

Composed by North Market Street Graphics,
    Lancaster, Pennsylvania
Printed and bound by Lakeside Book Company,
    Harrisonburg, Virginia
Designed by Maria Carella